Mischief, Murder and Merlot

J. C. Eaton

BEYOND THE PAGE
PUBLISHING

Mischief, Murder and Merlot
J. C. Eaton
Copyright © 2022 J. C. Eaton
Cover design and illustration by Dar Albert, Wicked Smart Designs

Beyond the Page Books
are published by
Beyond the Page Publishing
www.beyondthepagepub.com

ISBN: 978-1-958384-22-0

Praise for the Books of J. C. Eaton

"Engaging characters and a stirring mystery kept me captivated from the first page to the last."

> —Dollycas, Amazon Vine Voice, on *Divide and Concord*

"Well-crafted sleuth, enjoyable supporting characters. This is a series not to be missed."

> —*Cozy Cat Reviews* on *Death, Dismay and Rosé*

"A sparkling addition to the Wine Trail Mystery series. A toast to protagonist Norrie and Two Witches Winery, where the characters shine and the mystery flows. This novel is a perfect blend of suspense and fun!"

> —Carlene O'Neil, author of the Cypress Cove Mysteries,
> on *Chardonnayed to Rest*

"A thoroughly entertaining series debut, with enjoyable yet realistic characters and enough plot twists—and dead ends—to appeal from beginning to end."

> —*Booklist*, starred review, on *Booked 4 Murder*

"Filled with clues that make you go 'Huh?' and a list of potential subjects that range from the charming to the witty to the intense. Readers root for Phee as she goes up against a killer who may not stop until Phee is taken out well before her time. Enjoy this laugh-out-loud funny mystery that will make you scream for the authors to get busy on the next one."

> —*Suspense Magazine* on *Molded 4 Murder*

Books by J. C. Eaton

The Wine Trail Mysteries

A Riesling to Die
Chardonnayed to Rest
Pinot Red or Dead?
Sauvigone for Good
Divide and Concord
Death, Dismay and Rosé
From Port to Rigor Morte
Mischief, Murder and Merlot

The Sophie Kimball Mysteries

Booked 4 Murder
Ditched 4 Murder
Staged 4 Murder
Botched 4 Murder
Molded 4 Murder
Dressed Up 4 Murder
Broadcast 4 Murder
Railroaded 4 Murder
Saddled Up 4 Murder

The Marcie Rayner Mysteries

Murder in the Crooked Eye Brewery
Murder at the Mystery Castle
Murder at Classy Kitchens

Acknowledgments

We are so fortunate to have such a strong behind-the-scenes team of readers and tech wizards who never turn us down when we besiege them with last-minute emergencies, read-throughs and a zillion other issues that seem to crop up in the world of writing. We could not do this without you. Gale Leach, Larry Finkelstein (U.S.), and Susan Schwartz (Australia), we are in your debt.

And to the Cozy Mystery Crew of authors Esme Addison, Ellen Byron, Becky Clark, Vicki Delany, Tina Kashian, Libby Klein, Olivia Matthews, Elizabeth Penney, Shari Randall, Linda Reilly, and Raquel V. Reyes, thank you for your encouragement and continued support. We are honored to be part of the crew!

Of course, none of this would be possible without our amazing agent, Dawn Dowdle, from Blue Ridge Literary Agency. Boy, did we luck out!

And to our editor, Bill Harris, and the phenomenal staff at Beyond the Page Publishing, we are genuinely appreciative of all you do.

Finally, we thank you, our readers, for bringing our acerbic and quirky characters into your lives!

Chapter 1

Norrie Ellington's Apartment in Nolita, New York

At least Belinda Kuentz was happy. Happy? If her shrieking was any louder, I would have lost an eardrum.

"Oh my gosh, Norrie! I just saw your text. I must have turned my phone off. Oh my gosh! The answer is yes. Yes! I can be packed and at your place by tonight. The text didn't say when you'd be leaving. Oh my gosh." And then, in an even louder voice that was thankfully not directed at me—"Do you hear that, Mom? I'm out of here! I'm renting Norrie Ellington's apartment again. I'm out of here!"

The mid-October sun hadn't even crested the apartment building across the street from mine in Nolita when Belinda gifted me with her wake-up call.

I was barely coherent. "Huh? Tonight? Hold on a second, I'm not fully functional. I'll call you back in a few minutes. Like ten or fifteen."

"You're the best! The absolute best. I'm twenty-six and my mother thinks I'm fourteen. You're a lifesaver. Talk to you in a few—I'm coming, Mom—" And with that, the call ended and I stumbled to the bathroom and the coffee maker, in that order.

I'm the best, all right. The best sucker on the planet.

Belinda Kuentz, a client manager for a major bank on the Upper East Side, hadn't had much luck securing a rental in her price range. Heck, who did in Manhattan? Or Brooklyn, for that matter. She was stuck living with her parents until she could find a few roommates to make a permanent move feasible. That's where I came in. I sublet my apartment to Belinda a little over a year ago so I could babysit my family's winery in Penn Yan, New York, while my sister and her entomologist husband tracked down elusive, and most likely disgusting, insects in Costa Rica and Madagascar. I thought I was done with the favor, but apparently not.

With a quick rinse-off in the shower and half a cup of McCafé down my throat, I grabbed my cell phone and tapped Belinda's number.

She answered immediately. "I didn't even think about the time. I'm sorry if I woke you, especially on a Sunday, but when I saw your text, it was like Lewis and Clark discovering the Pacific Ocean."

"Um, I wouldn't go quite that far. Listen, Belinda, I want to be sure you understood what I wrote. It's only for a month. Maybe six weeks. This time my sister and brother-in-law will be on some godforsaken island in Central Visayas. That's the Philippines." *I know because I had to look it up when Francine told me.* "Someone had nothing better to do than to spot what they believed was a new species of the short-horned grasshopper. Now Cornell University's Experiment Station is all over it and are financing the study. My sister swore it will only be for a month but I'm giving it six weeks knowing her and her husband. Six weeks is a relatively short time. I'm not sure if it's even worth it on your part."

"Oh, it's worth it, all right. Besides, I never got the chance to polish the knobs on your kitchen cabinets. It's been plaguing me."

To say that Belinda left my apartment in good shape would have been an understatement. The woman was absolutely obsessive about cleaning. When I returned home, following my year in exile, as I prefer to call it, open heart surgery could have been performed on my kitchen floor. That's how fastidious Belinda was. Then again, I gave her a spanking good deal on the rent. All she had to cough up was a portion of the taxes, half the association fee, and her utilities. A steal by Manhattan standards.

"I'll be leaving in a week, so anytime you want to drop over and pick up the key would be fine. I've got some screenplay revisions due in four days so you'll know where to find me."

"I'll come by after work today. Oh my gosh, Norrie, I can't begin to thank you. I need a break from my folks. All my mother does when she's not nagging is drop hints that I need to meet someone and get married. As if I had a 'Sell By' date stamped on my forehead."

"Yeesh. That does sound bad. Okay, then. Catch you later."

I shuddered at the thought of having to live with my parents, even though they weren't the nagging type. They purchased Two Witches Winery on Two Witches Hill on Seneca Lake in Penn Yan, New York, before Francine and I were born. For the next few decades, they cultivated a variety of grapes and produced award-winning wines. When they retired to Myrtle Beach in South Carolina, they bestowed the winery on us. About the same time my great-aunt Tessie left us her fully owned and paid-for apartment on the outskirts of Little Italy in Manhattan.

It was serendipitous really. As a burgeoning twentysomething screenwriter, New York City was the ultimate destination, and having my own place was a prize beyond belief. Besides, Francine was meant to run the winery, not me. She was the one who knew all the ins and outs from following the vineyard guys around as a kid and later working in the production lab when she was in high school.

As for me, my time was spent reading, daydreaming, and writing short stories that eventually morphed into screenplays. I lucked out by getting a contract with a Canadian film company and many of my romances and mysteries can be seen on the Hallmark Channel if you manage to stay up late.

When Francine twisted my arm about overseeing the winery for a year, mainly because I was the silent partner, I couldn't turn her down. But honestly, I thought I was done with all of that when she and Jason returned in July. Ha! I should have known better. Some men are lured by sexy women, but not my brother-in-law. Dangle an atrocious insect in front of him and he's in seventh heaven. Funny part is, who knew Francine shared the same passion.

Belinda's call, and subsequent visit to get the key, was four days ago. Since then, I had gotten most of my packing done and double-checked my flight status from JKF to Rochester, New York. So far, so good. A nine-nineteen a.m. departure and a one-hour, twenty-one-minute flight. I decided to Uber it to the airport since Francine told me the cost was covered under Miscellaneous Expenses from the grant. However, that didn't mean flying first class.

She and Jason were going to pick me up at the airport because Bradley, the hunky lawyer I'd been dating long-distance, had to be in Buffalo for some sort of complicated family trust situation that his boss dropped on him. He swore he'd be done by the following Wednesday and I planned to hold him to his word.

I hadn't seen Francine or Jason since July when they returned from Madagascar so I looked forward to catching up on the drive back to Penn Yan. Too bad that didn't happen. A few days before my flight Francine called.

"Norrie, I'm so sorry to drop this on you but—"

"Oh, hell no! Do not tell me your one month to six weeks tops is now six months!"

"No, no, nothing like that. It's just that we got word from Jason's department head that we'll need to confer with a few entomologists on Maui before we get to the Philippines."

"Maui? Like in Maui, Hawaii? *That* Maui?"

"Uh-huh. Seems they're having a situation with flying cockroaches. Not enough geckos to eat them, I suppose. Anyway, since Jason did a related study on the hissing ones in Madagascar, they wanted to pick his brain on this situation."

I'll like to pick the nearest can of Raid and take care of the whole thing.

I kept still and let my sister keep talking. "Anyway, we need to fly out tomorrow. Cammy will take care of Charlie during the day until you get here. True, it's not in her usual line of duty as the tasting room manager, but she offered to help us out. She'll probably spoil that Plott hound more than you did. Not to worry. We've got the fence locked, so he can get in and out of his doggie door but he won't wander off. Oh, and don't worry about picking up after him. The vineyard guys will do it."

"Maui, huh?" For some reason, I was fixated on Hawaii.

"It's not as if we'll be sunning ourselves on the beach. It's a work thing."

Some work.

"Okay. Okay. I'll book an airport shuttle to Penn Yan."

"Wait. You don't have to do that. It's all been arranged. Godfrey Klein's going to pick you up. Theo and Don from the Grey Egret Winery next door wanted to but it's a Sunday and they'll be swamped in the tasting room. Anyway, when Jason told Godfrey about the change in plans, he offered to get you. Said he couldn't wait to catch up. Wants to tell you about his latest study on nematodes."

"Nemo what? Never mind. I'll get an earful from Godfrey. Um, he didn't happen to mention anything about me, did he?"

"Godfrey? Like what?"

Like me giving him a kiss on the lips that came out of nowhere.

"Never mind. I sort of involved him in a few wild-goose chases to catch killers."

"Oh, *that.* He did tell Jason that since you left, his blood pressure returned to normal and his sleep patterns improved."

"Good to know." *I will never do anything on impulse again.*

"Funny, but Theo and Don mentioned the same thing, although Theo said things were a bit boring with you back in the city. Good heavens, Norrie. What did you rope everyone into? I mean, I knew about those murders but I thought the Yates County Sheriff's Office dealt with them."

"Oh, Deputy Hickman dealt with them, all right, but things sort of landed at my feet and I had to shuffle them along."

"I don't even want to know what that means. Listen, we'll only be gone a month, give or take a week or two. Not enough time for any trouble to brew, even if Halloween is on the horizon. Which reminds me, the Seneca Lake wineries will be hosting a Hallow Wine Weekend. I'll let Cammy give you all the details. It's a new thing and should be lots of fun."

"I'm holding you to it."

"Oh criminy, with all the packing, prepping and last-minute change of plans, I almost forgot to tell you something. A very strange woman stopped by last evening and dropped off some sage sticks for you. She's a friend of Glenda's from the tasting room so that might explain it. I left the sage sticks on the counter next to the flour canister. The woman said you'd know what to do with them. When Jason answered the door, he thought it was the Grim Reaper."

"Nope. Only Zenora. Formerly Mabel Ann. She's a research librarian at Cornell. Even has her own office." *In the depths of the basement, but that's beside the point.* "Did she say anything else?"

"She told Jason the veil between the two worlds thins out in October and that you'd understand. Frankly, it gave him the willies."

Good thing he hasn't seen any of her rituals.

"Yeah, well, she and Glenda are kind of into a lot of that spiritual stuff."

"Wow. What else did I miss in the past year? Never mind. My brain wouldn't be able to process it right now. I like grounding myself in the here and now. That's why I like canning and freezing. It's very satisfying."

"Does that mean you made more jellies and jams to replenish the supply in the basement?"

"Uh-huh. And some casseroles, too. Mainly spinach and broccoli. Look for them in the freezer."

Only if the magnetic field surrounding the earth shifts.

I muttered something unintelligible and hoped she didn't hear me. Maybe Francine was a health food nut, but I was more of a pizza, hamburger, and nacho gal. Then I cleared my throat and spoke in a normal voice. "You'd better be back before Thanksgiving. I don't care if those grasshoppers devour a continent."

"Just keep out of trouble. And thank you, Norrie. We'll call you from Hawaii."

Hawaii. She'll call me from Hawaii. And the high point of my week will be figuring out what Zenora is so worried about.

Chapter 2

The crisp blue sky that had framed the Manhattan skyline had turned ugly and gray by the time my plane landed in Rochester a few days later. It was now late October, and as I looked around the airport, I noticed everyone was wearing heavy sweatshirts or fleece jackets. The jeans were standard.

Rochester. Ugh. A far cry from Maui.

The day before, Francine had called me from Hawaii insisting she wasn't going to have any beach time. We'll see . . . Anyway, it seemed she remembered something else. A writer from *Wine Enthusiast* was supposed to arrive this week to interview our winemaker, Franz Johannas, as well as the winemakers from the Grey Egret and Gable Hill Winery, regarding our Merlots. Apparently they were quite spectacular this year.

"Whatever you do, Norrie, don't say anything if you're asked about the wine. Let Franz do all the talking. In fact, steer clear altogether."

Anyone else might have been insulted, but I wasn't. Unlike Francine, my knowledge about winemaking was akin to a Jackson Pollock painting—little splotches of information that may or may not connect. I knew when to keep mum.

I left the baggage pickup area and walked outside, resigned to murky skies for the next few days. One thing about the Finger Lakes— rotten weather lingers. To make matters worse, a cold drizzle began to fall and my heavy windbreaker was stuffed somewhere in one of my two suitcases.

It was easy to spot Godfrey's car since he was behind the wheel of a New York State official vehicle that he undoubtedly borrowed from the Experiment Station. He was waiting at the curb and got out the second he saw me.

"Before you say a word, my car is in the shop. They had to order a special part for the alternator."

"I wasn't going to say anything. Well, more or less."

He gave me a hug and reached for the bags. "It's good to see you. Looks like you decided to let your hair grow longer."

"Not exactly. My beautician fell off her Peloton machine and broke a wrist."

"Ouch."

"What did I miss?" I asked as soon as Godfrey pulled away from the curb. "All I got from Francine was an update on her canning."

Godfrey gave me a quick look, then focused on the road ahead. "I hardly know where to begin. Hmm, Alex Bollinger's study on the swede midge was published in *Entomology Today* under research news and the *Entomologist's Monthly* magazine."

"There's a monthly magazine? Who would have thought?"

"Apparently Pemberly Books. And by the way, that magazine's been around for over a hundred and fifty years. Not like *People* or the tabloids."

"I'm sure that's a great honor for Alex, but insect studies don't exactly attract people's attention at checkout lines. Not like gossip from the Royal Family or the latest Hollywood scandal."

"Don't tell that to Arvin Pincus. His research project on spider mites attracted quite a bit of international attention."

"Um, not to sound uninterested in what the entomologists in your office have been up to, but I was thinking more along the lines of what's been going on around the wine trail."

Godfrey moved into the E-ZPass entrance for the thruway and breezed onto the highway. "I'm afraid my perspective is limited to vineyard pests and that sort of thing. So far, nothing extraordinary. But on a personal note, my studies on the nematodes paid off. You'd know them better by their common name: meal worms. Anyway, I secured an amazing grant from a major manufacturer of kitty litter."

"Kitty litter? You lost me."

"While most varieties rely on clay and chemicals, there are a few natural brands that only use ground corn or wheat. The problem is, those brands sometimes wind up with unwanted guests in the litter:

weevils, meal worms, gnats . . . all sorts of pantry pests. Manufacturing companies want to find a way to eliminate or reduce those infestations. That's where my studies come in. The makeup of the packaging can address it, provided it's nothing toxic."

"I see." I glanced out the window at the dreary autumn leaves, now in shades of brown and dark yellow. The fabulous fall foliage that splashed a color wheel around the Finger Lakes had retreated into a darker version of itself. No wonder the wineries went nuts between Halloween and Christmas to offer up their own eye-catching decorations. Hey, we had to keep the tourists here no matter the season.

Godfrey was still going on and on but somehow the subject changed to lepidoptera. I nodded as if I knew what the heck he was talking about and broke in. "I don't know about you, but I'm starving. I haven't had anything to eat since this morning and that was a leftover bagel without the cream cheese."

"Rats! I can't believe I didn't ask if you were hungry. I don't know what's the matter with me. Look, we're almost at the Canandaigua exit. There's a Panera Bread Company not too far off the road. What do you say?"

"Go for it before I chew my arm off."

One grilled cheese and a salad later, I began to feel human.

"The meal's on me," Godfrey said when the waiter arrived with our bill. "It's the least I can do for being so inconsiderate."

"Inconsiderate? You're like the most considerate person I know. Tell you what, let's do pizza this week and it'll be my turn."

"Deal."

In the few months since I'd been away, Godfrey hadn't changed a bit. Not that I expected him to. Thirtysomething, short, receding hairline, wispy brown hair, slightly round face, and an adorable charm I couldn't quite put my finger on. Cammy said it was most likely pheromones but that's almost as bad as believing in Zenora's otherworldly nonsense.

At this juncture in time, I was glad he and I were friends. Last thing I needed was drama in my life. I had enough of it writing my screenplays.

As Godfrey drove up the road/driveway to the old family farmhouse, I glanced at the winery to my right. The parking lot was packed and it looked as if there was a larger than usual crowd near Alvin's pen.

I squinted to get a better look. "Must be that goat is entertaining the guests. The only entertaining thing he does when he's near me is spit."

"I've never had a problem with him. He likes to be petted and loves ear rubs. Maybe it's a perfume or something you wear that he doesn't like."

"Nope. It's me. I've been around him perfume-less, sweaty, and freshly showered. He spat every time. Still, Francine and Jason think having a Nigerian dwarf goat is good for a family-centered business."

Godfrey cast a look to the right as well. "It's not Alvin. Some sort of display, but I can't see what it is."

"Probably a promotion for Hallow Wine Weekend. It's a new thing. I'll check it out later. Right now all I want to do is kick off my shoes and unpack the essentials. Then I'll mosey over there."

Godfrey insisted on carrying my bags into the house and was rewarded by Charlie, who gave him slimy kisses, but only after he jumped all over me with his wet, slobbering tongue.

"I missed you, too, boy," I said. "Enough to let you have most of the bed tonight."

Godfrey walked toward the front door and paused. "I've got to get going. I've got a few things to catch up on before I call it a day."

"But it's a Sunday."

"Shh. Don't tell the nematodes that."

I gave him another hug and thanked him again. "Pizza. Don't forget. I'll call or text."

"I'm holding you to it."

• • •

I was sure Cammy had fed Charlie, but to be on the safe side I gave him a cup of kibble before carting my bags upstairs and unpacking a few things. The room looked the same as it did when I last occupied it in July. Country-pleasant guest room with hints of its former teenage occupant. If it had been a hotel, I would have paid a premium for the lake view that allowed me to take in the far shore of Geneva and the rolling hills on the other side of Seneca Lake. Even under the dreariest conditions, it was breathtaking.

With my sweatshirts stashed in a dresser and my jeans hung on hangers in the closet, I was pretty well set. I grabbed the smaller bag with my toiletries and started for the bathroom when my phone vibrated with a text from Theo: *Join us 4 dinner tonight at 7:30. Charlie 2. Braised pork & mashed potatoes. 2 scared 2 guess what Francine left U.*

I texted back *With bells on* and added a smiley emoji.

"Tomorrow I'll make a Wegmans run," I said to the dog, "so we'll have some decent food around here. Thank heavens Theo and Don saved me from fruits, nuts, and beans. For now, you're still stuck with kibble and those dry organic biscuits. I'm too pooped to go shopping tonight."

It was four fifty-five according to my cell phone and the tasting room doors would close in five minutes. The winery, however, would remain open for another half hour for customers to make purchases while the staff began the cleanup process. At least it would remain daylight for another eighty or ninety minutes. I couldn't put it off much longer. I had to get over there and say hello. Besides, I was curious as all get-up-and-go as to what kind of display would cause so much interest. I doubted it was the usual pumpkins and cornucopia.

"Back in a bit, Charlie," I said. I gave the dog a pat on the head and rubbed his ears for good measure. Then I looked out the window again and swore I saw a body draped over a cauldron.

Chapter 3

As I approached the winery, my strides got longer and I was almost at a full run. A handful of people blocked the view of what I hoped wasn't another dead body. I'd seen my fair share of them since I was first cajoled into babysitting the place. Lots of chatter, but I couldn't make out what they were saying until I weaseled my way toward the front of the group.

"I've never seen papier-mâché done so realistically," a woman said. "From a distance, it looks like a corpse instead of a witch."

"Two corpses, actually," her friend replied. "Or should I say 'two witches'?"

They both laughed and trotted off as I vied for space amid three or four older adults and a handful of children. Sure enough, a large-size cauldron, the likes of which I've never seen, stood against Alvin's pen. An artificial LED fire-flame light was positioned inside the huge black kettle, which upon close inspection wasn't made of papier-mâché but, rather, fashioned out of what appeared to be lightweight metal spray-painted black.

A sign in front of the cauldron read *Join Two Witches Winery for Hallow Wine Weekend* and noted the dates for the last weekend in October. Six days from now, to be specific. If the display was any indication of the event to follow, I figured it would be a humdinger.

Relieved I didn't have to call the Yates County Sheriff's Office, I scampered up the steps to the tasting room. Lizzie, who had a few people on line at the cash register/computer, shoved her wire-rimmed glasses farther up her nose and waved. It looked as if she'd gotten a recent haircut. Either that, or a new product to keep her tight gray curls in place.

I waved back and proceeded to the tasting room, where Glenda and Sam were wiping down tables. "I'm back!" I shouted and rushed over to greet them. Both of them were sporting orange Two Witches–themed T-shirts that read *Stir Up the Hallow Wine Magic*.

"Norrie!" Glenda exclaimed. "We've missed you. How long are you staying? Please tell me it's at least until the new year. Your sister wasn't too specific and Zenora couldn't conjure up a vision."

The new year? I'll rent a boat and throw myself into the lake. Hmm, maybe I'll even take Zenora with me.

"Um, only for a month. Maybe six weeks if Francine and Jason can't find that stupid short-horned grasshopper right away."

"How'd you like the display out front?" Sam asked. "I borrowed the cauldron from the prop department at my college. I've got an in with the prop mistress. And no, I'm not dating her. She prefers older men."

"TMI, Sam, but the display is amazing. Very lifelike."

Sam ran his fingers through his wavy red hair. "I can't take credit for the papier-mâché figures or the lighting. Emma and Fred worked on that when they weren't making food in the bistro."

"Wow. I knew they were incredible chefs but I had no idea they were so artistically talented." I turned and faced the bistro, where the young couple were fast at work tidying up. "I'll give them a shout-out in a bit. Where's Cammy?"

Glenda pointed to the kitchen. "Where else? We had tons of customers and she's been going nonstop with the dishwasher. FYI, Roger's all pumped up about some lecture he's going to give at Hobart and William Smith Colleges on the French and Indian War. Thought we should warn you before he shows up to work tomorrow."

Roger, a retired educator, did his thesis on the French and Indian War and never let go. If he could transport himself back to the Ohio River Valley in the mid-1700s, he'd do it in a heartbeat.

"Um, thanks for the warning. I'd better hightail it into the kitchen and say hi to Cammy. I'll see you guys tomorrow morning."

"Morning as in when we open or morning as in when it's lunchtime?" Sam laughed.

"Ugh. You know me too well." With that, I walked directly to the kitchen and announced myself. Cammy all but dropped a tray of freshly washed wineglasses.

"Goodness, I wasn't expecting you until tomorrow." She rushed over and gave me a giant hug, all but taking the breath out of me. Her thick brunette hair was still in its usual bun, this time with a bright orange ribbon around it. "Boy, it hasn't been the same without you."

"Less excitement?"

"Well, less drama for sure. Although Glenda and Zenora have been muttering all month about unsteady energy and a slowly widening chasm between this world and the next as Halloween gets closer. Yeesh. Just what we need."

Glenda was our resident spiritualist and Zenora, well, the verdict's still not in. I was positive she belonged to some sort of coven on the lake but haven't been able to pin her down. Like Glenda, she's a kind soul who means well even if her purification and cleansing practices scare the daylights out of most rational people.

"Yeah, speaking of Halloween, Francine mentioned a new publicity thing: A Hallow Wine Weekend. She said you'd give me the details. I think I saw the first two by Alvin's pen."

"The cauldron and witches. Something else, huh? Believe it or not, Sam got the idea for it and Emma and Fred jumped in. All of the wineries on the Seneca Lake Wine Trail agreed to have eye-catching displays to tout the event."

"Is it like Deck the Halls Around the Lake or Wine and Cheese?"

"More like Little Mary Sunshine meets the Grim Reaper with a case of wine."

"Huh?"

"All of the participating wineries will take part in a Halloween costume contest. Customers who dress up will register and have their photos taken at one winery of their choice. Otherwise it gets too complicated. Then, that winery reviews the photos and selects the winner for a free case of wine."

"That sounds simple enough."

"That's just the start. Customers can buy tickets for Halloween treat food samplings at all of the wineries. Spooky finger food, to be exact. We're making chocolate-filled mummies that are essentially crescent rolls shaped like mummies with marshmallows for eyes that stick out of the chocolate. It should pair nicely with the red wines."

"Seems pretty benign."

"That's because I haven't gotten to the good part. Some nincompoop on the wine trail came up with the idea of a ghost story gathering at each of our wineries at dusk. Most of us have bonfires anyway so that won't be a problem, and people love the idea of sitting around a campfire. They just need to wear warm clothing. Finding a storyteller is another issue. Roger volunteered but we were scared to death he'd segue into the French and Indian War."

"So who did you wind up with?"

Cammy looked at me and didn't say a word.

"Oh, no. Not me. I'm not an actor."

"But you write screenplays."

"Romance mainly. Not horror."

"Norrie, our options are running out. It's only a few days away."

At that moment I felt like running out and catching the first flight back to Manhattan, but I couldn't do that to Belinda. Or the winery.

"Fine. I'll get my hands on some decent ghost stories that aren't hackneyed." *Or find someone I could convince to take my place.*

"I knew we could count on you." Cammy gave me another hug that pretty much engulfed me.

"I'll be here in the morning. Meanwhile, I'd better say hi to Emma and Fred before they leave for the day. Wow, those papier-mâché witches could've fooled me."

"Lizzie almost had a heart attack when they first went up. All but dialed nine-one-one."

I tried not to laugh. "At least it was only papier-mâché. See you tomorrow."

. . .

"I'm back, Alvin," I said as I walked past his pen. He snorted from the far side of the structure and dug a foot into the hay on the ground. No use trying. This was as close to sociable as it would get for us.

The cold drizzle that welcomed Godfrey and me at the airport finally let up, only to be replaced by an even colder wind as I hurried back to the house. At least I had located my windbreaker as well as Francine's closet full of seasonal coats, wraps, and parkas when I got inside. I doubted she would have had any use for them in the humid tropics of the Philippines.

Exhausted from starting my day at an unreasonably early hour, I sprawled out on the couch and channel surfed. I wasn't expected at Theo and Don's for another hour and forty minutes and was too tired to do anything else. Sometime between the six o'clock news and *Jeopardy!* I dozed off.

When I pried my eyes open, it was twilight. I'm not sure why, but I chose to trek down the hill to Theo and Don's rather than start up Francine's Subaru. And for some odd reason, I decided to take a closer look at the Halloween tableau that now beckoned visitors to our winery.

The faux flames were still going strong and I swore they carried the scent of crisp, burning leaves. As I got closer, I realized one of the figures was missing. The witch that was bent over the cauldron was no longer there and I wondered if it had inadvertently fallen into the pot. The thought that someone could have stolen it was disturbing, to say the least. But not as disturbing as what happened next.

I peered over the cauldron, and in that instant an arm reached out, grabbed my wrist and yanked with enough force for me to fall forward until my fingers splashed in a sticky gooey liquid that had somehow replaced the LED lighting in the cauldron.

"What the heck?" I tried shaking my hand, but whatever gooey substance it was trapped in had now made its way farther up my arm, and whatever force pulled me wasn't about to let go. I shook, I cursed, and I thrashed about until I slid from the couch onto the floor of the living room, landing unceremoniously on my rump.

The remote was also on the floor, a few feet from me, along with Charlie, who gave my hand a few more licks. *So that explains the gooey substance. Yuck.*

I got up, snatched the remote and clicked to the Weather Channel for the time. Seven ten. Whoever said catnaps were restful and restorative had to have his or her head examined. My vivid sojourn into dreamland was nerve-piercing and downright scary. I hadn't had a nightmare like that since grade school.

"It's the exhaustion," I said to Charlie, giving his head a good rub. "I'd better wash up and get over to Theo and Don's. Once I've had a good night's sleep, everything will be back to normal. Only, it wasn't. Which might have explained why Zenora dropped off those sage sticks.

Chapter 4

"We're taking the Subaru," I announced. More for my own sake than Charlie's. I once watched an episode of *The Twilight Zone* where someone had a hideous dream and it came true the next day. No sense taking chances.

The dog jumped into the passenger seat and proceeded to lick his paws as I started up the familiar engine. Francine and Jason had insisted I use their car last winter because it had four-wheel drive and a set of new snow tires that Walden's Garage was more than glad to put on. And while my trusty Toyota plodded along, it was no match for their newer vehicle. Now I was back behind the wheel of an old friend.

First the murky drizzle, then the cold wind, and now what? Snowflakes? Not particularly surprising in late October but annoying and out of place until Thanksgiving in my book. I pulled in front of Theo and Don's house and let the dog out of the car. He immediately scampered up the steps to their front porch/deck and sat in front of the door.

Like the Grey Egret, the house had that woodsy lodge feel going for it. The wraparound front, side, and rear deck added to the charm. It was "needed space," according to Theo, as it had to contain Don's grill, smoker, and spare grill, "just in case."

A quick rap on the door and the three of us were all hugs. Meanwhile, Charlie sauntered past us and plopped himself down on a throw rug near their fireplace while Isolde, their Norwegian forest cat, looked down at him from her perch on a new cat tree.

"Oh my gosh, that braised pork smells incredible," I said to Don. "I don't know how you do it."

Theo gave him a nudge. "He has a very talented sous chef. Come on, we can talk and eat at the same time. I'm starving."

Five or six forkfuls into the meal and we began to converse in full sentences rather than sounds or one-word exclamations.

I took a second helping of the mashed potatoes and plunked it on my plate. "Looks like the wineries are going all out with Hallow Wine Weekend. Cammy told me about the events. By the way, I need to check out your display. Ours literally gave me a night fright. I fell asleep on the couch around six and dreamt one of the witches' hands pulled me into that cauldron."

"That comes from being overtired," Don said. "My nightmares usually consist of unpaid bills or plumbing disasters. Anyway, I doubt our display will send shivers up anyone's spine. It's a huge papier-mâché pumpkin with two felted grey egrets standing on top of it and holding a banner from their bills that reads *Join the Hallow Wine Fun!* Theo's mother got someone in her senior retirement community to make the birds in their sewing and felting shop."

I swallowed another mouthful of the potatoes. "What about the pumpkin? Who did that?"

"Believe it or not, the art teacher from the school the Ipswich twins attend. Stephanie mentioned how that lady was designing their display and we asked if she would take on another project. Apparently, ours wasn't too complicated so she agreed in exchange for some of our wines."

"I guess those deadly Winery of the West meetings pay off after all or we never would have known about that," Theo said.

"Oh, no. I forgot all about those meetings. Please don't tell me we've got one this week."

The guys looked at each other and held back from laughing. "Thursday, as usual," Don chirped. "It's going to be at the Ipswiches' winery this time since Madeline is getting the floor in her patio room redone. Lucky for me it's Theo's turn. I got stuck at the last one listening to Rosalee complain about how the changes in barometric pressure were wreaking havoc on her joints."

Theo reached under the table and gave Charlie a tiny piece of the pork. "Yeah, well, I had to listen to her dissertation on hemorrhoidal creams versus ointments the meeting before that. It's an image I still can't get out of my head."

I chuckled. "Rosalee's got to be in her eighties. Those are hot topics for her."

Rosalee Marbleton was one of the vineyard owners who comprised our small group of six neighboring wineries. The group was started years ago as the West Side Women of the Wineries who wanted to offer each other support in a business that was a combination of farming, chemistry, and sales. When Theo and Don purchased the Grey Egret, the group was renamed the Wineries of the West so it could keep its acronym—WOW.

My sister and Stephanie were the youngest members with middle-aged Madeline Martinez and Catherine Trobert filling in the remaining slots. Meetings were usually held at Madeline's Billsburrow Winery so no one would get confused as to where the next meeting was to be held. It was hard enough to keep up with the gossip and rumormongering that took up most of the time. Still, it was an invaluable source of information if one was lucky enough to separate hearsay from fact.

"The Hallow Wine Weekend should go off without a hitch," Theo said. "It's that interview with Donovan Brin that's had our winemakers on edge all week. Lena's afraid one slip of the tongue and some horrible quote will go down in *Wine Enthusiast*, marring our winery for generations, and Julien's not much better. The last time I went inside the winery, the two of them were poring over prior issues of the magazine and groaning."

"Donovan Brin. Why does that name sound familiar?"

"Maybe because his face is plastered everywhere in the city. You probably weren't paying attention. He's the quintessential expert on wines and cultural trends. The guy holds a degree in journalism from Syracuse University and is a certified sommelier with heaven knows how many degrees in viticulture and vinification. He's authored a few books about wines and has appeared on all sorts of talk shows. One recommendation from him and that wine's an instant best seller."

"And if not?"

Don glanced at Theo and shuddered. "We're talking Merlot. Do you have any idea how many years it took for the industry to recoup losses after that 2004 movie *Sideways*? One lousy remark about Merlot and sales plummeted everywhere."

"I wasn't even ten years old in 2004 and you guys weren't much older. Why? Was the Merlot bad in 2004?"

Don shook his head. "Not bad. Just overly abundant. Like weeds. Of course, they were talking California Merlot and our situation is entirely different. This year's vintage is fabulous. Soft and velvety with a richness that stays on the tongue. And all three of the wineries he's featuring have garnered awards for it, which explains Donovan's interest. Still, the interview process can be daunting. Thankfully Lena, Julien, Klaus from Gable Hill and your winemaker, Franz, are slow and deliberate thinkers. They know what it means to choose their words carefully."

No wonder Francine wants me to steer clear of the interview.

"He's *that* intimidating?"

"He's *that* influential."

"Hold on a second." I grabbed my phone and googled Donovan Brin. The photo showed him holding a 3Musketeers bar with one bite missing. "He looks like a mousy fifty-year-old in dire need of a trim. Lots of wild bushy hair around his ears."

Theo laughed. "The mousy fifty-year-old has a net worth that puts all of us to shame."

"And a string of love interests if you believe in those tabloid tales," Don added.

Now my interest was piqued. So much for the nuances of Merlot, I wanted to know more about any and all salacious scandal surrounding Donovan. "Like what? What? And don't look at me like that, I can use that information for one of my screenplays. All I would need to do is give it the family-friendly version. I'm working on a new proposal and can use all the fodder I can get."

Don finished the last bite of the braised pork on his plate and hesitated about another helping. "How about some more pork instead? Or the potatoes? I'm tempted, but I'm more tempted to dive into an apple pie we took out of the freezer and smother it in vanilla ice cream."

"Well," I said, "when you put it that way, I'll help clean up so we can get to the pie sooner. But you still have to tell me what you know about Donovan. And I don't mean his degrees or wine reviews."

"You'll have to talk to Theo if you want the down-and-dirty scuttlebutt. He's the one who's glued to social media."

Theo widened his eyes. "Oh, please. You're as bad following those threads as I am. I'm just more vocal about it."

"Aargh. Will someone just tell me what you know?"

Don stood and grabbed a few dishes. "Fine. Married. Divorced. Remarried. No children. Mistress and girlfriend. Is that enough for Miss Busybody?"

I smiled. "It's a start, but geez, how does he juggle three women? Or is he getting a second divorce?"

"Maybe you can ask him yourself when you meet him this week."

"Very funny. Besides, I promised Francine I wouldn't say a word. Then again, that was about the wine. She didn't mention anything about other topics."

"Stick to Hello and Goodbye. Much safer that way. We want the guy to give our wineries lots of accolades. And put Merlot back where it belongs—on everyone's dinner table."

"Besides," Theo said, "I'm sure Donovan has enough drama going on in his life without having us add to it."

Theo didn't know it at the time, but his offhanded observation was the understatement of the year.

"Do either of you know how long Donovan will be here?"

"At least through the Hallow Wine Weekend," he said. "It was in the *Finger Lakes Times* a few days ago. Donovan will most likely kill two birds with one stone—write about the Merlots and do some sort of a travelogue thing about the wine weekend. The public clamors for those holiday events. Oh, he's staying at Belhurst Castle. Probably one of their suites, but the article didn't say."

"Did the article say if he was bringing the wife, the mistress or the girlfriend?"

"The article didn't, but the WOW rumor mill might have an inkling. You know how Madeline and Catherine can't keep their noses out of anything. Besides, what difference does it make as long as we come out looking pretty good. Just remember—Hello, Goodbye and Nice Meeting You."

"Good grief, Theo, you're worse than Francine."

Don broke out laughing. "Who do you think coached us on the topic?"

Charlie and I returned home with our bellies stuffed. He'd managed to procure little pork tidbits from all three of us, as did Isolde. At least none of us shared the ice cream or pie with those furry four-legged beggars. And while there was a lot to be said about going to sleep on a full stomach, it didn't bode well as far as restful slumber was concerned.

Again, I had the same nightmare about the arm in the cauldron. If it wasn't so darn unnerving, it would have made for a great short story. And while I wasn't about to burn those sage sticks Zenora had dropped off, I did the next best thing—I stuck them under my pillow for the following night.

I told myself I didn't believe in all that hogwash, but what harm could a scented pillow do? Especially if the veil between the two worlds was thinning.

Chapter 5

The next day, I made it a point to let Franz know that he, and his assistant winemakers, would have full reins when it came to speaking with Donovan. At a little past ten, I stopped by his office in the winery and noted the same *Verboten* sign that led directly into the production area. In bright red and black, one would have thought we were dealing with nuclear waste and not award-winning wines.

"Norrie! When did you get in?" Franz asked. He adjusted his horn-rimmed glasses and tossed a wisp of his reddish hair from his forehead. "It's good to see you."

Just then, Alan walked in from the lab and gave me a hug. He was the spitting image of Franz, with one exception—he was a good two feet taller. When seated, people always mistook them. The same couldn't be said for the other assistant winemaker, Herbert, a good-looking Black man who was our intern before we offered him a full-time position as an assistant winemaker. Like his cohorts, he was serious, focused, and professional.

"Yesterday. I'm trying to catch up. Congratulations on the Merlot. Francine, Don, and Theo told me Donovan Brin from *Wine Enthusiast* will be interviewing us. I mean, *you.* Your department. You're the ones who are responsible for this year's fabulous vintage Merlot."

Franz smiled and cleared his throat. "We're only part of the formula. We're not responsible for the soil, the nutrients, the weather, or the root stock. Not to mention the vineyard management. We're the chemists, so to speak. Our role is to oversee the maceration, fermentation, and extraction of color and flavor from the grapes. And, of course, the aging."

Oh, no. Please, not another lecture on fermentation. Or worse yet, maceration. Nothing like listening to someone drone on about the leaching of grape skins into a must. I'll poke my eyes out with the nearest fork.

"Well, whatever it is, I'm sure you'll do a great job with that interview. Um, do you have any idea when it is? Francine didn't say and Theo and Don weren't too sure."

Franz clicked the mouse on his computer and squinted. "It's this Wednesday, but I'd better double-check the time. Give me a second. It's in an email from Mr. Brin's assistant. He listed the complete interview schedule, including the dates and times for the Grey Egret and Gable Hill." He scrolled the mouse for a split second and looked up. "Here it is—eleven thirty. He's interviewing at Gable Hill tomorrow and will be at the Grey Egret on Thursday. According to his note, he intends to go directly to the winery and tasting room first."

Wonderful. That means I get to escort the womanizer over here.

"That's great. Thanks."

"Before I forget, we planned on posting some larger off-limit signs in front of the building today in anticipation of the Halloween Wine Weekend. Some of our visitors think they can traipse all over the place, and with the wines fermenting in the barrels, last thing we need is contamination. It's best to keep the merrymaking in the tasting room and vicinity."

"My sentiments exactly. John sent me an email this morning. They're roping off the rows of grapevines for the same reason and will actually have some of their vineyard workers on patrol during the weekend. Even though the first crushing of the grapes started in mid-August, they're still harvesting. No sense mucking that up. I love these events but they do bring out the loonies."

Alan laughed and I could see a slight smile on Franz's face.

"Well, I'd better get going. Let me know if you need anything. I'm only going to be here for a month. Six weeks tops."

Franz looked at Alan and then back at me. "I hope the grass-hoppers were informed of this as well."

"Trust me. I'll take out a national ad in all of the newspapers in the Philippines if that's what it takes. Six weeks tops!"

With a quick wave, I was out the door and on my way to the main building and tasting room. Although Francine was the poster child for organization, I still dreaded going into the office and booting up the computer. Inevitably I'd find scads of emails that would ultimately translate into to-do lists. At least I didn't have to deal with the winery website. Two Witches hired a web designer to keep it updated and eye-catching, but what I didn't know, until I read the note she taped to the computer monitor, was that she had started a monthly newsletter.

"Oops—One more thing, Norrie. And my apologies for cutting it close. Good news is that it should be right up your alley. We now have a monthly newsletter on Mailchimp. The details are in the folder in the upper right-hand drawer. I usually mail it to recipients the third week of the month. Maybe you could highlight Hallow Wine Weekend or ask John in the vineyard if he'd care to jot down a few thoughts about this year's harvest. Anyway, it doesn't have to be long. Have fun. Love, F."

Cutting it close? That thing needs to be sent out ASAP.

I figured our vineyard manager had enough going on without me adding to his misery. Mailchimp was essentially a cut-and-paste template so I didn't think it would be that hard for me to post a few seasonal photos and encourage our readers to make the trek to the Finger Lakes. With my screenwriting editing done and only a proposal to embellish, I figured I'd bask in a sea of free time. Now, apparently, I'd become the editor of a newsletter. Okay, maybe the featured writer, but still . . .

I sifted through the correspondence on the desk and followed the age-old practice of "toss it" or "file it." In this case, it was mostly toss it. Bradley called about an hour later and sounded awful. He was still stuck in Buffalo with no sign of making it back home until the weekend.

"Hey, at least we can enjoy the madness of Hallow Wine Weekend together," I said. "Plus, you'll get to sit around a bonfire and listen to me read ghost stories to our visitors. It's part of the program."

"Is Zenora going to be there?" I swore there was a nervous edge to his question.

"Not that I'm aware. Besides, it's Halloween weekend. She and Glenda are probably going to attend whatever wacky thing their friends have cooked up."

"Geez, I miss you. And here I thought we'd have all this time together."

"We will. Once the weekend festivities are over, we can make the most of these long autumn nights with nothing to get in our way."

I should never say things like that. It's like tempting the universe to interfere.

When my call with Bradley ended, I moseyed over to the tasting room and asked if anyone needed a break. There was a steady stream of customers but we had more than enough staff to handle it. Of course, that would change toward the end of the week when the city crowds made their way up to the Finger Lakes.

"We've got it covered," Roger called out as he motioned for two couples to join him at his tasting table. "We'll have to catch up later."

I nodded and headed straight over to the bistro, where Fred and Emma were preparing paninis. I hadn't had one of their savory bacon, tomato and avocado sandwiches in months and I was all but salivating when I got there.

"With or without cheese?" Emma smiled.

"Without. Listen, I just found out from Franz that the writer from *Wine Enthusiast* will be here on Wednesday. The interview is for eleven thirty so I'm figuring we'll offer him and his assistant lunch when they get done. Whatever you do, make it spectacular. It's not what I'd call bribery, exactly, but if we can dazzle them with our food, it'll put Donovan in a good mood and that will translate into a favorable article."

Fred walked over and laughed. "Is that a tried-and-true formula?"

"It wouldn't hurt."

Fred winked. "Shall do."

I waited while Emma prepared my panini, then took it back to my office, where I spent the next hour and a half muttering expletives at

Mailchimp before finalizing the "one-more-thing" newsletter from Francine. Satisfied I was done with writing for a while, I scrolled through my own emails and spied one from Renee, my producer in Canada. It was sent a few hours ago so it wasn't as if I'd been sitting on it for days. Something I'd been known to do.

The subject line was innocuous enough but the same couldn't be said for the message. It read, "Forget the beachy romances. Out. Out. Out. We need you to write a mystery romance. Preferably with murder. Quaint village setting. It's what the advertisers are looking for. Everyone's switching gears. How fast can you get it delivered?"

How fast? What station on the crazy train is she at?

So much for "all the time in the world" and my proposal for lustful adventure in the Caribbean. Now it would be more like "Love gets stabbed in the back." The message was too unnerving for me to reply. Instead, I pushed speed dial and waited for Renee to pick up. She was in Toronto this month so we were in the same time zone.

Three rings and Renee answered by announcing her name. I rolled my eyes.

"Renee, it's Norrie. I just got your email. Last month you insisted on beachy romance. If I remember correctly, you even used words like *salty*, *sand*, and *soft waves*. It was an alliteration alphabet soup. What's going on?"

"A change in advertisers, that's what. Keating and Keating Insurance, a *global* company, as they like to remind everyone, is now yanking our chains. You're not the only one shocked beyond belief. Patrice and Pauline Whitstone could hardly form words in their mouths when I spoke with them yesterday. And Dennis Dayton kept muttering, 'What am I supposed to do with the hundred and eight pages I've written?' I was tempted to tell him but I bit my tongue. Anyway, the stable of actors is ready to make the switch. It's now in your hands. Well, all of your hands if Patrice, Pauline, and Dennis can pull it together. We need at least seven movies for next year's lineup."

I took a breath and let it out slowly. "Quaint as in English countryside or quaint as in mountain, lake, or seaside towns?"

"Stick to this side of the pond. And hustle it up. We're already behind schedule."

"I'll do what I can. I'm back to babysitting the winery again. Probably until Thanksgiving."

"Wonderful. It should be very peaceful for you to get some writing done."

Oh, no. Another invitation for the universe to muck things up.

I told myself that with the exception of this weekend's shindig, it should be clear sailing until Deck the Halls Around the Lake in December. And, if that lousy grasshopper was sighted, that event would land on Francine's lap, not mine.

"Um, yeah. Very peaceful."

"Thanks, Norrie, I knew we could count on you."

Take a number and get behind my sister.

Chapter 6

I phoned Stephanie at her house the next morning when I was certain the twins were well into their school day. If Donovan adhered to his schedule, he had already completed the interview at Gable Hill. "Good morning! Sorry to bother you but can you give me the heads-up about Donovan? Is the guy a prima donna or what?"

"Hello to you, too, Norrie. The winemakers are getting interviewed. You're off the hook. Besides, they're the ones conversant with the Merlot."

"They are. This is purely speculative."

"You mean gossipy?"

"I wouldn't go quite that far."

"Okay. I wouldn't call Donovan a prima donna, but he's certainly sure of himself. We only spoke for a few minutes before I passed him along to Klaus. I would have insisted Derek handle things but he had a dental appointment, and since he canceled the last one, I was insistent he go. I don't need us to spring for dental implants because my husband is too lazy for his teeth cleanings."

"Uh-huh. What about Donovan's assistant. He or she?"

"She. Thirtysomething is my guess. Very businesslike. Hardly engaged in conversation. Took a few notes."

"Okay, I'm thinking she's probably not one of his love interests."

"Not you, too? My tasting room staff's been all over the tabloids reading about him."

"Just curious, that's all. I've got to come up with a new plot line for a screenplay. It was going to be romance but now they want murder. In a quaint setting."

"And you need more ideas? After last year? Yeesh."

"What I need is to get back to Manhattan. At least I'll have more time with Bradley while I'm up here. That is, once he gets back from Buffalo. That law firm of his sends him all over."

"What about Godfrey? Anything going on there?"

"Nah. We're friends, that's all. Which reminds me, I was supposed to call him about pizza this week. Anyway, I'll see you on Thursday. Would you like me to bring any cookies or something?"

"Thanks, but we're all set. Check out our display when you get here. It's a hoot!"

"Sure thing."

I phoned Godfrey the minute I got off the phone with Stephanie because I knew if I didn't, I'd forget. We agreed to meet at Uncle Joe's for pizza at seven thirty tomorrow. I'd be able to tell him about Donovan and he, in turn, would most likely tell me about some new insect study or worse yet, a boring ongoing study.

As it turned out, I wasn't wrong. The following evening Godfrey was still fixated about the kitty litter pests and even brought photos to show me. Not exactly the most appetizing thing before diving into a sausage and green pepper pizza, but it was Godfrey, after all, and I was used to it. And I supposed he was used to me babbling on and on about whatever winery thing had me tangled up at the moment.

"For a guy who supposedly has a wife, a mistress, and a girlfriend, I don't see the attraction," I said as I took a second bite of my pizza. "He was straight out of that old Carly Simon song 'You're So Vain,' only he was no Warren Beatty. Not that it's all about looks, mind you, but the guy sort of dismissed everything around him as if he had better things to do."

Godfrey wiped the sides of his mouth with a napkin and took another slice of pizza. "Maybe he had so much on his mind, he was busy processing everything. I do that sometimes."

"You do that *all* the time, only you're nice about it. Anyway, Donovan did say that his panini was rather tasty and that he was looking forward to immersing himself in the culture of our wine trail. The *culture* of our wine trail. Can you imagine? He made it sound like he was observing an indigenous tribe straight out of the Amazon basin."

"It couldn't have been that bad. What was Franz's take on the interview? That's what matters."

"You've met Franz. It was impossible to pry anything out of him. He didn't even mention how Donovan reacted when he tasted the Merlot. If I didn't know any better, I'd say Franz was prior wartime military—name, rank, and serial number."

Godfrey winced. "He must have given you some indication of how it went."

"He used the word *engaging*. Like that's supposed to mean something."

"Did he seem satisfied?"

"We're talking about Franz. He's the ultimate perfectionist and control freak. And since he wasn't the one writing the article, satisfied wouldn't be in his vocabulary. Anyway, he didn't grouse or mutter expressions in German so I figured it was okay. I'll have to get Theo and Don's take tomorrow on their interview. Donovan's supposed to be at the Grey Egret early in the morning so I'll get the details when Theo goes over to Stephanie's for our WOW meeting."

"I thought those meetings were at Madeline's winery."

"They were. I mean, they are. But she's getting her floors redone."

"I see." Godfrey smiled and bit off the tip of his pizza slice.

"Oh, I forgot to mention the assistant. All business. Stephanie gave me the rundown yesterday and she was right. The woman hardly said a word and took copious notes about what, I have no idea because I was on my best behavior to only offer up information on a 'need-to-know' basis."

Godfrey all but choked on his pizza. "I've never known you to hold back on anything."

"Trust me, it's a learning process."

• • •

Maybe it was a full stomach from the pizza or Zenora's sage sticks under my pillow but I got a decent night's sleep and woke up with a higher than usual energy level. I took advantage of it by jotting down thoughts and a rough plot point for the mystery romance Renee insisted I write.

Then it was a quick shower and I was off to Stephanie's winery for our ten thirty WOW meeting. Gable Hill was the next road over, and technically within walking distance if I felt like traipsing past a pond and over a field. I didn't. I drove the Subaru and pulled up near the entrance. That's when I saw the Grim Reaper. Dressed in a long black cloak and hood, that I imagined someone other than Stephanie had sewn, he brandished a large silver scythe and peered out at me from his creepy skeleton skull. Yep, her Hallow Wine Weekend display was a hoot, all right.

The sign beneath him read *Reap the magic of Hallow Wine Weekend at Gable Hill Winery*. I chuckled and headed inside. A petite girl with spiked blond hair directed me to their banquet room, where the WOW meeting was being held. Catherine, Madeline and Theo were already there, plates filled with assorted scones and dried fruit from the credenza behind the large rectangular table.

A moment later, Stephanie wheeled in a tray with coffee, tea, and hot apple cider. Funny, but I never tired of the aroma of nutmeg, cinnamon and apples. "Hey, everyone," she chirped. "Good to see you. Where's Rosalee?"

"Right behind you, if you'd turn around. I nearly had a heart attack when I saw your display. I hope no one's sending me a message. I get a little sensitive at my age."

"No message," Stephanie said and laughed. "Believe it or not, Derek had that old fake skeleton from his college days. Don't ask. All we had to do was tie the arms down and substitute wire so we could have the thing hold the papier-mâché scythe. With the long, black hood no one can tell. We also thought about purchasing a real scythe from MSC Industrial Supplies but worried that some nutcase might get ahold of it and do some serious damage. You know how some of our guests can get. Especially if they've had one too many tastings around the lake."

A series of groans followed as we helped ourselves to the hot beverages. Madeline proceeded to conduct the meeting as usual with old business about the Deck the Halls Around the Lake event and a review of this weekend's festivities.

"How did the interview go?" I mouthed to Theo.

"What?" He shrugged.

I mouthed my words again, only this time I exaggerated them.

"Oh, for heaven's sake," Rosalee said. "Norrie wants to know how the interview went at Theo's. What interview? What did I miss? Frankly, I'm sick of these emails. I just wish someone would put everything in a letter and mail it to me."

Catherine, who was seated next to her, patted Rosalee's arm. "I'm afraid those days are gone. Soon they'll come up with something else and we'll all complain that we miss the emails."

Theo leaned across the table and looked at Rosalee. "Our winemakers had that interview with *Wine Enthusiast* this morning. Lena said she and Julien were able to bounce off of each other so it moved along. Said Donovan was pretty much what she expected but she was convinced his assistant gave her the evil eye."

Stephanie took a sip of coffee and held on to her mug. "I thought it was my imagination but I swore she gave me a cold stare that would put the Ice Queen to shame. At least she's not the one writing the article. Or taking photos, for that matter. Donovan mentioned a photographer from the magazine arriving this weekend to take a number of shots. If we're lucky, one or two of them will feature our wineries. Usually those magazines stick with vineyards and lakes."

"Will they send all of you a preview copy?" Catherine asked.

Theo shook his head. "Doubt it. We'll see it when everyone else does. According to Donovan, it will be in the December issue. Along with 'the cultural backdrop to our success.' His words, not mine. I suppose it'll be up to the editors when they match the text with the photos. Gee, I wish I knew when this weekend that photographer will make his or her rounds."

I bit into a walnut and cranberry scone and followed it with a large sip of coffee. "It won't matter. Last time a magazine sent a photographer, it was *Finger Lakes Life* and all they wanted were close-ups of the grapes. What a snoozer."

"I wouldn't worry about the photos," Stephanie said. "It's what Donovan says about our Merlot that matters."

"I just want to get the weekend over with, even if Donovan decides to take a bath in our giant cauldron."

"Party pooper." Theo laughed.

"More like stressed-out screenwriter who has to come up with a mystery before she gets the axe." Then I looked at everyone seated at the table. "The production company I write for has a new advertiser who wants them to produce mystery romance in quaint settings. Caribbean seaside romance is out."

"I'm sure you'll think of something, Norrie," Madeline said. "Meanwhile, we need to get back to our agenda."

I must have zoned out for the rest of the meeting because, before I knew it, Theo kicked my ankle and I jumped to attention. "Well, this has been fun, everyone. Have a great weekend."

As I stood to leave, Catherine grabbed my wrist. "Please tell me you'll be here for Christmas. Steven is definitely planning to spend the holidays with us and you'll finally get to see each other."

Yeesh, talk about a Halloween nightmare. Poor Catherine had been trying to fix me up with her lawyer son for months. Steven was in Francine's class and hardly knew I existed. It was just as well. I already had a boyfriend, and unlike Donovan, didn't need to add to the collection.

"Oh, Francine and Jason will be home way before Christmas. *Way* before."

The second *way* was more for my sake than hers. I'd only been back four days and I was already roped in to telling ghost stories for the wine weekend. Unfortunately, I had no idea one of them would come to fruition.

Chapter 7

At first I thought the sound was from a car backfiring on the street, but when I heard it again in rapid succession, I realized it was a cannon going off in the vineyard to keep unwanted birds from devouring the last of our grapes to be harvested.

I rolled over in my bed and glanced at the digital clock—7:39 a.m. An ungodly hour to get up, even if the sun had started to rise. And while I knew the vineyard workers were already on the job, I wasn't. That is, until the landline rang a few minutes later.

"Norrie, it's John."

Halloween Wine Weekend hadn't yet started since it was Friday morning at the crack of dawn. Literally. I figured he couldn't be calling to tell me visitors had managed to trample through the vineyards, but it was quite possible Alvin had gotten out of his pen and John wanted to alert me.

"Did Alvin escape?" I asked. My voice was raspy and I cleared my throat.

"No, Alvin's fine. Listen, about your display with the two witches and the cauldron—"

"Don't tell me someone stole one of the witches. Take a good look. Maybe one of them fell down. Do you see two figures in front of the cauldron?"

"That's why I called. There are three figures. Two standing and one leaning into the cauldron."

"Aargh. The weekend didn't even start yet and you're calling to tell me there's an inebriated person in there?"

"I wouldn't call it inebriated. More like dead. There's a dead person in the cauldron and I've already phoned the sheriff's office."

Nothing like the words *dead person* to snap someone wide awake without a cup of coffee. John continued to talk but all I processed was "dead body."

"Like I was saying, Travis went up to Alvin's pen to add some hay and grain and that's when he noticed the body. It was leaning over the cauldron. At first he thought it was part of the display but then he remembered there were only two witches, not three."

"Not again. Not another dead person. Please tell me you think it was a heart attack or something."

"Or something. Impossible not to notice the dagger shoved into the man's back. Definitely a male victim."

"What man? Who?"

"I have no idea. And do not ask me to check his pockets for an ID. I heard you and Theo did that when you found that body in the woods a few months ago. Besides, the sheriff's office has a deputy on the way. I phoned them before I called you."

"They didn't happen to mention which deputy, did they? Never mind. I can guess. Grizzly Gary will be marching over here like a stormtrooper. Oh my gosh, I'd better throw on some clothes and get over there. Is there much of a scene?"

"Only Travis and me. And Alvin. I had Travis give him some extra hay to keep him occupied. That goat tends to paw his front legs like a bull when he's stressed."

"Okay. I'll be there right away."

"Hey, one more thing. Whoever did this covered their tracks."

"What do you mean?"

"I had Travis check the security cameras around the building entrance and Alvin's pen. Someone sprayed them with what looks like shaving cream. So much for identifying who was responsible. And no strange vehicle on the premises either. Too bad we didn't have a dusting of snow. The sheriff's office could have photo'd the tire tracks. Our unknown assailant planned it."

"You can say *killer*. Even if it takes the Yates County Sheriff's Office a few days to make an official determination. A knife in the back is pretty intentional as far as I'm concerned."

"A dagger. It's a dagger."

"What's the difference?" I asked.

"Daggers have points for stabbing, knives have edges for cutting. And knives don't have handles or cross guards. And before you ask, I've been to the Renaissance Festival on more than one occasion."

"Do you hear that? I can hear it from here. It's a siren. I'm on my way."

I raced to brush my teeth, splash water on my face and throw on a heavy sweatshirt and jeans, pausing only to feed Charlie and make sure he had water. I opened the front door with the intent of jogging down the hill when something occurred to me.

"Two more minutes aren't going to make a big difference," I said to the dog as I grabbed my cell phone and selected Cammy's number from my list of contacts.

If I thought I was groggy at the crack of dawn, Cammy was worse. "Who is this? Who died?"

"It's Norrie. Listen, can you get in early and make a new sign for our front display?"

"Huh? Someone ripped off our sign?"

"Not exactly. But we need one that reads *It's a crime to miss Hallow Wine Weekend.*'"

"It's not even eight. What's wrong with the one we have?"

"We're going to need one that explains why there's yellow crime scene tape all around the cauldron and the witches."

"Yellow crime scene tape?"

"I know. I know. My mind is jumping all over the place. It's the first thing I thought of when John woke me up to tell me there's a dead man keeping the two witches company."

"What? A dead man? In our Hallow Wine display? You could have started with that. I'll get dressed and come right over. Should I call the tasting room staff?"

"Probably a good idea, but they don't need to get here early," I said. "Tell them to try to act natural when we open up for business at ten."

"*If* we open. What if the sheriff's office shuts us down for their investigation? Even if someone had a stroke, they'd investigate."

"It's not as if anything happened inside the winery. Everything was locked up for the night."

"Are you there now? What's it look like? Any sign of a struggle?"

"I'm on my way over now but John didn't mention anything like that, only the fact our security cameras were covered with shaving cream or some sort of cream."

"It has to be murder. The only question is, did it happen on Two Witches property or was the body dumped into our display?"

"Um, not the only question. We need to find out who the dead guy is. Then we can worry about how he got here."

"Not *we*. The sheriff's office. *They* need to find out."

"Good grief. I'd better get a move on. I can see the blue and red flashers coming up our hill. And holy crap, why is their siren still blaring?"

"I imagine so everyone else in the vicinity will know we've got something brewing and it isn't wine."

"Very funny. See you in a bit."

As soon as I ended the call with Cammy, I charged out of the house and down the hill as if I was back in school and running on the girls track team. I was winded and nearly out of breath when I reached the parking lot and nearly collided with a familiar face from the forensic team.

"Eugene, right?" I asked as he got out of his van.

The technician all but recoiled when he saw me. "I was told you were back in New York."

"Yeah, well, I'm here for the time being. Look, before we mosey over to where Deputy Hickman and my vineyard manager, John, are standing, can you do me a tiny little favor? And I promise, I'll keep it to myself."

Eugene looked as if I had asked him to level a small city. "I have to follow protocol."

"I'm not asking you to change the way you secure evidence. Just let me in on who the victim is if you find a wallet or ID on the guy. No one has to know."

"I can't do that. A victim's identification is secured information, and until the sheriff's office discloses it to the public, it has to remain secure. Next of kin need to be notified first."

"You know as well as I do that the man didn't wind up dead in my display cauldron as a result of natural causes. Heck, take a look from here. There's a giant dagger sticking out of his back. A dagger, not a knife. For all I know, it could be a relative."

Eugene rolled his eyes and it wasn't pleasant. "Then you'll be notified by the sheriff's office."

I let out a long and extremely audible sigh before hoofing it directly to where John and Deputy Hickman, aka Grizzly Gary, stood. The deputy looked craggier than usual, with slight grayish brown stubble and his usual furrowed brow. Standing a good six feet tall, the guy certainly projected a formidable presence, unlike his assistant, Clarence Eustis, with his cherubic face and equally passive demeanor.

"I'm back in town," I said to Deputy Hickman. "In case you were wondering. Francine and Jason are in the Philippines." *Or on some beach in Maui.*

"Oh, trust me, Miss Ellington, I figured as much. As soon as the call came through about a dead body at your winery, I had a gut feeling you were here." He let out an obnoxious groan and continued. "The coroner will be here any minute to examine and remove the corpse along with Eugene's assistance. And speaking of my forensic technician, do not try your strongarm tactics on him to eke out information. Capable technicians are difficult to come by, let alone maintain. After the last incident involving your winery, he all but transferred to Seneca Falls."

I turned my head and glared at Eugene, who was now fixated over the body, taking photos. "You're not going to remove the display, are you? Hallow Wine Weekend begins tomorrow. How about if we just tell Eugene to lift any fingerprints or DNA, or fibers, or whatever it is, and leave the cauldron and papier-mâché witches alone? In fact, I can just—"

"Stay right where you are and leave him alone."

A second later, I heard a car door slam and turned to see Theo racing toward us. Deputy Hickman put the palm of his hand on his forehead and held it for a moment. "I should have known your cohort would arrive. What do you do? Keep him on speed dial for this sort of thing?"

"I, um, er . . ."

"Never mind. I'll deal with it."

Grizzly Gary strode toward Theo and called out, "Good morning, Mr. Buchman. As you've surmised, we didn't gather here for an early morning prayer service, although it certainly wouldn't hurt. I suppose by now, you know the drill. Someone from my office will be over to your winery in the next day or so to ask your employees if they've seen or heard anything. In the meantime, refrain from prying around."

Then he marched over to where John stood. "I understand someone from your crew was first on the scene. I'll need to speak with that person."

"Travis should be in the barn, getting the grape harvester ready to roll. He left a few minutes ago. Want me to send him here or did you or your assistant want to go there?"

The deputy rubbed the back of his neck. "I'll send Clarence down for a statement. Shouldn't take that long."

Clarence's rigid stance loosened. "On my way, Deputy Hickman. I'll take the car if it's all right with you."

"It's not. That barn is spitting distance and this damp morning air isn't doing my bones any good. I may need to sit in the car with the heater on."

While Grizzly Gary and Clarence continued their conversation, I walked closer to the cauldron, careful not to disturb the coroner or, heaven forbid, set Eugene off. That's when I saw Stephanie's large papier-mâché scythe, sharing the cauldron with the dead body.

"That scythe belongs to the Grim Reaper," I announced. "And last I knew, he was holding it with both hands in the display at Gable Hill Winery."

Chapter 8

"What?" Deputy Hickman shouted. "Are you sure?"

"Of course I'm sure. They had to use duct tape on the tip so it wouldn't fray. Besides, why on earth would we have a scythe in a flaming cauldron?" Then I inched a tad closer to Eugene and mouthed "Who is it?" when Deputy Hickman turned to say something to John.

Eugene widened his eyes and turned his attention to the gurney that another man from the coroner's office wheeled over. From my vantage point, all I could see was the body of a man clad in tan pants and a dark windbreaker leaning into the fake flames that someone had the good sense to turn off.

Theo and I exchanged glances as Eugene and the coroner, a fiftyish man with a brush cut and broad shoulders, proceeded to remove the body and place it on the gurney, careful to leave the dagger imbedded in the small of the man's back.

"Shouldn't there be a lot of blood dripping down?" I asked Theo. By now he and I stood next to each other watching the grim—no pun intended—scenario unfold.

"Depends how long the body's been there. I don't think there's much blood if the body's been dead for over eight hours. Or maybe it's ten hours. I'm not sure. It was in one of Don's thriller novels."

"What if the dagger isn't the weapon? What if it's an afterthought? For the effect."

"Geez, Norrie, it's not a Hollywood movie."

I looked around to make sure no one could hear us. Deputy Hickman was now conversing with Eugene and the coroner but I still kept my voice low. "Maybe whoever was responsible did it to throw everyone off."

Theo shook his head. "Not for long. Not after the autopsy. And the toxicology report. Heck, they might have a clue after the preliminary tox screening."

"It has to be a homicide. Don't you think? People don't up and die leaned over into a Halloween display. And if they were passed out and not dead at first, then the dagger did the trick."

"Where did you get your training in forensic pathology?"

"I'm just saying—Oh my gosh! Take a look! It's Donovan Brin." The pitch in my voice rose until I was all but shrieking. Eugene and the coroner had positioned the gurney to the opposite side, giving Theo and me a full view of its occupant. "It's Donovan Brin," I announced again, unable to stop myself from repeating his name.

Deputy Hickman immediately turned to face me. "You know who the victim is?"

I nodded and swallowed the lump that suddenly formed in the back of my throat. "He's, I mean, he *was* the writer from *Wine Enthusiast* who came here to interview the winemakers from our winery, Theo and Don's winery, and the Ipswiches' winery regarding this year's Merlot. It was a wonderful vintage. Velvety. Not that heavy oaky taste that everyone comes to expect, but more in line with a softer, more subtle flavor." It was that moment when I knew the shock of seeing Donovan's lifeless body had somehow gotten to me. If it wasn't for Theo shaking my wrist and whispering, "Get a grip," who knows how long I would have rambled on and on about Merlot.

Deputy Hickman must have figured as much because he didn't say a word other than to repeat Donovan's name and write it on a pad. I stood motionless as the gurney was loaded into the van and the coroner and his assistant took off, leaving only Eugene "to process the scene." His exact words.

Then, the fog that had taken over my brain evaporated and two thoughts immediately sprung to mind. I looked at Eugene and crossed my arms. "You're not going to dismantle our display, are you?" It was more of a threat than a question. "I mean, you already have what you came here for, don't you?"

Eugene didn't say a word but he did answer my question. He walked back to his car and returned with enough yellow crime scene tape to wrap around the entire building. I nudged Theo, careful to keep my voice low. "I planned for this. Cammy is going to make a new sign that says 'It's a crime to miss Hallow Wine Weekend.' Hopefully our visitors will think the crime scene tape is meant to be there."

"Hopefully your visitors won't be turning on the news."

"Oh, rats. Not the news. That's all we need."

Just then, John approached us. "The deputy gave me the all clear. I've got to get back to work. Someone from his office will get my full statement later. Meanwhile, I anticipate a throng of lookie-loos once word gets out. I'll make sure our rows are roped off. Keep me posted of any new developments, will you?"

"Sure thing."

I couldn't possibly imagine any new developments, but then again, I couldn't imagine seeing Donovan head-first in a lightweight metal cauldron flanked by two papier-mâché witches.

With John headed back to the barn and the coroner and his assistant on their way to the county morgue, that left Eugene poring over the evidence and Deputy Hickman poised to chat with Theo and me.

"Miss Ellington, need I remind you that if and when the news crews show up at your winery, you are to direct them to my office for all information. No speculation. No commentary. No nothing."

"Uh-huh. No nothing. Um, can you ask Eugene to remove Stephanie's scythe? It really doesn't fit in with our display, and I'm sure they want it back."

Deputy Hickman had just opened his mouth when a call came in. He closed his mouth and rolled his eyes simultaneously before he took the call. All Theo and I could hear was, "Tell her I'm aware of the matter and someone will be over there shortly. Tell her not to touch the rest of her display. What? She thinks it's a death threat? Tell her—"

That very second, Theo's phone went off and he mouthed "Don." I caught part of his conversation in between straining to hear the rest of Deputy Hickman's. "Seriously?" Theo furrowed his brow. "Someone stole one of our felted egrets from the display? Are you sure it didn't blow over and it's lying on the ground somewhere? Sure, I'll hold. What? Yeah, I do know what's going on at Norrie's. Donovan Brin's body was found in her cauldron. Keep it to yourself for the time being. I'll be back down the hill in a few minutes." Then he turned to me. "A missing felted egret is the least of anyone's problems."

At the sound of the word *egret*, Deputy Hickman stopped talking to whoever had phoned him and said, "What's this about a missing display egret?"

Theo shrugged. "The Grey Egret Winery display is now down to one bird. It's not exactly something I'd call the sheriff's office to investigate. We're used to all sorts of pranks and petty thefts around the wine trail. Besides, looks like you've got other, more pressing matters." He leaned toward the cauldron and stared as the deputy returned to his call.

"Yes, yes. Tell her to snap a photo with her phone and send it directly to my email. Yes, Gladys. Go ahead and give her my email address. Okay, fine. And remind her again not to touch anything."

He ended the call and stood still for a moment. Then, "I'm sure you couldn't help yourselves from listening in. That was the sheriff's office secretary, Gladys Pipp."

"Um, I figured as much," I mumbled.

"Stephanie Ipswich phoned our office. She's convinced someone tampered with their Halloween display, turning it into a death threat of sorts. Hold on, the photo's on its way. You might as well look since I believe this is all connected."

A second later, he held out his phone and I gasped. Theo tried not to laugh but it was impossible. Instead of their Grim Reaper brandishing a scythe, he was now choking the daylights out of one of Theo and Don's felted egrets.

"That's our egret, all right. I hope no one's trying to send us a message. Seeing Donovan's dead body was enough to curdle my morning coffee. Boy, if this doesn't top the cake, I don't know what does. Stephanie's scythe winds up in Norrie's cauldron, our egret gets choked to death by a Grim Reaper, and, well, how many ways can you say *murder*? Either this is one hell of a Halloween prank gone bad or there's a diabolical killer out there with a sick sense of humor."

"Slow down, Mr. Buchman," Deputy Hickman said. "Before you go off concocting theories, let me remind you that the victim's death is considered *suspicious* at this juncture in time. It has not officially been deemed a murder. That's why we rely on evidence. Just because there's a dagger thrust into the man's back does not automatically equate it with the murder weapon."

I nudged Theo's ankle. "Isn't that what I said?"

The deputy continued, "Let me remind both of you again. This is an active investigation. And while you have identified the victim, you are not to share that information. Our office will provide it to the news media once the family has been notified. In addition, since all three neighboring wineries seem to be involved, we will be sending deputies to speak with your employees later today regarding anything they may have seen or heard."

The wind picked up a bit and I rubbed my arms together. "I think it was a deliberate cross-contamination of evidence meant to prevent your office from finding out where Donovan was—" And then I rephrased what I was about to say. "Where Donovan died."

"We have a well-trained and capable forensic crew. I'm sure they will be able to piece together all of the evidence. Oh, and one more thing—Do not barrage Gladys Pipp with questions. She's a civil service county employee, not your personal news source."

Meanwhile, Eugene continued to poke around the display. I was positive he took fiber samples from the witches but at least he didn't demolish the tableau. Deputy Hickman turned away from us and approached Eugene. "Let the office know when you're done here. I need to send you to Gable Hill Winery to dust for prints."

"Understood," Eugene replied.

With that, Grizzly Gary tromped back to his car and drove off. Presumably to pick up Clarence first.

"Cross-contamination of evidence? That's not a thing, you know. Food can be cross-contaminated. Food to food. People to food. And equipment to food. That's been drilled into every restaurant and winery."

"Grizzly Gary knew what I meant."

The sheriff's car was partway down the hill when another car drove up—Cammy's.

"I have to tell Cammy it was Donovan," I said to Theo. "How can I *not* tell her? You know I'm not very good about lying."

"Yeah, it's a dilemma. If you tell her, you tell all your employees. And then what?"

"Okay, fine. I'll tell her the body *looked* like Donovan's but no official identification has been made."

"She wasn't born yesterday."

"Who wasn't born yesterday?" Cammy hurried to where we stood. "I heard you guys all the way over from my parking spot. Wow. Donovan Brin murdered. And dumped in our Hallow Wine Weekend display."

Theo poked my elbow. "That takes the pressure off. Cammy heard the news without you telling her. I'd call that serendipitous."

"Uh, speaking of serendipitous," Cammy answered, "what do you call the lineup of news vans? Take a look behind you. They're turning up our hill."

I flinched. "Oh, crap. I call that indigestion."

Chapter 9

"Eugene's still here," Theo said. "Direct the news crews to him."

In that second, Fred and Emma came out the front door of the winery and stood, mouths wide open, at the scene in front of them.

"I thought we heard voices outside," Fred said, "but we had the radio on and were busy getting everything prepped in the bistro. The view from our window faces the upper end of the vineyard so we didn't see anything. Still, Emma was insistent something was going on out front. Holy cow! Why is there crime tape all over the display? And a slew of news vans pulling up?"

I motioned for them to walk closer to the cauldron, but not so close as to give Eugene hives, which probably wouldn't have taken much. "Travis found a dead body in there when he went to replace Alvin's hay."

Fred bit his lip and, in that instant, I could have sworn the color in his face turned ashen. He reached for Emma's hand and she took it. "Oh, no. Please don't tell me it's someone Emma and I know. I can't believe we were totally oblivious to all of this."

Emma, who had also lost coloring in her face, looked at the cauldron. "The body must have been in there when Fred and I got here at five but we didn't notice. The flame was out and it was shadowy in that corner." Then she dropped Fred's hand and moved toward me. "You don't think whoever did that was still here, do you?"

"No, Alvin would have pitched a fit and you and Fred would have heard him. But, it's quite possible that ornery goat heard the culprits and scared them away. And I'm saying culprits because I don't think one person could have done this. A body is too heavy."

Fred nodded. "Makes sense. We must have already been inside when Travis showed up with Alvin's hay."

"Listen, I'm sure Deputy Hickman will piece together a time line so tell him everything you noticed, or didn't notice, when he or whoever he sends speaks with you. Um, whatever you do, don't say anything to the reporters. We've been given the riot act by Grizzly Gary to keep our mouths shut. Refer them to the Yates County Sheriff's Office or the forensic crew."

Suddenly Eugene chirped up. "Do not refer them to me. I'm a forensic technician, not a spokesperson for the office."

"Then who can we speak with?" a voice bellowed out.

I turned and realized it was a channel 13 WHAM reporter, the insignia plastered across the front of his black windbreaker and a microphone in his hand. Behind him was a cameraman recording everything. It wouldn't have been so bad if it was only channel 13, but oh no. It's like vultures that discover carrion. Once one news crew gets a whiff of it, the others are right behind. In this case, channel 10 and channel 12 also decided to attend the party.

The only saving grace was that we didn't open until ten, a good two hours away. I approached the first two reporters and pinched my shoulders together to exude an air of confidence and authority. *That*, or a pain in my back muscles.

"Good morning. I'm Norrie Ellington, one of the winery owners. I take it you zoomed in on an incident from the sheriff's office scanners. Please be advised that none of us are at liberty to disclose any information regarding said incident."

"More than an incident," the blond thirtysomething reporter from WHAM said.

Underneath his windbreaker, I could see a black shirt and deep teal tie. "A body was discovered on your property, and if I'm not mistaken, this isn't the first time."

"As I said, I am not at liberty to discuss the matter."

"But a body was discovered. The sheriff's office doesn't issue alerts at random. And again, if I'm not mistaken, that crime technician appears to be dusting for prints."

"He's following protocol. They dust for everything."

Theo squelched a laugh. "She's right. About not being able to engage with reporters. But feel free to take photos of our wineries and promote the Hallow Wine Weekend, which begins tomorrow."

The reporter walked away but not before having his cameraman take a few shots of Eugene still poring over the evidence.

"Emma and I better get back to the bistro," Fred said. "We've got cookies to bake and a few salads to make."

Cammy nodded in agreement. "Me too. Not salads. Signs."

A nanosecond later, the three of them disappeared into the building.

Theo gave my shoulder a squeeze. "I'll take that as my cue to head down the hill. I know it will be a madhouse, but what do you say we meet after work at Port of Call? They're not taking reservations so we'll have to hang out at the bar, but frankly that's what I had in mind."

"I know what you have in mind and I'm in. I want to see if anyone leaks any information about this morning's wake-up call, too."

"Interesting choice of words. The news media will refer to it as a suspicious death, but trust me, someone knows something and Port of Call is a good starting point. I still can't shake the feeling I have about the prop staging surrounding Donovan's death. Why go to all that trouble? And you know what the worst part is?"

"All the nutcases it will bring out?"

"Nope. All the suspects. It'll be like one big knotted ball of yarn that gets more tangled as soon as someone tries to unravel it."

"As long as none of us are on the suspect list, let that yarn unravel. Um, are you sure Don will be up for Port of Call?"

"Don's always up for eating there. He's totally into their fall menu and has been mumbling about the seasoned squash soup with roasted croutons. Too bad Bradley's stuck in Buffalo. When did you tell me he'd be back?"

"Tomorrow night. Maybe sooner if he can wrap things up. Who would have thought family law could be so complicated."

"Ever watch *Dr. Phil?*"

I chuckled. "Geez, I hope the sheriff's office sends Clarence over to us to interview the staff. Grizzly Gary may scare away the customers."

"No kidding. I think he even scares Clarence. I wouldn't worry about it if I were you, they've got lots of deputies chomping to get into a possible murder investigation."

"They can join the club. I don't think we can sit still on this one. Hmm, what do you think about asking Stephanie and Derek to join us tonight if she can get her mother-in-law to babysit?"

"Good idea. We can scope out the crowd, eavesdrop, and commiserate at the same time. See you later."

Theo made a dash for his car and I darted inside the winery to let Cammy know I'd be back in a bit once I showered and changed. As I walked into the winery kitchen, the chemical aroma of markers burned my nose. "Smells like my third-grade classroom," I announced.

"Good. Enjoy the nostalgia. I'm moving at breakneck speed on this new sign. By the way, all of the tasting room staff is on board today. Don't worry, I'll give them the party line about a hapless victim who may have succumbed to a medical issue. Donovan's identity will remain under wraps until I get the all clear."

"Yep. We can act as shocked and surprised as everyone when they announce it on TV. Probably tomorrow. Today they'll have to hype it up with the 'grim discovery of a corpse at one of the wineries.'"

"No kidding."

"Too bad you missed the prelude." I went on to tell her about the swapping out of decorations and she nearly lost it when I described one of the Grey Egret's birds being choked to death by Stephanie's Grim Reaper. "I have to admit, that part was hilarious," I said. "If it wasn't for the murder, I'd be pointing a finger at Eli Speltmore. I don't care if he is twelve years old. Hmm, maybe not the murder, but what if he and that little cohort of his, Stuart Landrow, did get on their bikes before the body was dumped? I wouldn't put it past them. Those two are reckless and fearless. Hmm, give me a second."

Since Eli's father, Henry, was the president of the Seneca Lake Wine Trail Association, I figured it was definitely my duty to inform him of the unfortunate incident, now under investigation. Without wasting a minute, I selected his home number from my contact list and waited for someone to pick up.

"Norrie? Is that you? For a minute I thought I misread my caller ID. Are you in town visiting?" It was Delia, Eli's mother.

"Not visiting. Babysitting, probably until Christmas. Maybe sooner if there's such a thing as a true Christmas miracle."

"I'm sure Eli would love to see you but he's in Pittsford at my sister's house. I drove him there Wednesday after school. Frankly, I couldn't take the chance of him getting into mischief during the Hallow Wine Weekend. Besides, he's way ahead in his studies and two days won't make that much of a difference, especially since we worked it out with his school and my nieces' school so it would count for visitation days."

Nope. The kid's got a darned good alibi.

"Um, that's wonderful. Actually, I called to let Henry know that we had a rather unpleasant incident at our winery this morning. A dead body was found in our cauldron decoration out front."

"A dead body? A dead body?"

Next thing I knew, Delia shrieked, "Henry, pick up the phone. It's Norrie Ellington and they found a dead body in front of her winery."

I spent the next five minutes trying to explain what had occurred. And the three minutes after that imploring Henry not to shoot off an email to all of the wineries without first conversing with the Yates County Sheriff's Office. When the call ended, I was wiped out and Cammy was laughing herself silly.

"At least we know it wasn't Eli," I said.

"You better hope Henry doesn't jot down his thoughts and push a group Send button."

I shuddered. "I need to get home and take a shower. I'll be back down here to help with the tastings. It'll be a circus no matter what, but once word gets out about Donovan's body, it'll reach epic proportions."

"As long as it doesn't reach Zenora right away, we'll manage."

"It's Friday. Term paper time. She'll be stuck at Uris Library all day."

Cammy smiled. "Today, yes. But she's off on the weekends."

• • •

I arrived back at the tasting room an hour later, wearing the traditional outfit: Hallow Wine–themed sweatshirt and jeans. Even from the doorway I could see the place was full and it wasn't even eleven. Lizzie, who was at her regular spot at the cash register/computer, waved me over. She adjusted the frilly collar of her top so that her pearl necklace could be seen.

"Heavens, Norrie. What a horrid way to start the day. Especially with an event weekend. Do you have any idea what happened? Who the victim was? All Cammy said was that a man's body had been found and that the sheriff's office was investigating."

I crossed my fingers behind my back and lied like a pro. "No idea. Possibly a stroke. Maybe he was with a large group of people and they didn't know he was missing."

"I guess that would explain why his car wasn't in our parking lot. Nancy Drew would have picked that up immediately. I'm not going to be much help when those deputies show up to speak with us. Everything was as normal as could be yesterday when we locked up."

"They may ask about seeing or overhearing anything suspicious."

"Like I said, a very normal day."

At that moment, a middle-aged woman approached and handed Lizzie a bottle of Cauldron Caper for purchase.

"That's my favorite," I said. "Perfect for Halloween festivities. The blend of Cabernet Franc and Cayuga pairs nicely with all sorts of foods."

"I just fell in love with the label. Funny, but I seem to buy books the same way."

Lizzie rang up the sale and nodded. "Surprising oneself can be terrific fun."

I thanked the woman, told her to enjoy the wine, and headed toward the tasting room, nearly colliding with Glenda and a full water pitcher.

"It was on the radio," she said. "But I already knew."

"Huh?"

"Zenora texted me. Said she felt death in the air. Wanted me to perform a cleansing ritual."

"No ritual. And tell her it wasn't in the air. It was in our event display."

Just then, Roger brushed a wisp of his graying hair from his forehead and motioned me over. He had a full table of customers so I was thankfully spared lying to him.

"Fill me in when you get a moment," he whispered as he uncorked a bottle of Witches Brew. "Cammy was more secretive than John Bradshaw and Thomas Knowlton combined."

"Who?"

"Spies during the time of the French and Indian War."

Then he quickly held up the bottle and announced, "An enchanting blend of Riesling, Chardonnay, and Pinot Gris."

As I moved away from Roger's table, Sam came out of the kitchen carrying a tray of clean wineglasses. "Yeesh, another dead body, huh? Did you get a look? I tried coaxing more out of Cammy but forget it. All I know is to expect someone from the sheriff's office to grill us today."

"Um, yeah. That's all I know."

My back was to the entrance but Sam's wasn't. He put the wineglasses on the nearest table and moved his head in the direction of the door. "Isn't that Donovan Brin's assistant from the other day? He must be lagging behind her. Say, I thought he already interviewed you. Do you think he wants to speak with any of us?"

Not unless he located Zenora and he plans to be chatting from the grave.

Chapter 10

I shrugged, hoping Sam wouldn't ask me anything else that pertained to Donovan. "Uh, I don't see him so I'm guessing not. I'd better walk over and see if I can help her."

"Okay. Hey, let us know if you hear anything."

"Uh-huh," I mumbled as I walked over to the tall, shapely brunette in black slacks, white mock turtleneck and beige fleece button-front coat. Like the first time I met her, she wore her long hair tied back in a French knot and sported the same rectangular red-silver glasses that were trending right now.

Donovan had introduced her as his assistant but didn't offer up her name. Neither did she. No effort whatsoever for a friendly meet-and-greet. I attributed it to a strong work ethic but the image of the Ice Queen still stuck.

"Norrie Ellington, right?" she asked as soon as we were face-to-face.

"Yes. We met the other day. Sort of. I didn't get your name."

"Adrienne Stafine. I'll make this brief. Has Mr. Brin been to your winery today?"

You may want to elaborate on the phrase "been to."

"I haven't seen him inside the building."

Adrienne stared at the tasting room tables and then looked over both shoulders. "It's not like him to miss our morning meeting and not text me. Or return my text, for that matter. I've already been to Gable Hill and the Grey Egret. No sign of him. And apparently he hasn't been spotted here either."

At the word *spotted*, I winced and hoped she didn't notice. "I thought he had completed his interviews." *Not exactly a lie.*

"So did I. I've been with Mr. Brin for three years. If he intended to acquire more information, he wouldn't do it without my note-taking. He's a polished journalist and knows just what to ask, but let's just say his note-taking skills are subpar. That's where I come in."

"Is that all you do? Take notes?"

Oh my gosh. It sounds as if I'm asking her if she's sleeping with him.

Adrienne remained expressionless but I could feel the heat rise in my cheeks. "Um, what I meant was, do you outline the articles for him or prepare rough copy for him to review?"

She shook her head. "Let's just say my role is a combination of court transcriptionist and ghost writer." Then she looked around again. "This is very disconcerting. Mr. Brin definitely left the hotel. His rental car wasn't in the lot this morning. I had to arrange for my own rental this morning. It wasn't easy. I can't believe how many tourists flock to this area." She let out an annoyed sigh and glanced over her shoulders again to where a group of seven or eight people entered the winery. "I suppose that's why Mr. Brin chose to write a cultural piece in conjunction with the Merlot article," she went on. "But it would have been nice if he informed me he was taking in the local culture."

"I'm sure you'll find out his whereabouts soon enough."

"Let me give you my cell phone number. Call me if he comes in, will you? I should have thought to do that at the other two wineries."

"I'll make sure they know as well."

"Thank you."

Adrienne turned and started for the door when my brain kicked in. "Uh, before you go, was Mr. Brin worried about anything? Was he overly anxious? Deadlines can do that, you know." I thought of Renee and twitched. *"Change everything to a quaint little town with a cozy murder."*

"That's an odd question to ask. Why? Do you think something awful happened to him?"

"What? No. Not at all. But sometimes when people have pressing issues, they take scenic drives around the lake. It does wonders to calm them down."

I can't believe what's coming out of my mouth.

"I can't think of anything that made him anxious. Upset and annoyed maybe, but not anxious. Then again, he did act differently when we returned from California last month having visited a few wineries in the Napa Valley. Mr. Brin did a feature article on some of the organic wineries: Frontanac, Clear Meadows and LaVerna Vineyards."

"Different how?"

"He became fixated with one of the apps on his phone. I don't know which one, but he checked it all the time. He's never done anything like that before. I thought maybe he was checking the status on some of his stocks because it was a quick look-and-see. He didn't spend much time on the site. And last night, when I walked over to where he was seated in the hotel lounge, he had the phone in his hand and immediately tapped it shut. Acted as if it contained the nuclear codes."

"Maybe it was one of those dating sites."

Adrienne's jaw dropped open and the amused look on her face gave me the answer before she did. "I doubt it was a dating site. Mr. Brin doesn't seem to have a problem in that regard."

"Not to pry"—*of course I'm prying*—"but I thought he was married."

"Married, but not committed. And please don't let that go any further."

"Um, I think social media and the tabloids already have."

"It's impossible for anyone to retain any privacy these days."

"Tell me, when *was* the last time you saw him?"

"In the hotel lounge yesterday evening. We were going over his article about the Merlot. I don't know how much longer he stayed in the lounge but I booked an evening spa treatment and left after an hour or so. When I returned to my room, I went right to bed. Honestly, I can't imagine where he could be. Don't forget. Call me if he ambles in here."

I think his ambling days are done.

"Absolutely."

She made a beeline for the door without further conversation. Honestly, I was grateful for that. Each encounter with someone made it more difficult for me to continue this ruse. But maybe I didn't have to. I located Cammy in the kitchen and motioned for her to keep quiet. Then I dialed Gladys at the sheriff's office.

"Hi, Gladys. It's Norrie. Hope you're doing well. I guess Deputy Hickman told you I'm back in town. Grasshoppers this time. In the Philippines. Don't worry, I know what you know. Maybe more. Is Deputy Hickman aware Donovan Brin had an assistant working with him? Her name is Adrienne Stafine and she's been in here looking for him. That's after she checked out Gable Hill and the Grey Egret. Not that I would dare tell him what to do, but Deputy Hickman really should have a chat with her."

"Whoa. Now I know what I've missed the past few months. Thanks, I'll pass that along. He's currently at Belhurst Castle, where the victim was staying. Our office is working with the Ontario County Sheriff's Office and the Geneva Police Department. You know how these shared jurisdiction cases go."

"Ugh. Slow. That's how they go. Listen, our staff is getting antsy. They know a body was found in our holiday display but so far I've been able to keep the identity hush-hush. But they're going to put two and two together. Especially since Donovan's assistant is on the hunt, so to speak."

"I really want to help but I don't want to risk losing my pension. Until the next of kin is notified and an official announcement is given to the media, I can't breathe a word and neither can you. You can't disclose what you know. Not even to your staff. Especially your staff."

"Okay. Well, can you tell me when we can expect Deputy Eustis or whoever your office sends to interview our people?"

"That I can do. Hold on a second. Let me look at my notes."

The line was quiet for a minute and then Gladys spoke. "I have you down for three this afternoon. Deputy Hickman is aware this is a busy time for the wineries but hopefully, the one-to-one interviews won't take long. Oh, looks like our forensic crew is back. I need to have a word with them."

"Okay, thanks, Gladys."

"Got the answer I needed," I said to Cammy. "Interview time at three. That's usually a lull time for us but I'm not counting on it. At least we can work around it with the tasting tables."

"No worries. What's this about Donovan's assistant? I've been back here running the dishwasher."

"She's out looking for him. My take is whoever killed him drove Donovan's car. Find the car and we find the killer."

"Not *we*, the sheriff's office. Besides, *we* don't even know what kind of car he rented."

"We don't, but I guarantee Theo and Don do. Theo's always scoping out those things. I'll be sure to ask when I see them tonight at Port of Call. Care to join us?"

"I wish I could but I promised my aunts I'd help out at their restaurant. Rosinetti's is usually packed on Friday nights. With or without Hallow Wine Weekend. And don't worry, I'll have my ears tuned to any gossip that may pertain to Donovan. Once that Geneva crowd loosens up, you'd be surprised at the stuff they say."

"There's one more thing but it's probably unrelated. The assistant said Donovan was obsessed with an app on his phone when they got back from California. I mentioned online dating and she nixed that one."

"Probably online betting. It's legal in most states. Or maybe he was checking his bank accounts. When my aunt Theresa's checking account got hacked and the bank gave her a new account and new routing number, she checked it every hour on the hour for a year."

"I doubt it had to do with his bank but I'm not ruling anything out."

• • •

Deputy Eustis stepped into our tasting room at a few minutes past three. I had just finished restocking the blends when I noticed him a few feet from me. "Quick," I said. "Let's talk in the kitchen."

"I can't divulge any information. It's all in the hands of the lab. And speaking of which, Eugene asked me if I'd remind you not to tamper with their evidence."

"He could have asked me himself."

Clarence rolled his eyes. "There's no polite way to say this—You scare the daylights out of him."

"Fine. I'll keep away. But isn't he done collecting evidence?"

"Sometimes they require more. That's all I'm saying."

"Okay, fine. Speaking of evidence, I had a little chat with Adrienne Stafine, Donovan's assistant. Donovan may have been into something that he didn't share with her. Your office should check his laptop and his cell phone. They could still be in his room at the Belhurst."

"Thank you for the information."

"Well? What are you waiting for? Call Gary and ask him before those devices wind up with Ontario County's law enforcement. The body was found in Yates County. We should have dibs on everything that goes with it."

"It doesn't necessarily work that way but we are the lead agency on this case."

"Whatever. Call him. I'll wait."

"You see, this is exactly why you make Eugene nervous."

"The man works for Deputy Hickman. How can I possibly make him nervous?"

"First of all, Eugene works for the county and takes his orders from the supervisor in charge of the forensic lab. Oh, never mind. I need to get these interviews underway. And I'll text my boss about the laptop and cell phone." He wrung his hands together then shook them. "Please tell me you don't have any other demands."

"Um, just one more thing. Has your office determined where Donovan was killed? I mean, sure, he wound up in our cauldron, but any moron could tell you the body was staged. And while you're at it, has your office determined the cause of death? We all know the dagger was just for show."

"We don't know what was for show, what was for real, and what-was-what yet. Good grief. The corpse was only discovered this morning. Now, may I please get on with the interviews?"

"Sure. Sure. Follow me to the banquet room. If you want a coffee or anything, let me know."

"Thanks, but I'm good."

The interviews moved like clockwork, and before I knew it, Clarence approached me to let me know he had finished. And to let me know they didn't find a laptop or a cell phone in Donovan's room.

"They're probably in the rental car," I said. "Did your office find that? It's a bigger piece of evidence."

Then I bit my lip. "Sorry. I didn't mean to be sarcastic. Seriously, I wager those rental cars come with GPS tracking systems in case the renter decides to drive one of them off to another state."

Clarence took a step toward me. "Hey, I know it's kind of scary to find a dead body in front of your place of business, but trust me, this isn't our first suspicious death investigation."

Or mine either.

Chapter 11

Madhouse didn't come close to describing Port of Call on the Friday night before Hallow Wine Weekend. Packed tables and two layers of people around the bar made me question if this was such a good idea. With the wraparound deck now closed for the season, all the activity was indoors.

Faux pumpkins and leaves, along with mini skeletons, graced the mantel of their giant fireplace. In addition, orange fairy lights were strung across the beams in the ceiling, giving the place a cozy fall atmosphere. The usual candles on the tables were now ensconced in glass pumpkins and the aroma of nutmeg, cinnamon, and vanilla permeated the giant room.

It was a little past seven and I had serious doubts there'd be a spot wide enough for all of us to alight. I stood on tiptoes scanning the place for Theo, Don, or the Ipswiches. Just then, an older man in his fifties poked me in the elbow. "I think that woman in the corner is trying to get your attention."

I turned and sure enough, Stephanie was seated at a corner table and waved me over.

"You'd better hurry," the man said, "before there's a mutiny and someone else grabs that spot."

"Thanks." I nudged, bumped, and elbowed until I got to Stephanie.

"Hurry up and sit. If you're wondering, Derek is home with the boys. He promised them a Friday night Halloween movie and pizza. It had better be one of those funny movies, too. The last thing I need is those two in our bed all night."

"Have you seen Theo or Don?"

"Three yards away. If both of us wave our arms, maybe they'll see us."

"I'll do better." I stood and waved both hands until I saw Don wave back.

"I don't know how we're going to pick up any scuttlebutt in this crowd," he said when he reached our table. "All I hear is noise. Heck, I can't even make out what music is playing."

Stephanie propped an elbow on the table and leaned on it. "At least we can hear each other. No news on our end regarding those interviews. Clarence Eustis was here about an hour after we opened. Very pleasant gentleman."

"Very closemouthed, too," I said. "He got to our place around three."

Don rubbed his temples and looked at both of us. "We got stuck with the new assistant deputy. It was as if she followed a high school theater script and needed a prompter. The worst part of today was when Donovan's assistant showed up looking for him. I'm not proud of this, but I hid in the office with the door locked. Theo wasn't much better. He barricaded himself in the kitchen and told the staff 'to deal with it.'"

Stephanie chuckled as she gave her long blond hair the classic flip. Then she looked at the ceiling. "Good thing I'm not devout because I lied through my teeth."

Theo laughed. "Forget the WOW moniker, our three wineries should now be dubbed the Liars Club."

"I think that was already taken," I said. "Listen, I've got an idea. While we wait for someone to take our orders, how about we go up to the bar in twos, order our drinks, and mosey around to see if we pick up anything Donovan related."

"Great." Don shoved his chair back and recited his order—just in case. Stephanie didn't waste much time either.

"Roasted Cornish game hen with brussels sprouts and pine nuts." Three seconds later, it was only Theo and me at the table.

"In theory, this was a good idea," I said, "but I'm not so sure about the practicing end of it."

I told him what Adrienne said about Donovan checking an app on his phone and how cloak-and-dagger he was about it.

"It could have been anything. Don't read too much into it."

A few minutes later, Stephanie and Don returned with their drinks and the unmistakable look of loss on their faces.

"Maybe you two will have better luck," she said. "Did they take our orders yet?"

I shook my head as I stood. "Order me the same thing—Cornish game hen."

"Don't get crazy and order mounds of squash," Theo said to Don, giving his shoulder a squeeze. "Come on, Norrie, maybe we'll have better luck than Nick and Nora Charles over here."

No sooner did I stand when something, or should I say, *someone*, caught my eye. Long brunette hair draped over her shoulders, the highlights sparkling from the candle's glow. No trendy red-silver glasses but no doubt in my mind who she was.

She sat catty-corner from us across the table from a classy-looking dark-haired woman whose silver pashmina with intermittent gold tassels spelled "expendable cash." If Stephanie joined them, it would be *Charlie's Angels* all over again.

"A, A, Adri—"

"Are you all right?" Theo crinkled his nose and waited for me to say something. Unfortunately, I couldn't choke the words out fast enough.

"What? What's the matter with you?"

"Shh!" I finally got my voice back. "Don't look obvious but that's Donovan's assistant diagonally across from us. I know it's her. Sit back down."

Then I looked at Stephanie. "Take out your phone and pretend you're taking a photo of Theo and me. See if you can zoom in on her."

"Got it!"

A second later, a tall waiter stood over our table and asked to take our orders. When he left, I turned back to Theo. "Do you think she knows Donovan bit the dust?" Then I looked at Stephanie and Don, "What about you guys?"

Don looked at the table where the women were seated and then at the photo Stephanie had snapped. "Hard to say. People react differently at bad news. Are you sure it's her?"

"Oh, I'm sure. This is awful. What if Deputy Hickman told her? How does that make me look? I lied to her today about Donovan. I might as well have an embroidered *L* on my shirt like Hester's *A* in *The Scarlet Letter*."

"Before you go off the deep edge, Miss Prynne, you didn't have a choice. You were directed to keep your mouth shut."

"Drat." I took a big swallow from the water glass in front of me. "I can't believe it was the one directive from Deputy Hickman I actually listened to. A lot of good it did. Maybe I should take a bolder move and—"

"Don't!" Theo and Don said at once. "Last thing we need is for her to come unglued and create a scene. I watch the news. One minute there's a quiet timid person sipping on a latte and next thing you know, they turn into Mr. Hyde."

"Fine. I'll try another approach. Too bad Gladys has gone home for the weekend. Without her, I'm cut off from the inside news."

I took out my phone and called the non-emergency number at the sheriff's office. A deputy whose name I didn't recognize answered.

"Hello. This is Norrie Ellington from Two Witches Winery. I called earlier today to inform Deputy Hickman that the victim found on my property was in the area with an assistant and the assistant has been looking for him. The victim. Not Deputy Hickman."

Don bent his head down and rubbed his forehead as I continued. "Anyway, I wondered if he made contact with her because she's at Port of Call seated at a nearby table. I'd hate for her to waste time filling out a missing person report tomorrow."

"I can't divulge that information in a crime investigation."

"Okay. Fine. Let me reiterate. I know the victim's identity. I identified him. Not officially but *visually*, if you know what I mean. Now, I can walk over to where the assistant is seated and give her the grim news, but that could be problematic. It might result in a rather unpleasant reaction in a crowded restaurant on Halloween weekend. Gee, I'd hate to see your office swamped with a zillion frantic calls about a ruckus and a hysterical woman. Or, you can just tell me and neither of us will breathe a word of this to Deputy Hickman."

"Hold on."

"Good grief, Norrie," Don whispered. "You should fill out an application for the CIA. Either that, or forget screenwriting, go right into acting."

A second later, the deputy was back on the phone. "I'll only say this once. Yes, the victim's assistant was notified at her hotel and brought in to identify the body at a little past five this evening."

"And?"

"That's all I'm at liberty to say. Have a good evening."

I looked at the dumbfounded expressions around the table. "She was brought in to ID the body. And now she's out dining like the Merry Widow. Maybe she killed her boss and that's her accomplice sitting across from her. Face it—two able-bodied women are just as capable of moving a dead body as two able-bodied men."

"That could be the new slogan for the human rights march in Geneva this spring," Don said.

"Very funny. I wish we knew who the woman having dinner with her is. Wait! I have an idea." I moved my chair closer to the table and lowered my voice. "Stephanie, pretend to take a photo of me but zoom in on the mystery woman instead."

She removed her phone from her bag while I grinned like the Cheshire cat. "Too bad these phones don't come with facial recognition software."

Don grabbed a breadstick and took a bite. "I was only kidding when I mentioned the CIA."

Stephanie took a sip of her white wine and smiled. "All set. I took a burst. Lots of photos. Of course, I don't know what good it's going to do. Anyway, I'll forward them to you."

"This is crazy. Adrienne and I both know Donovan's as dead as a doornail."

Theo put his hand on my wrist and gave it a squeeze. "Adrienne doesn't know you were there when the coroner removed the guy's body from the cauldron."

"You're right. Guess I'm off the hook." I turned my head slightly to get a better look at Adrienne and her dinner companion. "I'm no expert when it comes to reading body language, but I've seen people conduct bank transactions that displayed more emotion. This is so frustrating."

"Oh, for heavens sake, Norrie," he said. "Just get it over with. Walk over there, pretend you don't know Donovan is dead, and ask her if she was able to contact her boss. She'll either tell you he's resting comfortably at the county morgue and introduce you to her friend, or she'll tell you she identified a body and it wasn't his."

"Oh, it was him, all right."

Don grabbed another breadstick. "Go for the acting skills while you're at it. Feign shock. Place a palm over your chest and say, 'Oh, no! That was *his* body in our Hallow Wine display?' Then let her fill in the details."

"Arragh. It's better than sitting here waiting for our food to show up."

I took a deep breath and prayed to the gods I wouldn't muck it up. Then I skirted around people and tables until I stood behind hers. "Adrienne, right? I thought that was you. Were you able to locate your boss?"

Adrienne's body stiffened and she opened her mouth slightly. Her eyes were fixed on her dinner companion and neither of them said a word. I could have nuked an egg in the time it took for her to reply but I wasn't about to move.

"Not as of yet."

Okay. I can play along.

"Have you filed a missing person report at the sheriff's office?"

"There's a forty-eight-hour wait."

"Right. I forgot about that." Then I leaned toward the woman in the silver pashmina. "Norrie Ellington, Two Witches Winery. Unfortunately, we were on the news today since someone was found dead on our premises. Most likely a tourist with a medical issue. Happens all the time. I mean, in general, not in our winery. People have medical issues, they overindulge and well . . . anyway, it's very distressing. Especially at this busy time of year with Hallow Wine Weekend starting tomorrow."

"Yes, that's what brought me here. I'm Whitney Fontana. I host the *Wines in Our Lives* podcast out of Valhalla, New York. I happen to be staying at the same hotel as Adrienne and her boss. We met in the lobby when they first arrived. I told her not to be too overly concerned about his whereabouts. Writers sometimes go off on their own when they're following a story."

Adrienne fiddled with the end of her paper cocktail napkin until tiny pieces coated the table like confetti. "Whitney convinced me to join her for dinner tonight. It was better than staying in and ordering room service."

"I see. Well, um, er, hopefully you'll have news of your boss pretty soon." Then I smiled at Whitney. "Ask for me if you decide to visit us tomorrow or Sunday. I'll make sure you get to taste a number of our wines and not the usual flight."

"Thank you. I look forward to it."

I didn't know how much longer I could stand the charade so when I spied the waiter bringing our entrées to the table, I couldn't get out of there fast enough. "Nice chatting with both of you. Enjoy your meal." I dashed back in such a hurry I nearly knocked over a nearby tray at another table.

"Well, Mata Hari, what did you coerce out of them?" Theo asked.

I reached for my wineglass before I was fully seated. "No doubt in my mind. Deputy Hickman told Adrienne to keep her mouth shut about Donovan's death. You couldn't pry it out of her with a pair of hot tongs."

"Ew!" Stephanie winced. "Who's the other woman at her table?"

"Whitney Fontana. A wine podcaster from Westchester County. She said she's staying at the Belhurst, too. Said that's where she met Adrienne and Donovan."

Don cut into the roasted game hen and moved a juicy slice of meat toward his mouth. "Maybe Adrienne didn't admit to identifying Donovan's body because it wasn't his."

Chapter 12

Stephanie's fork hit the floor and she gasped. "My gosh. I never considered that. Hmm, it does make sense, though. That deputy you spoke with never said Adrienne identified Donovan. He said she was brought in to identify the body. That's all."

"You think? Maybe that's why she acted as if he was missing. But I saw the body and I swear, it was Donovan."

Theo stabbed a brussels sprout. "How can you be sure? And don't get into ugly graphics while I'm eating."

"Um, well, the clothes for one thing. Tan slacks and a navy windbreaker with a dagger poked through it. Donovan wore tan slacks and had a dark windbreaker when he was at our winery to interview Franz."

"That's the fall uniform in the Finger Lakes—light-colored slacks and a dark windbreaker. Or vice versa. Did you notice anything else?"

I nodded. "Body type. The dead body was the same average body type as Donovan's. And the same hair color."

Don slapped a palm across his forehead. "It doesn't mean it was Donovan."

"It does if the diamond-stud earring I saw in the dead body's left ear matches the one Donovan wore when he interviewed us."

"Norrie may be right," Stephanie said. "It's too coincidental."

"Yeah, *way* too coincidental. Face it, if anyone knows what Donovan looks like up close and personal, it's Adrienne. And my money's on Grizzly Gary telling her not to breathe a word until next of kin are notified. Along with his usual line: Don't leave town yet."

Theo popped a slice of the Cornish game hen in his mouth and followed it with a sip of wine. "It doesn't matter anyway. Once the family is informed, all the news channels will be blasting out the gory details in time to make our wine weekend complete. My take is the noon news tomorrow. In time to usher in Halloween fun."

"Forget fun. What about our chances for Merlot fame?" Stephanie tossed a lock of hair from her forehead and sighed. "Without Donovan, we might as well just spring for an ad in one of the Finger Lakes magazines and call it a day."

"Not so fast. Okay, granted, maybe the timing is off, and maybe it's a tad tactless, but Adrienne told me herself she was the ghost writer. Heck, she's got all of Donovan's questions and our answers on *her* laptop. The article can be written posthumously." Their three jaws dropped at once. Thankfully they'd already swallowed whatever bites of food they had in their mouths. "Okay, okay. I know it sounds mercenary, but how many chances do we get to appear in *Wine Enthusiast*? Adrienne can write the article. Heck, she can add her name, too, for that matter."

Don shook his head. "Only if she agrees."

"Or if we're very charming and persuasive."

"I see three 'charmings' at this table and one Norrie." Theo laughed.

"Hilarious. Once the weekend is over, I'll drop by the Belhurst Castle and chat with her. Trust me. She's not flying back to the city any time soon. Not if Donovan really was murdered. She'll move from body identifier to murder suspect before you can say 'Welcome to the Finger Lakes.'"

"What about the podcaster?" Stephanie sat taller in her seat and looked across the room at their table. "I say we might as well go for the full treatment."

"I agree. She's on Seneca Lake to cover Hallow Wine Weekend and none of us are shy when it comes to promoting our wineries. I'll call her tomorrow morning around breakfast time and see if I can firm things up."

"Mercenary. Plain and simple," Don said. "Count us in."

"That doesn't make us horrible, does it?" I asked.

Theo shook his head. "Nah. Opportunistic maybe, but not horrible. Hey, we didn't kill Donovan and plant his body in a cauldron. Come to think of it, we're victims, too. One minute on the road to fame and glory and the next—"

I rolled my eyes. "On the curb waiting for Deputy Hickman to make his next move."

We consumed our food and downed our wine without further conversation. At least for a few minutes. When I turned to look at Adrienne's table again, they were gone.

"One good thing," I said, "Zenora hasn't made an appearance. She's like a homing pigeon when there's bad news floating around."

"Good grief, Norrie!" Don exclaimed. "When will you learn to keep quiet about these things? Don't look now, but I swear that's her. The woman in that hideous orange and black cloak. And what's she holding? It looks like a bundle of firewood. All neatly bound together with cloth."

My delicious Cornish game hen settled in my stomach like a chunk of granite. "Yeesh. It's Zenora, all right. And I think those are long sage sticks. She's not alone. Glenda's right behind her. Orange hair this month, not the holographic spectrum from earlier this summer. I wonder what they want. They've got to be looking for me. This isn't someplace they frequent."

"Are those Halloween costumes?" Stephanie asked.

I shook my head. "Nope. Normal attire. Geez, I thought Zenora would be working late at Uris Library tonight."

A second later, Glenda hovered over me. "Cammy said you'd be here. Zenora was in the middle of helping a student research the adjuncts to Linear A and B from the ancient Minoans when she had a horrible vision. Told the student she thought she had a touch of the scourge and he took off without saying a word. She drove to my house and, well, here we are."

Terrific. Now I have a touch of the scourge.

Zenora leaned over the table and acknowledged everyone. Then she looked directly at me. "The air is thick with death."

"I already know. The entire Finger Lakes knows. It's been on the news. Not every day a body shows up in a Halloween cauldron."

Zenora pressed the sage sticks close to her chest and inhaled.

"Death is lingering. Don't tempt it. Be very careful this weekend. And consider a ritualistic cleansing of your house and the winery. That's why I brought these." She thrust the sage sticks at me and next I knew, I was cradling them.

"Let Zenora perform the cleansing tonight," Glenda said. "Best to stay one step ahead of unearthly forces."

"No. Not tonight!" I tried not to shriek but it was difficult. The anxious look on Zenora's face was a combination of disappointment and fear, compelling me to offer up an alternative. "I have a better idea. A much better idea. Tomorrow night, beginning at dusk, I have to tell ghost stories around a bonfire. It's part of Hallow Wine Weekend. Can't we add the sage sticks to the bonfire? Much more efficient if you ask me."

Zenora and Glenda looked at each other before Zenora spoke. "It will offer some protection."

"Some is better than nothing," I chirped. "I mean, it's best to have the pure energy circulate around our guests. I'll give these to our vineyard manager since he's the one building the bonfire."

"Don't worry," Glenda said, "I'll make sure to bring more tomorrow so there'll be enough for both nights. Zenora and I will be able to join you for the first night but the second night falls on Halloween and we're taking part in a ceremony to usher the dead into the next world."

Stephanie widened her eyes. "Huh?"

Zenora took a step closer to her. "The veil that separates the living from the dead becomes a porous thread, making it easier for those souls who haven't left this world to move on."

Like a cruise send-off but without the confetti and champagne.

"Well, I don't know about you guys, but I'm ready to move on," Don said. "Tomorrow morning's going to hit us in the face like a bag of rocks and it won't be over until Monday morning."

I motioned for the waiter to bring our bill. "Not Monday morning. It won't be over until we figure out who murdered Donovan."

And suddenly, I gasped. I had inadvertently let the cat out of the bag without realizing it.

"Donovan?" Glenda asked. "Donovan Brin, the writer who was in our winery to interview Franz? *That* Donovan?"

"You can't breathe a word of this to anyone." I stood and faced her, shoving my chair into the table. "Yes, that Donovan. If word gets out that our winery leaked the information before it was officially disclosed to the public, we'd be in all sorts of deep you-know-what for interfering with a suspicious death investigation."

"A suspicious death investigation?" Glenda clutched the amethyst pendant from around her neck and held it firm in her grasp. "We figured someone had a stroke or something and wound up in our cauldron. All of us thought the sheriff's office sent a crew to the scene to determine who the person was and how he or she got there. In fact, none of us were fazed by the crime scene tape. Those deputies plaster it all over the place."

"You can't say a word. Not to anyone. Not until Donovan's name is released to the media."

Zenora grabbed my arm and shook it. "You have to find out who murdered that man so he can cross over to the next world, preferably while the veil is thin."

"He may have to cross over with a thick veil because no one can solve a murder investigation in forty-eight hours. I don't care what they do on TV. I write that stuff, too, you know."

Now complete with quaint little villages . . .

"It's up to the sheriff's office," Don announced. "They're the ones conducting the official investigation."

Stephanie snickered. "Only on paper. I'm with Norrie's friends on this one." Then she looked at me. "Think you can manage to talk Adrienne into penning that article on our Merlot, Whitney into giving us a podcast and the yet-to-move-on spirit of Donovan Brin into giving up his killer?"

"Only if Zenora comes up with something stronger than sage sticks."

Chapter 13

The list of disasters-yet-to-be was growing but at least I didn't have to face the bonfire nightmare alone. Since the Grey Egret and Two Witches Winery shared the same hill, Theo and Don had the bright idea that we could do one combined bonfire. And while they were more than willing to have their vineyard crew assist with the gathering of wood and the building of the bonfire, they weren't all that keen on telling the ghost stories themselves.

"You're the one with the imagination and the flair for the dramatic," Theo told me when we first discussed the idea a few days ago. "Meanwhile, Don and I can stoke the fire and keep the crowd under control."

Now, with Zenora's disquieting image of the dead waiting to cross over, I was relieved they'd be there along with Bradley, who was expected back from Buffalo around that time. True, we couldn't exactly hold up a sign saying *This way to the afterlife. Keep moving*, but maybe the scent of burning sage would hurry them on.

When I got home from Port of Call that night and greeted Charlie, I was convinced I'd get a good night's sleep before Hallow Wine Weekend started. Aargh. So much for wishful thinking. While my body screamed "sleep," my mind wouldn't turn off, and next thing I knew, I found myself listing motives for Donovan's murder when it would have been far easier to count sheep.

If that wasn't bad enough, when I finally did fall asleep, I dreamt Donovan's wife, mistress, and girlfriend had taken over our cauldron, making Macbeth's witches look like Disney princesses. And while the witches' prophecy about Macbeth becoming King of Scotland came true, so did Don's. I woke up like a bag of rocks hit me in the head. At least I didn't oversleep.

Charlie must have sensed I was in a hurry because he took care of business and gobbled his kibble while I ate a cup of granola and washed it down with iced tea, even though I would have preferred to linger over a cup of coffee.

"You've got to stay inside your fence," I said. "Too much road traffic today. Be a good boy and you can join me tonight at the bonfire."

Since it was daylight with no precipitation in sight, I walked to the tasting room rather than start up the Subaru. The forecast was in our favor for once, promising crisp cool air and abundant sunshine all weekend. I expected the news channels to make a big deal out of our unfortunate discovery, but as of early this morning nothing more was said except that a dead body was found on our property and that the sheriff's office was looking into the matter. No identification given and no talk about the victim.

It was such a benign announcement coming from all of the channels that I wondered if the coroner's report revealed a heart attack or stroke. If that was the case, then maybe it really was pranksters who put Don and Theo's egret into the hands of the Grim Reaper and thrust a dagger into Donovan's back, thinking he was part of our display. Then again, they would have realized the body was real. Too bad Gladys was off on Saturdays because now I had to wait until Monday morning.

The crime scene tape surrounding our display, coupled with Cammy's new sign, made it look as if this is what we had designed all along. Hallelujah. I bounded up the steps and into the winery, announcing myself as the door closed behind me.

We were an hour from opening, and according to Lizzie, Cammy was in the kitchen, fast at work with Glenda, preparing the remainder of the crescent roll chocolate-filled mummies. Sam and Roger had already set up the food sampling table and were now embellishing it with seasonal decorations.

"Have any of you seen the Halloween cocktail napkins?" Sam asked. "I need to put them on the table."

"They're over here," Lizzie called out from the front of the winery.

"Someone must have set them down near my cash register this morning."

"Wow. Is that apple pie I smell?" I breezed past Lizzie, Sam, and Roger on my way to the bistro. The cinnamon was the first spice to hit my nose, followed by ginger, nutmeg, and cloves.

Emma looked up from her worktable behind the bistro. "Good morning, Norrie. I could hear you clear across the room. We're making apple-filled pastries as well as baked apples with honey and cloves. Fred just put another tray in the oven. Hold on, I'll get you one that we baked a few minutes ago."

The flaky crust gave way to a delectable filling that combined chucks of Granny Smith and MacIntosh apples, seasoned just right.

"I may never leave the bistro. This is incredible."

Emma beamed. "Wait until you see what's on the lunch menu for Hallow Wine Weekend: hot roasted turkey sandwiches with butternut squash, pumpkin curry, and baked mac and cheese with mushrooms."

"Whoa."

"By the way, any news on the unfortunate person who died here yesterday? Was the sheriff's office able to identify him? Sorry, but Fred and I couldn't offer much help to the deputy yesterday."

"No official word, yet. To be honest, I hope it stays that way until we get through this event."

"I know what you mean. Anyway, I need to chop more apples for the pastries. Stop by at lunch."

"Stop by? I may plant myself here permanently."

We both laughed and I trotted back to the tasting room in time to help Sam bring clean wineglasses to the tables. When we opened a short while later, Glenda, Roger, Sam, and two college students working part-time were at their tables with another one handling the food sampling. Cammy was the designated photographer for the event, taking photos of those customers who came in costume and wanted to enter the event's contest. We had worked it out so she would use her iPhone and forward the photos to the winery email, where Lizzie would put them in a special file.

My role was the gopher. I hustled back and forth replenishing supplies, carting used wineglasses to the kitchen and running the dishwasher.

The small alcove between the banquet room and the tasting room served as the backdrop for the photos. Earlier in the week Glenda and Cammy decorated it with corn stalks, mini pumpkins, and large faux acorns.

Surprisingly, only a handful of people mentioned the dead body and all of us recited the party line: probably a medical issue. By a little past eleven, the room was packed with customers waiting their turns at a tasting table while they perused the wine and gift racks.

There was no slowdown at Cammy's alcove, either, with an abundance of witches, medieval maidens, pirates, and TV personas. One person clad in a taco bodysuit got my vote, but it was still early in the day.

Periodically, I checked my emails and found one from Godfrey. "I left you a message on your landline. Your voicemail box is full. Empty it, will you? Anyway, I won't be able to make tonight's bonfire. I have to cover for Alex Bollinger. He was supposed to speak at a Kiwanis dinner in Canandaigua about his recent cockroach study, but he picked up a stomach bug. Don't want to go into details. Anyway, I'll make it for Sunday's event. Have a happy Hallow Wine Weekend."

I don't know what part of the email was worse: picturing someone talk about cockroaches at a Kiwanis dinner or visualizing Alex's stomach upset. It was a toss-up for sure. I replied, "Tell Alex I hope he feels better and good luck tonight. You'll do great. See you tomorrow!"

At a little before noon, after I snagged another apple pastry from the bistro, I began to relieve workers so they could grab something for lunch. First at Roger's table, then at Sam's, followed by the part-time worker tables. Glenda told me she'd eaten a giant breakfast so she wasn't hungry and that I should relieve Cammy at the photography area.

"I'll make it quick," Cammy said.

"Take your time and eat. Everything's moving smoothly. I only hope I can say as much when it comes time for the bonfire. I don't know why, but I have a creepy feeling about it. Not that I believe in premonitions or anything, but Zenora really freaked me out last night at Port of Call."

"Zenora can freak out Freddy Krueger. I wouldn't worry about it."

"I'm trying not to. I have other things on my mind right now. Like I said earlier this morning when we chatted, I'm anxious for Whitney Fontana to stop by so I can convince her to do a podcast. Not to mention twisting Adrienne's arm."

"I know. Unless you can talk Donovan's assistant into writing that *Wine Enthusiast* article posthumously, Two Witches, the Grey Egret, and Gable Hill may have to wait another year for an opportunity like that."

"And there's no guarantee that next time around our Merlot will be so extraordinary. Each year is different and we have no control over things like the weather."

"Or who enters our winery. Turn around and take a look."

I'm afraid I didn't want to know.

Chapter 14

"Oh, heavens, no! Grizzly Gary. What are the chances people will think his uniform is a Halloween costume?"

"Slim to none." Cammy patted my arm. "Have fun."

With that, she made a beeline for the bistro and I headed over to Deputy Hickman.

"Good day, Miss Ellington. I won't keep you long in the middle of your festivities, but I do need to have a word with you."

"Um, sure. We can go into my office."

Deputy Hickman refused to take a seat, which was really awkward. I wanted to get off my feet but couldn't do that with him standing in front of me.

"I'll make this brief," he said. "The man's body in your cauldron was identified as Donovan Brin by a source close to him."

"I already told you that. I was the one who identified him yesterday morning."

"Yes. Glancing at the cauldron before shrieking and screaming out his name is not deemed a viable identification. However, we were able to substantiate it."

"With his assistant, right? Adrienne Stafine."

"I'm not at liberty to confirm that."

"Oh, come on. Who else could it be? She was the only one up here with him. The photographer isn't expected until sometime today. And I don't even know who the photographer is. Someone from *Wine Enthusiast*."

Deputy Hickman flipped a few pages in his notepad. "I expect the news channels to bombard your winery once the name is released so I'll caution you again. No theorizing. Refer them to my office. They're like hyenas feasting on a kill when it comes to a story."

"When will the hyenas, I mean the media, get the name?"

"Tomorrow. There are a few formalities that have to be taken care of first."

"That means his next of kin was contacted. The wife, right?"

Grizzly Gary rubbed the back of his neck and sighed. "She was notified by the authorities in Westchester County where she resides, but that's not why I paid you a visit. Or why I intend to stop by the Grey Egret and Gable Hill."

"Uh-huh."

"The preliminary examination by the coroner showed no signs of bodily injury, with the exception of a stab wound in his back. The coroner determined that wound occurred after Mr. Brin was already dead. We believe whoever was responsible used that dagger to send a message."

Isn't killing the guy enough of a message?

"I'm not sure I understand."

"The juxtaposition of objects in all three of your displays may mean something. We're not sure. Since Hallow Wine Weekend ends tomorrow, we are directing the wineries involved not to remove their displays."

"How can we remove it when there's crime scene tape all around it?"

"I simply needed to be clear, Miss Ellington. The coroner has labeled the death *suspicious*. We do not expect the results of the preliminary toxicology screening for another twenty-four hours. And even then, the results will most likely need further review and testing."

"Let me get this straight. You think Donovan was poisoned but you won't know until the lab figures it out. Worse yet, you think whoever did it used our displays like some sort of a puzzle for the authorities to solve? How am I doing so far?"

"Splendid, if you can keep all of that to yourself. There are a number of unanswered questions and the investigation is in its infancy."

"Um, since you have your notepad out, I've got two pressing questions myself. Where's Donovan's car and—wait—the next thing is more of a statement. Donovan was a big guy. One person couldn't have dragged his body to that cauldron by himself. Or herself. I think we're talking a tag team at the very least. Maybe his assistant knows more than we think."

"*We* don't think anything yet. *We* are still gathering evidence. And let me remind you again, in case you had any thoughts about snooping around, *Don't!*"

"I can't help it if I'm observant."

"Let's not get into semantics. I've got to head down the hill to the Grey Egret and then over to Gable Hill. I came here first because, quite frankly, I was most concerned about you."

"Don't worry. We've got lots of sage sticks on hand."

He gave me a quizzical look and then exited the room without another word. I was about to leave it at that when something crossed my mind. I raced out and caught him just as he opened the winery's main door and started down the steps.

"Wait! One more thing. I know you've spoken to Adrienne. Please tell me you directed her to stay in town. This has nothing to do with the murder. I mean, *the suspicious death.* It has to do with that article for *Wine Enthusiast.* Business, that's all."

"Off the record, understood?"

I nodded.

"Miss Stafine will be remaining at Belhurst Castle at least until the beginning of the week."

"Thank you."

Just then, two stocky men dressed as ghouls brushed past him and Grizzly Gary wasted no time getting into his car.

"Thank goodness we don't have to contend with a sheriff's car parked right out front," Lizzie said when I got back inside. "I could see it from here whenever the door opened or closed. Makes our patrons wonder if there's trouble in here."

"I know what you mean. Hmm, speaking of which, I'm going to give Theo and Don the heads-up. Then Stephanie."

I shot off two text messages before returning to the tasting room. It was early afternoon and I had hoped Whitney would show up, but so far, no luck. I hadn't counted on Adrienne making an appearance, but then again, what was she supposed to do? Sit in her room all weekend waiting to be grilled by the sheriff's office?

Ice Queen or not, the woman had to be curious about Hallow Wine Weekend. And she did have a rental car. Maybe luck would be on my side after all.

An hour and forty minutes passed and no sign of either one of them. I moseyed over to the bistro for a cup of their baked mac and cheese and gobbled it up in seconds. Then I started back to the tasting room when a woman with spiked reddish hair and an all-weather coat tapped me on the shoulder. She looked to be my age with freckles and a few ear piercings. "Are you Norrie? The lady at the register said I'd find you here."

Lizzie must be more observant than any of us.

"I'm Norrie. Can I help you?"

"Ronny Morgan. I'm the photographer from *Wine Enthusiast.* I meant to be here much earlier but my flight had engine trouble and we were stuck on the tarmac for two hours. I flew in from Charlottesville and drove from the airport in Syracuse."

"Not Rochester? That seems to be the usual airport."

"Maybe, but I was able to secure a rental car in Syracuse so I booked my Delta flight to that airport."

She looked around the room and grinned. "This place is really hopping. I can feel the energy already."

"Have you stopped by the other two wineries in the article?"

"Not yet. With a name like Two Witches, I had to come here first."

At least the name paid off for something. When Francine and I were in school, we were teased mercilessly about being the two witches. We begged our folks to change the name but they refused. Especially since the hill was Two Witches Hill and they couldn't very well change the name of a county road. Even if it wasn't much more than a glorified driveway.

"Great! Please feel free to take all the photos you'd like. If you need one with people tasting our Merlot, we can arrange that. Just let me know. Listen, you must be hungry. Our bistro is phenomenal and lunch is on us. Come on, I'll introduce you to the chefs."

"Thanks. By the way, have you seen Donovan? I wanted to run a few things by him."

"Um, not lately." *And not alive.*

It was getting worse and worse keeping quiet about Donovan. I almost wanted to grab a megaphone and make an official announcement. The only thing keeping me from doing that was the thought of Grizzly Gary locking me up in the county jail for interfering in a crime investigation.

With no real leads as to who could have killed Donovan, and no motive, it was like taking a hike in quicksand. I did, however, have one thing in my favor. Adrienne told me Donovan was alive and well Thursday evening in the hotel lounge. That meant I could construct a time line of sorts. Especially if Rosalee's friend still worked at Belhurst Castle.

"Must be he's at one of the other two wineries whose Merlot he's featuring," Ronny went on. "I'll catch up with him one way or the other. Say, was his assistant with him when he interviewed your winery?"

"Adrienne?"

"Uh-huh. Adrienne Stafine. Kind of hard to miss with her looks."

"Yeah, she was with him. All business."

"Hmm, I didn't think she'd continue working for him but I guess I was wrong."

"What do you mean?"

"Adrienne's been looking for another position in the industry but hasn't had much luck. I shouldn't say this, but I think Donovan's been blackballing her."

"Whoa. That's a pretty strong statement."

"Listen, everyone on staff at *Wine Enthusiast* knows how talented she is when it comes to writing. At a wine release in California last month, she told me she didn't know how much longer she could stand working with him. Used words like *officious* and *egocentric*. If he hasn't been blackballing her, then I'd bet money he's giving her lousy recommendations."

"That's awful." *Not to mention a darned good motive for getting him out of the way.*

Ronny nodded. "All the more reason I'm glad I work independently. Especially with status climbers like Donovan around. Word at the magazine is that he'd step over bodies to get the story he wants. Frankly, I'm surprised he's covering the Merlots. That story was supposed to go to Raisa James. Somehow she wound up covering something just over the border in Pennsylvania. That's why I try to stay on his good side even if it means walking on eggshells around him. Last thing I need is for him to insist another photographer cover his story."

"Wow. Thanks for the inside scoop."

"I probably shouldn't have been so loose-lipped, but after years of putting up with Donovan, it finally got to me. Too bad you had to be at the receiving end."

"Like I said, knowing the background helps. Follow me. That's Fred and Emma, our chefs, over there. Come on, I'll introduce you. Make sure you come back tonight for the event's bonfire. You can't miss it. We're doing it with the Grey Egret and I'll be telling ghost stories."

"Is that a passion of yours? Storytelling?"

"Not ghost stories, but I do write screenplays for a Canadian film company. I'm just babysitting the winery for a few weeks so my sister and her husband can chase down disgusting insects."

"Huh?"

"He's an entomologist. I prefer not to think about it."

Ronny laughed, and once I introduced her to Emma and Fred, I darted back to my office and phoned Rosalee.

"Don't tell me you're calling to announce another dead body on your property," Rosalee said when one of her employees got her to take my call. "I heard it first thing on the news. Probably an inebriated person with low blood sugar. I've heard of people going into diabetic comas."

"Uh, I don't think it was that. Listen, I may find out more if you can give me the name of your friend who works at Belhurst Castle."

"What does Belhurst Castle have to do with anything? And her name is Ada Mae. She works the front desk Wednesdays through Sundays from three to nine. Doesn't like working mornings."

Join the club.

"I wish I could tell you more, Rosalee, but I've been given a gag order from Deputy Hickman."

"You told me enough. I'm not daft. I can figure it out. The victim was staying at the Belhurst. Hmm, seems a certain writer for *Wine Enthusiast* was also staying there."

"Shh! Don't even say it out loud."

"Don't worry. I'm not one of those gossipers. Good thing you didn't get my sister Marilyn on the phone. Since she retired, she's become the voice of the Finger Lakes. I'd better be quiet. She's helping out here today and she snoops around like crazy."

"Thanks, Rosalee. I'll keep you posted. Good luck with Hallow Wine Weekend. By the way, who's telling the ghost stories at your bonfire?"

"Marilyn. Who else? She'll scare the daylights out of everyone for sure. I figure she'll either wind up telling horror stories or detailing her last colonoscopy. Either way, our guests will get the true horror treatment for sure."

I squelched a laugh and thanked her before ending the call. Then, I dialed Belhurst Castle and asked for Ada Mae.

"This is Ada Mae. How may I help you?"

"This is Norrie Ellington from Two Witches Winery and I need you to help solve a murder."

Chapter 15

Ada Mae gasped. "A murder?"

"It appears that way. I'm a friend of Rosalee Marbleton's and I'm trying to piece together some information."

"A murder you said?"

"Uh-huh. I'm surprised sheriff deputies from Yates and Ontario counties haven't spoken with you about it."

"Oh, they spoke with me yesterday but they didn't say anything about a murder. They asked if I had seen anything unusual on Thursday and retrieved a guest's room key from the manager."

"You can't breathe a word of this to anyone, although I'm sure the news media will make an announcement any day now. By any chance did you happen to see if anyone joined Mr. Donovan Brin while he was in the lounge Thursday night? He's a writer for a wine magazine and he's here with his assistant, a young woman. I know the lounge is visible from the front desk. Perhaps something caught your eye."

"Mr. Brin? Was he—Oh, dear. Can you tell me what he looked like?"

I described Donovan as well as Adrienne. Ada Mae acknowledged she saw them both and that Adrienne left the lounge at a little before eight. Said she knew the time because that was when she took her gastro pill.

"Did anyone else join Mr. Brin when Adrienne left?"

"Not in the corner where he was seated. But a stocky middle-aged gentleman with wavy brown hair and black rectangular glasses had words with him as Mr. Brin exited the lounge."

"Words, what words? And what middle-aged gentleman? Was he one of the guests?"

"Oh, dear. I couldn't say if he was one of the guests because I don't register all of them. But I did catch snippets of their conversation."

"Like what? What snippets? This is really important."

Ada Mae took a breath that sounded more like a hum. "I don't know who said what, because I only heard the words. They were faced away from me."

"That's okay. What did you hear?"

"One of them said something about false advertising and deceiving the public. And the other one said, 'It's going to end now.' Then they left. I could still hear them talking in the corridor but it was all garbled."

"Did Mr. Brin return to the lounge?"

"Not while I was still here. I get off at nine. Guests who need assistance after I've gone home push a button for the manager on duty. But the bartender is on duty until one. Give me a moment, I can tell you who worked that night."

I waited a few seconds and Ada Mae was back on the line. "Marsha Whitman. She works Mondays through Thursdays."

"Thanks so much, Ada Mae. You were a terrific help."

"Tell Rosalee hello from me."

"Shall do. And thanks again."

When the call ended, I had more puzzling questions than before. However, I also had another suspect I could add to my very scant list— the middle-aged man with the wavy brown hair. If the last time Adrienne saw Donovan was around eight, then perhaps the last person to see him alive was the brown-haired man. Then again, who knows who Donovan could have spoken with after that encounter? Especially if he went back to the hotel's bar. I knew I'd need to chat with Marsha, but it would have to wait until Monday since I was on ghost story detail for the next two nights.

While I was still at my desk, I grabbed a piece of computer paper from the printer and jotted down a list of people who had been in Donovan's circle for the past few days. That included Adrienne, who pretty much had a solid motive for giving her boss the send-off; Whitney, whose stay at the Belhurst seemed a tad too coincidental; and now the wavy-haired man who had words with Donovan. I also penciled in Ronny. Given what she told me about Adrienne, I doubted there was any love lost between Ronny and Donovan. And while she did say she flew in from Charlottesville, she could have lied. Heck, she could have been in cahoots with Adrienne.

The list was ridiculously short but Donovan didn't wind up in our cauldron by himself. He had help. And I needed to find out who before Two Witches became noted for murders rather than wine.

That, in and of itself, should have been plenty of motive for me to stick my nose into the investigation, but when Lizzie knocked on my door with a cryptic note someone had dropped off by the cash register a few minutes ago, I knew whoever wrote it wasn't messing around. Lizzie told me she had no idea who placed it there but that I should "use my best Nancy Drew deduction skills." Ugh!

The note was printed on plain white paper in Times New Roman and it read, "When Donovan's name gets plastered all over the news, back off or all fingers will point to you."

I couldn't call the Grey Egret fast enough. Luckily, Theo answered the call after three rings and told me they had gotten the exact same note. They were about to call Stephanie and me but it was too frenetic in their tasting room.

"What kind of diabolical message is that?" I asked him. "Someone's idea of a prank?"

"More like someone's idea of a threat. Look, it's nuts around here but we'll try to give Stephanie a call in a bit. We'll touch base sometime between five thirty and dusk when the bonfire starts. Meanwhile, I wouldn't worry about it."

"Think I should call Deputy Hickman?"

"Only if you want to add more chaos to this event. We can call him later. It's unnerving, but it's not a death threat."

"Thanks. That's reassuring."

Theo chuckled. "Anytime."

I tromped back into the tasting room hoping to chat with Cammy but once again, Lizzie approached me. "Stephanie Ipswich is on the phone. Sounds hysterical." I followed Lizzie to her spot at the cash register, where the ancient landline phone was located. A wall phone, of all things. I picked up the receiver and got an earful before I could say a word.

"Is that you, Norrie? Someone dropped off a horrible note at our hostess station. I think it constitutes blackmail, or some sort of threat."

"Did it say back off or someone will point a finger at you for Donovan's death?"

"Yes, but how do you—"

"The Grey Egret got the same note and so did we. Someone must have overheard us last night at Port of Call."

"I don't know how anyone could have heard anything with all that noise in there."

"I asked Theo if he thought we should call Deputy Hickman but he didn't think it was such a good idea."

"He's probably right. We don't want to call any more negative attention to our wineries. At least not until this weekend event is over. Besides, what's the sheriff's office going to do?"

"I'll tell you one thing, whoever's behind it doesn't want us snooping around. What better way than to threaten us? Listen, while you're on the phone, have you seen Adrienne or Whitney today?"

"No, but I've been so busy in the kitchen I wouldn't have noticed Elvis if he walked in."

"Too bad you've got your own bonfire to deal with. Theo and I plan to talk before the bonfires get started."

"Let me know if anything more comes up."

"Okay. And just think, Halloween isn't until tomorrow."

Stephanie groaned before ending the call.

If I had any great hopes of Whitney showing up to discuss a podcast, they fizzled out by a little before five. Our staff looked totally whipped and Cammy told me if she had to take one more photo of someone in a costume, she'd puke.

With sunset at a little past six and twilight not until after seven, it didn't give anyone a whole lot of downtime if they wanted to attend the bonfire. And, with the exception of Roger, who had a prior commitment, Lizzie, whose bedtime was shortly after dusk, and the part-time college students, who had other plans, everyone on staff planned to be at the bonfire.

At least Cammy and I had the good sense to think ahead. We ordered four giant pizzas from Cams in Geneva and had them delivered to the winery at six thirty. The entire tasting room crew dug in along with Fred and Emma. I made sure to put slices of the meat-lovers pie aside for John and his crew, who were getting the bonfire going.

"Are you ready to scare the daylights out of our guests?" Sam asked. "No wimpy stuff. I'm looking for some blood-curdling, bone-rattling stories."

I winked. "You'll get them. I dug up an old copy of terrifying Spanish ghost stories, left over from my high school Spanish class."

"Are you sure it's not a copy of the homework assignments you turned in?"

"Laugh now, but all of you will be shaking in your boots later."

I didn't realize it at the time, but as it turned out, I was the one shaking, and I wasn't alone.

Chapter 16

I darted home after chomping down on two veggie-laden pizza slices. Charlie needed to be fed and I wanted to grab a warmer jacket. That, and my crib notes for the bonfire. Twenty minutes later, I headed down the hill with Charlie at my side. I had him on a long leash because I wasn't about to take any chances of having him run into the woods after some nocturnal animal.

"You need to be a good boy tonight. No whining or pestering people if they brought food."

Who was I kidding?

Cammy had suggested we supply marshmallows and even went as far as putting handfuls in small plastic bags for anyone who wanted to toast them. The sticks were easy: We had an abundance and John had no problem stacking an extra pile of them off to the side of the bonfire for those folks who enjoyed this campfire tradition.

John estimated twenty to thirty people and set up rows of wooden benches that we used from time to time for other winery events. Twilight was slowly descending, and as I looked across the lake, I could see scatterings of bonfires from the eastside wineries. Ours was well underway with flickers of orange and blue flames but not quite bright enough to make out the faces of our guests. In spite of the autumn cold, I could feel the bonfire's heat from three or four yards away. It made me question why I ever thought I needed to drag out my fleece-lined jacket.

True to his word, John had added the sage sticks to the bonfire's logs and the aroma was unmistakable. If nothing else, Zenora could rest assured the air around us would be purified. I owed the vineyard guys for all their extra work and made a mental note to buy them lunch next week.

At least fifteen or so people, including Fred and Emma, were already seated when I got there. Small clusters of guests walked from our parking lot to the spot between the wineries and the woods, and as

I looked closely, I realized Don and Theo were among them. I immediately headed their way.

"You two walked all the way up here from your winery?" I asked.

Don shook his head. "Seriously? That's a quarter mile at least. We parked near your winery entrance. I had enough exercise for one day." He bent down and patted Charlie, who immediately rubbed against his leg. "Listen, Theo and I can hang on to Charlie while you do your ghost story thing. He'll be fine."

"Are you sure?"

"Of course."

I handed him Charlie's leash and reminded the dog once again not to be a pest. "I know what you mean about getting enough exercise today," I told Don. "Come on, Cammy's got a stash of marshmallows she's handing out. I don't see Glenda or Sam but I'm sure they'll be here soon enough."

"If I'm not mistaken, I think that's Glenda to the right of the bonfire. Holy cow. Take a look. That's not a ritual I remember from the Boy Scouts."

I closed my eyes for a brief second, praying Don was mistaken, but unfortunately, he wasn't. Glenda and her friend Zenora stood a few feet back from the fire pit, dressed in long black cloaks with astrological symbols on the fabric. Both of them had their hands raised to the air and it wasn't to lead anyone in a high school cheer.

Their motions rivaled a bat when it spread its wings and took to the air. And while their feet were anchored to the ground, their hips swayed, and their upper torsos gyrated.

"What a great way to start the program!" someone shouted.

I turned to face the crowd, now estimated closer to thirty people. "I'd better get this thing started or who knows what they'll do," I said to Don and Theo. Without wasting any time, I thanked Zenora and Glenda and motioned them to the seats in front. Stupefied, they moseyed to the benches and sat, much to my relief. Next, I introduced myself and welcomed everyone to the first bonfire night of Hallow

Wine Weekend. I could see a few flasks in the crowd and reminded our guests not to drink and drive. "If you need a designated driver, see one of us after the program."

Rather than face any lawsuits, many wineries, like ours, contracted with local drivers. Better safe than sorry. By now, the soft hues of twilight were gone, replaced by a dark crescent moon sky with a handful of stars peeking out.

"Feel free to toast marshmallows," I continued, "as we begin with the first chilling story of the evening." It was a Mexican urban legend, and it probably went further back than that, but I recounted the tale of La Llorona, the crying woman who haunted rivers, streams, and lakes in search of the children she drowned.

"Just stay out of the water," Theo announced. It was followed by "Hey, that's *Jaws*."

Next, I moved on to el chupacabra, the tale of a blood-sucking beast that roams the woods from Mexico to Canada. For now, Glenda and Zenora were seated near the bonfire. But for how long was anyone's guess.

In gruesome and gory detail, I described the chupacabra beast, including the rustling sound it made while moving about the woods. Then, without warning, something soft brushed against my neck from behind and I let out a shriek that caused everyone to follow suit.

I jumped, ready to flee for my life, when I turned to see Bradley behind me.

"Holy hell, Norrie. You scared the daylights out of me. I thought you'd know it was me."

"Oh my gosh." I threw my arms around his neck and kissed him. Then I cleared my throat and said, "Sorry, everyone. It was only my boyfriend." That pronouncement was followed by comments like, "Is he the chupacabra?" and "Someone ought to buy him earplugs."

After a few seconds of more jabs, I finally finished the ghost story and gave everyone a five-minute marshmallow-toasting break. That's when Zenora approached me, telling me she had a premonition of a dead woman's body in our woods.

My stomach did a flip-flop. "Are you sure it was our woods as opposed to, well, anyone's woods?"

Zenora nodded. "Yes, these woods. Adjacent to the vineyards."

"Lots of woods are adjacent to vineyards on this lake."

"But not within yards of your house. I saw your house in the vision, too."

Wonderful. Why couldn't she see this week's lottery number?

"As long as the dead woman's body isn't in my house, I say we continue with tonight's program."

Zenora took my wrist and looked straight at me. "I don't know if she's dead yet. It was a premonition. She may still be alive. At least for a little while."

"Geez, that's worse than the ghost stories I told."

"The veil between the worlds is getting thinner and thinner. By midnight tomorrow it will be transparent."

"So, um, one way or another, it's curtains for this woman in your vision."

Zenora rubbed her arms together and nodded. "If she departed recently, her soul may still be lingering in your woods."

Near the body, no doubt.

"Zenora, do all of your visions come to fruition?"

"Not all of them. Some are merely warnings of what could come to pass."

"Well, maybe this is a blinking yellow light. You know. Caution. Look, if we hear of a missing woman, I'll point Deputy Hickman to our woods. Preferably in daylight. It's pitch-black and way too risky to get flashlights and traipse through the woods in search of a possible body. Lots of brush, logs, and rocks. Not to mention scary night creatures like bats. Meanwhile, I'll remind our guests to steer clear of the woods." *As if any sane person needs to be reminded.*

Zenora returned to her seat on the bench and continued to rub her arms together while Glenda put a marshmallow on a long stick and approached the bonfire. It was my cue to continue with the program.

"Beware forced marriages," I said, "or you may wind up like the ghost of Tenerife." The audience was still as I detailed the sorrowful ending of one Catalina Lercaro, one of Spain's most famous apparitions. "The poor woman threw herself into a well rather than face an arranged marriage. Now her apparition moves through the shadows, haunting all those who inhabit the island. But Catalina isn't the only restless soul. As we enjoy Hallow Wine Weekend, remember, All Hallows' Eve is tomorrow and the curtain lifts between the earthly world and the afterlife. Beware the bony hands of death that may reach out and—"

A sudden shriek and I looked behind. Three dark figures emerged from the woods, faces illuminated from beneath their mouths. More screams from our guests followed by a few people getting up from the benches. I took a closer look and bellowed, "It's all part of the program! No reason to freak out!"

No wonder I hadn't seen Sam in the crowd. Unbeknownst to all of us, he arranged for two of his college classmates to join him in giving all of us a scare. Cammy raced over to him and kicked his boot. "I could've had a heart attack. Good thing Lizzie goes to bed early."

Just then, the audience applauded. And not one of those required applauses that usually follow boring lectures. They were cheering, clapping, and whistling.

"We're really glad you enjoyed tonight's ghost stories," I said. "Our event bonfires continue tomorrow night. We hope you'll select another one of our wineries and attend theirs. Ours will be a duplicate of tonight's. Be careful walking back to the parking lot. Our vineyard staff will be off to the side with flashlights, but please don't run, no matter how scared you are."

A few laughs followed as the attendees stood and started down the road to the winery. I approached Sam and his buddies, not sure if I should read them the riot act or congratulate them for pulling one over on us. "Holy mackerel. That was a classic ending for sure, but next time, give me the heads-up, okay?"

Sam nodded. "I kind of figured if you knew in advance, you'd give it away by checking out the woods."

"Hmm, you're probably right. Are you guys up for doing this again tomorrow? It really was a classic ending."

Sam looked at his friends, both a good foot or so taller than he was, and they nodded in agreement. "It's a go. Should be fun. Oh, before I forget, Chad found this woolly scarf in the woods when we scoped out a hiding place." He reached under the long black trench coat he had on and handed me a wadded-up silver pashmina with intermittent gold tassels on the edge.

"What's the matter? You look like you've seen a ghost. And it's not the lighting from the bonfire."

I took the pashmina from him and stood motionless. Long enough for Zenora's words to sink in. My mouth had suddenly become dry and I coughed a few times. As I looked around, most of the crowd had now left their seats and were trekking down the hill. "I think this is Whitney Fontana's pashmina. The podcaster I met Friday night at Port of Call. She was wearing one that looked just like it."

Sam shrugged. "It could have come from anywhere. The wind blows like crazy around here. Scarves arc a dime a dozen."

But not expensive pashminas.

"I suppose you're right. Anyway, thanks for adding some excitement to this event. And if you plan on something more frightening tomorrow, let me know. Okay?"

"Sure thing. It was a hoot, all right."

Sam and his buddies took off as Bradley, Cammy, Don, and Theo approached me. I held out the pashmina and made eye contact with each of them. "Sam's crew found this in our woods. The last time I saw it was on Whitney Fontana's back when we were at Port of Call on Friday." Then I quickly explained to Bradley who Whitney was, before I continued. "I expected to see her today at our winery but she never showed, even though she gave me every indication she would."

I moved closer to the bonfire so we'd have more light. "Holy crap. This better not be Zenora's premonition. How many dead bodies can anyone deal with in a single weekend? And how many calls do I need to make to Deputy Hickman?"

"Whoa." Bradley put an arm around me. "We don't know there's a dead body in those woods and we hardly have enough evidence to call the sheriff's office."

Theo handed me Charlie's leash and the dog took a few steps toward me before making himself comfortable on the ground. "Bradley's right," he said. "There are no missing person alerts because I get them on my phone and so far, nothing. And as far as that pashmina goes, we don't know how long it's been in the woods or where it came from. Deputy Hickman would blow us off in a nanosecond."

"Not if Whitney hasn't been seen in her hotel."

I took my cell phone from my pocket and had Siri get me the phone number to Belhurst Castle, then added it to my contacts. With fingers crossed, I prayed Whitney was sitting comfortably at the bar with a nice glass of Merlot in her hand. If not, I'd owe Zenora an apology.

Chapter 17

It was after nine and Ada Mae was no longer on duty at Belhurst Castle. Thinking fast, I had the automated system transfer the call directly to the bar. As I waited for someone to pick up, I saw Travis and Robbie from the vineyard move closer to the bonfire. They had offered to hang out until it died down. Time and a half helped, I mused. To be on the safe side, the crew had had truckloads of water brought to the scene earlier in the afternoon.

A second later, a male's voice was at the other end. "Belhurst Castle. Lounge and bar. How may I help you?"

"This is Norrie Ellington from Two Witches Winery. I'm calling to speak with one of your guests: Whitney Fontana."

"Sorry, but the only guests in here are middle-aged and senior men. I can forward this call to her room and you can leave a voicemail."

"Thanks." I left her a brief message with no expectation she'd return the call.

"You all heard that," I said. "Whitney's AWOL. I'm thinking maybe—" And then another thought crossed my mind. I clutched the pashmina to my chest and charged toward Glenda and Zenora, who were still watching the bonfire. Charlie was at my heels, as if this was some sort of game.

"Zenora! Can you still do that thing where you hold an object in order to locate its owner?"

"You mean the visualization and reconnection?"

"Yeah, yeah. Whatever you call it."

"It's a practiced art. I'm still honing my skills."

I shoved the pashmina at her. "Well, hone away. Sam and his friends found this in our woods while they waited to make their grand scary entrance."

Zenora gasped and wrapped both arms around the pashmina while Glenda stood wordlessly watching.

Bradley, Cammy, Theo, and Don inched forward but didn't say a word. None of us took our eyes off of Zenora, who moved the woolen cloth across her arms, her neck, and her head. Finally she spoke. "The life is gone from this pashmina. What was once wool is now dust. All I sense is cold, dank ground."

"Maybe that's because the pashmina has been lying on the ground in the woods. It's almost November. Naturally the ground is cold and dank."

Zenora shook her head. "The object gets its life from the wearer."

"Are you saying the owner's dead?" My stomach tightened and I was positive the temperature had dropped at least ten degrees.

"It's not an absolute science," Glenda said. "Zenora can't sense any life related to the pashmina. That could mean anything."

Cammy touched the scarf and shrugged. "I'll tell you what it means. It means it's getting late and cold. I say we worry about it tomorrow."

"Ditto!" Don shouted. "That's the best idea I've heard all night. And here's another one—if you plan to call Grizzly Gary, it can wait a day."

"Not like Stephanie," Theo added. "We better let her know what's going on when we get home."

Don rubbed his forehead. "Fine, but you do all the talking."

I looked around and, other than Travis and Robbie, the seven of us were the only ones left at the bonfire. In the distance I watched the remaining cars pull out of our parking lot and drive down the hill. I took the pashmina from Zenora as if it were cursed. "I'll put this in a safe spot in my house until tomorrow." *Preferably as far away from me as possible.*

Glenda tapped my arm and kept her voice low. "A fast sage-cleansing of your house before you turn in might be a good idea."

Just the thing to keep my romance with Bradley going.

"I'll keep that in mind."

We all said our good nights and went our separate ways: Bradley and me up the hill to my house, and everyone else to their cars. The only uptick to the night was that Alvin didn't have a conniption fit with the noises from the bonfire. Who says miracles don't happen?

When we were a good eight or nine yards away from everyone, Bradley pulled me close and the two of us kissed. I had Charlie's leash in the same hand as the pashmina, making sure to keep both of them away from us.

"I couldn't wait till we got inside. It's been too long already," Bradley said.

"Is that your car parked next to Francine's Subaru? Please tell me you're spending the night."

"Would I leave you alone in the house with that smelly pashmina? I don't think it had the life sucked out of it. I think some animal marked it."

"Ew!"

"Seriously, if it does belong to that podcaster, then we've got a lot of unanswered questions ahead of us."

"Us?"

"Yeah, us. You don't think this Hardy Boy is going to let you have all the fun solving murders."

"Murders? Let's hope it's only the one. Hey, you must be starving. I know I am. Come on, for once I thought ahead and I've got cold cut subs in the fridge."

"Fantastic."

Charlie positioned himself between the two of us and used his best begging skills to land tidbits of ham, roast beef and cheese before curling up on the rug by the sink.

"Are you as wired as I am?" Bradley asked when we finished eating. "Usually I'm winding down by nine or ten, but my mind's on overdrive tonight. It's been that way ever since you told me about Donovan."

"Yeah, speaking of which, Deputy Hickman believes whoever killed him left us clues in the form of moving objects around in our displays. Told us not to touch those displays until he gives us the okay."

"Am I the only one still laughing over the Grim Reaper choking one of the egrets?"

"No, Don and Theo thought it was pretty funny, too."

"About that, both your display and Stephanie's had parts of other displays added. What about Don and Theo's? Was anything added to theirs?"

"Yeah, as a matter of fact. They didn't notice it at first because whoever added it, taped it to the back of their giant pumpkin. And we didn't notice it either because it was so small. It was a black envelope that one of the witches held. It said 'Recipes' and had depictions of newts and eyeballs on it."

"Clever. Look, since we're wide awake, maybe we can puzzle this out and come up with our own clues."

"Like what?"

"I'm not sure but I do know that scythes represent justice and death. Believe or not, it was in one of my law classes."

"Okay. And since the scythe was found in our cauldron, along with Donovan, does that mean he got the justice he deserved?"

"It's as good a theory as any. What about Stephanie's display? What does death have to do with an egret?"

"I'm not sure. Let me google it and see what comes up." I grabbed my iPhone and sure enough, the egret was thought to represent good fortune. "Guess this one's a no-brainer—Donovan's good fortune has met its end."

"And the recipes?"

"Your guess is as good as mine. Maybe we're reading too much into it. What do you say we go old school? At least as far as motive is concerned. I'm not sure about means and opportunity."

"Heck, it's like building a case. We start with what we know and go from there."

"I already made a list of Donovan's inner circle for the past few days. We can easily convert it into name and motive."

Less than ten minutes later, I read back the stark reality surrounding Donovan.

"Adrienne—Revenge for stifling her career. Raisa—Revenge for stealing her story. Unknown middle-aged man at Belhurst—Anger over something. Ronny—loathing."

"Then there's his wife," I went on. "She's in Valhalla but that doesn't mean she couldn't orchestrate something from a distance. Her motive is clear as could be—cheating."

Bradley pinched his shoulders together and stretched. "Looks like you've got the entire lineup as far as motive goes. But factor in means and opportunity and we may be looking at a very different story. And then there's Whitney. Don't you find it coincidental she's from Valhalla just like the wife?"

"Oh my gosh. It kind of blew past me with everything else going on. So help me, if Whitney's body winds up in our woods, then the wife is going to become my prime suspect, even if she *is* six hours away by car."

"Slow down. Don't get ahead of yourself. Whitney's probably having a fun night out in one of the lakeside establishments. Besides, there's nothing to connect her to Donovan."

"Nothing that we know of. When she introduced herself to me Friday night, she indicated that she and Adrienne had met in the hotel. But given how circumspect they were, it very well could be that she and Adrienne knew each other prior. I don't care how angry Grizzly Gary gets, I plan to track that woman down as soon as I get into the tasting room tomorrow. After all, wouldn't you be concerned if you lost your pricey silver pashmina?"

"Let's hope that's all it was."

Another half hour of playing "whodunit" and we could barely keep our eyes open. Fatigued and no closer to figuring out whose motive had the most punch behind it, we gave up and turned in for the night.

With Bradley's warm body pressed against mine, any thoughts of Whitney and her silver pashmina evaporated into the night. Morning, however, was another story. The first thing I did when we woke up was to turn on the news and scan my phone apps for the announcement regarding Donovan. Deputy Hickman said his name would be released to the media today and I knew it would be splashed and splattered all over the place.

"No word about Donovan," I said to Bradley as he brushed his teeth. "I figured it would be on the news by now."

"Probably on the noon segments. That may be a good thing since your event attendees will be too busy with the festivities to be checking the news."

"All it will take is one loudmouth customer and we might as well hire a town crier."

"They haven't determined the cause of death yet so you can still go to the default setting—medical issue."

"I'll have to. It's the only line I've practiced."

"Try not to worry about it. Nothing you can do, anyway."

Bradley took off for his own house as soon as we downed our first, and only, cup of coffee. Even though it was a Sunday, he had paperwork to deal with and laundry to do. I told him I'd call if I found out anything more about Whitney. He promised not to miss the final bonfire and even offered to pick up marshmallows, but Cammy already had that covered.

At a little past nine, I walked into the tasting room and removed an old tartan scarf from my neck, an indicator that winter was fast approaching. Charlie had already been fed and I'd taken him for a decent walk around the vineyard and one other stop before showering. As for breakfast, I counted on Emma and Fred's culinary delights rather than cold fiber-infused cereal, compliments of my sister.

"Quite the bonfire," Cammy said when she saw me. "Let me guess. Breakfast at our bistro?"

"Uh-huh."

She laughed. "No wonder you're so early. Must be Bradley had to get back to Geneva."

"Yep, work and laundry. Can't compete with that. As soon as I grab a bite, I'm calling Belhurst Castle again. If Whitney's not in her room, I *will* call Grizzly Gary."

"I hate to think it, but finding that pashmina was unnerving. Not that I put any credence into Zenora's premonitions, but still . . ."

"Yeah, I know."

Chapter 18

I didn't realize I had eaten my entire sausage and cheese burrito until I looked down at my plate and realized only a few small clumps of scrambled egg and red bell peppers remained. Either I was really famished or my mind was elsewhere. I opted for the latter. It was a few minutes before ten and we were about to open for day two of Hallow Wine Weekend. Like it or not, I needed to speak with Deputy Hickman, even if it meant getting an earful about jumping to conclusions.

"Thanks, guys!" I shouted to Emma and Fred. Taking a deep breath, I plodded past the tasting room tables and gave thumbs-up to our crew. Then I retreated to my office, booted up the computer, and reached for the winery's landline phone. I was four or five digits in when someone rapped on my doorjamb and I put the receiver down.

"Come on in!"

Whitney breezed into the room and smiled. A dark teal all-weather jacket and cream-colored scarf replaced the infamous pashmina. "Sorry I didn't make it yesterday but I'd love to take you up on your offer and taste those wines."

"You're alive. Oh my gosh. You're alive."

"Huh? I should hope so. Why? What did you hear?"

"Not what I heard. What was found last night. Your silver pashmina in our woods. Not many people have pashminas that color. We tried reaching you at your hotel but you weren't there. Without a forty-eight-hour missing person report, it wasn't enough evidence to call the sheriff's office. Wow, I'm glad you're alive."

Whitney put her hand on her neck and swallowed. "I am, yes. But I wasn't in possession of that pashmina yesterday. I inadvertently left it in Adrienne's car Friday night. We drove from Belhurst to Port of Call in her rental. I tried reaching her yesterday when I realized it, but she didn't return my call. I figured her boss must have returned and they were working on assignments. I didn't hear otherwise."

Guess Whitney doesn't know Donovan bit the dust after all.

"Did Adrienne give you any indication of her plans, other than working?"

"No, it was mainly small talk Friday night. She mentioned that even in an industry like hers, looks are everything and that she had to worry about maintaining hers no matter the cost. I wondered if she had any work done, but it would have been way too intrusive to ask. Anyway, the topic moved on to wine venues we both covered."

"That's pretty benign. Too bad she never got back to you."

"In all fairness, I was out and about. Yesterday morning, while I visited another winery, I ran into an old friend and wound up spending the entire day with her. Not that I'm a party girl, mind you, but we hadn't seen each other in months. I didn't get back to my room until the wee hours. Do you think Adrienne's in some sort of trouble? I mean, how else could my pashmina wind up in the woods by your winery?"

"I'm not sure, but from what you told me, I really do need to call the local sheriff's office."

"Maybe she brought it inside the hotel, set it down, and someone else picked it up."

"I'm sure the hotel has surveillance. I don't think we should get ahead of ourselves."

What am I saying? I'm already ahead of myself.

"Listen," I said. "I have a decent relationship with our local deputy sheriff." *In what world?* "I'll phone him and let him take it from there. He may want to hold on to your pashmina for evidence. Is that all right?"

"Of course."

"In the interim, why don't you relax at our bistro? They have wonderful pastries and lattes if you want something light. Tell them who you are and that you're my guest. I'll be over as soon as I know something."

"Thanks. My head is spinning over this. And to think, I was

looking forward to tasting wines and coming up with ideas for podcasts."

I nodded. "I understand completely.*" Even if the idea of a podcast is on hold for Two Witches.*

No Adrienne meant no story in *Wine Enthusiast.* I wasn't quite ready to buy into Zenora's premonition about a dead woman's body. That pashmina could've gotten into our woods any number of ways. Then again, maybe Adrienne showed up to our winery yesterday wearing the pashmina. And maybe someone strong-armed her into the woods before she made it inside the building. The woods aren't that far away. But why? To prevent her from picking up where her boss left off with our story? But why? There's nothing controversial about Merlot.

As the seconds passed, I came up with more and more theories. Or *speculation* as Deputy Hickman likes to call it. I grabbed my iPhone and texted, *Whitney's alive and in our winery* to Cammy, Don, Theo, Stephanie, and Bradley. Then I dialed the Yates County Sheriff's Office from our landline and leaned back in my chair.

The deputy on duty connected me with Grizzly Gary, whose first remark came as soon as I explained the situation.

"What the heck is a pashmina? Are we talking some sort of skunk in your woods?"

I rolled my eyes and reminded myself that fashion wasn't his forte. "It's a fancy woolen scarf. Expensive."

I then went on to explain that Whitney was at our winery but I wasn't sure about Adrienne's whereabouts. Then I suggested that they might want to send a forensic team into our woods.

"There's no evidence of a crime, Miss Ellington. And there are no missing person reports for anyone with that name. In fact, the only missing person report was down in Branchport. Elderly man with dementia. He was found a half hour ago."

"Can't you do a preventative search?"

"I can understand why you might be concerned. Look, I'll give Ontario County a heads-up and see if they can spare a deputy to have a look-see at the Belhurst."

"Thanks. Listen, I already figured out Adrienne was informed of her boss's death but was told to remain silent. I ran into her on Friday night and she was awfully cagey. I think the one person who might be willing to offer up some information is Ronny Morgan. She's one of the photographers for *Wine Enthusiast*."

"I'll take that under advisement. Have a good day, Miss Ellington."

I plopped my elbows on my desk and put my head in the palms of my hands. Short of traipsing through the woods myself, there was little I could do. Especially during an event weekend. I stood and started for the door when there was another knock.

"Hey, hope I didn't disturb you." It was Ronny. Same all-weather coat but this time with a dark blue snood wrapped around her neck. I thought about buying one of those things when the winds in Manhattan got to be really crazy, but I never did. "Sorry to plague you," she said, "but the lady up front with the wire-rimmed glasses said you wouldn't mind."

"Sure. What's up? We missed you last night at the bonfire."

"That's because I'll be there tonight. I went to Gable Hill last night and it was pretty cool. Listen, I'm about losing it trying to find Donovan. I left him like a zillion messages and the same thing with Adrienne, but it's radio silence on their end. Do you know what's going on?"

I shook my head. "You know how these events are. Everyone's all over the place."

"Well, Donovan better be darn well satisfied with the photos I took because—what the hell—he hasn't been around to tell me what he wanted. Listen, here's my cell number. If either of them shows up, call me."

"Uh, sure thing."

"Say, some of your customers have really gone overboard with the costumes. I'll see if one of the tasting tables can showcase a few of them trying the Merlot."

"I'm sure they will. In fact, I'll head out with you and get it arranged."

I left Ronny at Glenda's table with a group of enthusiastic tasters and hustled over to Whitney in the bistro. Last thing I needed was for Whitney and Ronny to meet each other and put two and two together.

"How's your latte?" I was out of breath and panting.

Whitney took a quick sip and smiled. "Heavenly."

"Great. I spoke with Deputy Hickman from Yates County. He's going to speak with his counterpart in Ontario County, since they have jurisdiction for Belhurst Castle. Anyway, they'll work on tracking down Adrienne."

"That's a relief. All of this is troubling."

"And then some." I pulled a chair up to her table and sat. "There's really nothing you can do at this point. It would be a shame to waste the last day of Hallow Wine Weekend. Why don't you visit a few of our neighboring wineries and then pop in later to taste our wines? By then, I should know something."

"Good idea. Thanks, Norrie. And tell your bistro chefs and baristas they're amazing."

I walked her to the entrance, not because I was hospitable, but because I needed to dodge Ronny. I wondered if this was how Donovan felt, keeping his girlfriend and/or mistress away from his wife. Then again, it could have all been tabloid rumors.

With my eyes glued to the parking lot, I made sure Whitney pulled out and watched as she drove down the hill. Too bad I couldn't see which direction she turned. Then I hurried over to Glenda's table, where Ronny finished an impromptu photo shoot.

How much longer can I keep this charade up?

"I suppose I'll meander down the lake and take a few stock photos of the vineyards and such," she said as she adjusted her camera bag on her shoulder. "Then I'll swing back here and see if you've heard anything."

"It's the perfect day for it. Crisp autumn air and no rain or snow."

Ronny stood and bit her lower lip. "You don't suppose anything's happened to them, do you? Nah, never mind. If they were in an automobile accident, it would have been all over the news. Guess Donovan's just being Donovan. Catch you later."

She sprinted out the door before I was forced to lie again.

"Any news about the you-know-what?" Glenda whispered while a new crew of customers joined her table.

I shook my head.

"Zenora's quite distressed over this, you know. She feels compelled to be here tonight but she gave her word she'd attend a Samhain ceremony in Ithaca."

"Tell her not to worry. We'll be fine."

"She can always—"

"No, no. We'll be fine. I need to catch up with Cammy in between those photo shoots she's doing."

Glenda chuckled. "Either you need glasses or you're not very observant. Cammy pawned them off on one of the college students. She's in the kitchen making more pastry mummies."

Come on, channel 13 WHAM and every other darn Rochester station. Make the announcement about Donovan already. Even Sarah Bernhardt and Meryl Streep couldn't continue this act.

Chapter 19

"Great timing, Norrie," Cammy said. She set down a pastry sleeve with chocolate filling and admired her handiwork. "This is our last batch. I never want to see another chocolate-filled pastry mummy again. Well, not for a while anyway. By the way, in case you're wondering, I got one of the part-time college kids to take photos for me since I became bleary-eyed doing that."

"I know. Glenda told me. Honestly, I've got so much on my mind, I didn't even notice."

"I saw your text. Whitney, huh? What'd she have to say about the pashmina?"

"She left it in Adrienne's car. Boy, if it wasn't so cliché, I'd say the plot thickens. I called Deputy Hickman but he blew me off as usual. And if that wasn't bad enough, Ronny showed up. I spent the last half hour juggling her and Whitney so they wouldn't run into each other and start a conversation. Eventually it would get to Donovan."

"I didn't think they knew each other."

"No sense taking a chance. Darn it all, I don't know why those news stations are being so pokey. Grizzly Gary said it was released to the media."

"How do you think we should handle it when they do? People on the wine trail will get their news on their apps long before they go home and turn on their TVs."

"Okay, the first person who mentions it to me will get the following reaction." I slapped a hand on my chest and took a deep breath. "Oh my gosh! Donovan Brin. Dead? *He* was the body in our cauldron? Donovan? The writer for *Wine Enthusiast*? Oh my gosh!!"

Cammy's jaw dropped and she burst out laughing. "Sorry, but you need to tone it down a notch."

"This is really creepy, but now I'm thinking Adrienne may be the next body to surface."

"Or not. Slow down, Miss Marple. By the way, did you get a chance to look at the photos Lizzie forwarded you from yesterday? Lots of neat costumes. Some candid shots from Friday and yesterday were also there. Scroll past them."

"Geez, I've been so fixated on Donovan and now the bearer of the pashmina, I totally skipped over reviewing those costumes. I'll get to work on it right now. Looks like the tasting room is under control."

"Let me know which ones are your favorites."

"Sure thing."

I moseyed back to my office with every intention of looking at those photos when I realized something—even though I had sent Franz a text on Friday about a body surfacing in our cauldron display, I had neglected to inform him who it was. True, I was under a gag order of sorts, but still . . . John knew and Cammy knew. It wasn't right to exclude our winemaker from knowing the truth.

Franz was practically glued to the lab, and today was no different. Even though it was almost noon on a Sunday, he picked up the phone the instant I called. "Enlarging those *Verboten* signs worked. It's been very peaceful around here. Thank you for keeping the merrymakers in your tasting room. Have you heard anything more about Friday's unfortunate victim?"

"Not officially, no, but I have a good idea who it is. Or was. Actually, that's why I called. I shouldn't be telling you this, because Deputy Hickman insisted I keep it to myself, but the media's going to release the name any time now and I felt you should know."

"I'm not sure why it would be a particular concern for me. I'm not familiar with the wine trail customers."

"Not a customer. The writer from *Wine Enthusiast.* Donovan Brin."

"Mr. Brin? That's whose body was found? *Gott in Himmel!*"

"I know. Of all things. None of it makes sense."

"Did the man suffer a seizure? I must apologize. I've been so busy with the maceration process, I haven't paid any attention to the news."

"They labeled it a suspicious death. That's all I know."

"I wonder if any of this has to do with the phone call he got midway through our interview last week."

"What phone call?"

"It was his lawyer. I know because he said, 'It's my lawyer. I have to take this call.'"

I did a mental eye roll while Franz continued talking.

"Mr. Brin stood and walked to the corner of the office. That's when I heard him say, 'That shrew can wait until hell freezes over if she thinks I'm about to pay one more cent.'"

"Did his assistant give you any idea who Donovan was talking about?"

"In a manner of speaking. She looked up from her notes and mouthed 'Personal matter.' I don't suppose she's given you any indication about the article. From what I could ascertain, he was the one who asked the questions, but she was the one who would pen the article. Tell me, is she aware he's dead?"

"I'm not sure. She may have been informed by the sheriff's office and told not to say anything, or she really doesn't know. In either case, it doesn't matter because no one has been able to locate her."

"Ach du Lieber Gott!"

"I know. All of this is very strange. And if you're wondering, the sheriff's office is looking into it. And all of this just as we were about to be in the spotlight for our Merlot. Now the only notoriety we'll get is for another dead body cropping up on our property."

"Let's hope the woman is alive and well. And eager to make a name for herself by writing that article."

"Funny, but I had the same exact thought."

When I got off the phone with Franz, I texted Bradley. *New intel. I think the wife was divorcing him. See U tonite. Xx's*

Bradley texted back. *Marvin has contacts in Valhalla. Will check. Xoxo.*

Marvin Souza, Bradley's partner and head of their family law firm, had contacts all over the country. Contacts who wished to remain in Marvin's good graces. I crossed my fingers one of them might know something about an impending divorce. But divorce or not, it wasn't strong enough as a motive for murder. If Donovan had to cough up the payola to keep his soon-to-be ex-wife in the money, then why would she murder him? Unless she took out one heck of an insurance policy. Too bad Marvin wasn't in that business.

There was only one person who seemed to have a handle on Donovan's goings-on and I had booted her out of here less than a half hour ago. Now, I thumbed around for the cell number I'd written on a Post-it note and called her.

"Norrie. I didn't expect to hear from you so soon. Have you caught up with Donovan and Adrienne? I must have just missed them."

"Sorry, Ronny, but no. You wouldn't happen to know if Donovan and his wife were getting a divorce, would you?"

"Do you think that's what he's been up to? Dealing with Felicity? It wouldn't surprise me but geez, you'd think it could wait one more day. Bad enough they yanked each other's chains when we were in the Napa Valley last month on that piece about organic vineyards. But I figured they must have smoothed things out by the time we left."

"What makes you say that?"

"Donovan seemed relieved. You know, like when a writer's been blocked and all of a sudden the clouds lift."

I clenched my fist as visions of Renee holding up maps of quaint little towns sprung to mind. "Only too well."

"That's right. I suppose it happens to screenwriters, too."

"But you think divorce could have been in the works?"

"The word was certainly bandied around. Is that why you called? Someone said something about it?"

"More like idle gossip that reached my ears. We've got zillions of wine tasters in here and people talk. I was curious, that's all."

"Good thing no one paid attention at the fundraiser a few months ago at the Guggenheim. Felicity had one glass of Chardonnay too many and said she wished she could up Donovan's insurance policy and send him spiraling down past Kandinsky, Mondrian, and Picasso.

Talk about hyperbole."

Or wishful thinking.

"Like I said, I was curious, that's all."

"Well, let me know if he does waltz in."

"While you're on the wine trail, check out the roadside stands selling grape pies. They're the best."

"Sure thing. See you later."

Felicity rose to the top of my murder suspect list before I ended the call. Now it was simply a matter of substantiating the hearsay. Was she able to take out a hefty insurance policy on her husband? And who did she get to do the dirty work?

I did a mental lineup of suspects before forcing myself to open Lizzie's email and scroll through yesterday's costume contest entries. I promised Cammy I'd come up with my top three and she'd do the same for today's entries. Then we'd get everyone's feedback on Monday before selecting the grand winner. The name and photo would be posted on our website as well as the one for the Seneca Lake Wine Trail. Nothing like a wine giveaway to get the publicity going.

Marketing wines was a daily process and no one understood it better than the Seneca Lake Wine Trail Board. My mother said it reminded her of a furniture store that always ran a sale—Memorial Day, Fourth of July, Labor Day, Columbus Day, Veterans Day, Halloween, and so forth. Name the month and there'd be a sale. Same with the wineries. Pick a holiday, and there'd be an event.

"We've got to stay in the public's eye," my father told her, "because people have short memories. Our wines may be fantastic, but unless we lure people in to taste them, we're going to lose customers. And unless we promote our wine trail, no one is going to trek up here to visit one solo winery. Promotion and camaraderie go hand in hand."

It was a philosophy that worked, even if it meant scrolling through endless photos of pirates, princesses, cartoon characters, and superheroes. And while I expected to choose a winner, I never expected to have a clue to Donovan's murder jump out at me.

Chapter 20

I could understand why Cammy was bleary-eyed after taking photo after photo. Heck, all I did was scroll through them and I could hardly stay focused. Thankfully two costumes stood out and I made a note of them: nineteenth-century vampire and caterpillar cocoon. Godfrey would have selected the latter, no doubt.

Whoever set up the photo contest did have the foresight to identify the people. Entrants wrote their names and emails on numbered lines in a notebook. Their corresponding numbers were printed on half sheets of paper which they held up while the photographer took their picture. Really easy to figure out who was who.

With nothing more jumping out at me, I continued scrolling and yawning simultaneously. Cammy had mentioned she'd taken a few candid shots prior to the contest, and up until the second when one of them set my hair on edge, I pretty much glossed over them. But not this time. I blinked, rubbed my eyes, and took a closer look, astonished not so much as *who* I saw, but the circumstances surrounding it.

It was Adrienne. No doubt whatsoever. She stood sideways at our door while a heavyset man with black glasses and tight wavy hair leaned against the doorjamb, his arm held out, stopping her from taking another step. He matched Ada's description of the guy who had words with Donovan on Thursday night at the Belhurst. *Coincidence my you-know-what.*

I slowed down to see if there were any other photos of the two and sure enough, there was one more. It was pretty much the same photo as the previous one, only this time Cammy had managed to capture a side image of the man's chest and profile. He wore a tan Harrington jacket, the kind of all-weather design that was popular with golfers and tourists. I could easily see the small round logo affixed to the upper left of the coat, but I didn't recognize it as one of the wine trail insignias even though it was a circular cluster of grapes with the letters *LV* in the center. Definitely not Lake View Winery. Catherine's logo was completely different, and last I knew, they weren't changing it.

Unless she could have her son Steven's face plastered all over it.

I figured it might have come from any number of wineries in the Finger Lakes region, not to mention the Niagara Falls area. I tried to zoom closer, but when I did, the image became blurry. Given the guy's stance, it didn't appear as if it was happenstance Adrienne was stopped momentarily from proceeding out the door.

I don't remember when I started tapping my foot but it was going full steam as I looked closely at Adrienne. Cammy must have snapped the image a few seconds after Adrienne walked out of here on Friday. Had I not seen her that night at Port of Call, I would have bet money she was coerced into leaving with whoever the wavy-haired man was.

Okay. So maybe the timing was off, but still, he could have been gunning for her, in a manner of speaking. I emailed the photo to my personal email, snatched my iPhone and flew out of my office. This time I made sure to glance at the alcove. The college student was still doing the photo shoots. That meant Cammy had to be in the kitchen.

I all but collided into our guests as I raced to the kitchen door and flung it open. "Have you seen this man?" I asked. I waved the phone in the air just as Cammy finished putting marshmallow eyes on a mummy.

"Not from over here, I can't. Why? And take a breath, will you."

It was hard to be slow and deliberate when I wanted an answer five minutes ago. I handed her my phone and tried not to garble my words, which I have a tendency to do when I'm in a rush. "Rosalee's friend, who works at the Belhurst, described a man who looked like this. He had words with Donovan on Thursday night as they were leaving the lounge. Now—look! I'm positive it's the same man who intimidated Adrienne at our door. It must have happened Friday after she came in here looking for Donovan."

Cammy squinted and stared at the phone. "Sorry, but I don't recall seeing him. Maybe he never actually came in here. Maybe he was about to but Adrienne was already at the door."

"Geez, I wish I knew who he was. Or which winery that logo on his jacket is from."

"All I can think of is Lake View but I know theirs is different. Hard to confuse them. Lake View's is three wine bottles with grapes and glasses off to the side."

"I'll shoot off an email to our WOW group and ask if anyone recognizes it. Not that I expect an answer tonight. Everyone's probably as stressed as we are with the last night of Hallow Wine Weekend and another bonfire."

"By the way, Lizzie is bowing out tonight but Roger said he'd be at the bonfire. Said he'd be happy to share ghostly sightings from the Lehigh Valley that date back to the French and Indian War if you'd like."

"Ghosts, yes, but I'm afraid he'll go off on a tangent and next you know, everyone will be fast asleep as he drones on and on about battle strategies. At least we don't have to worry about Zenora. She's going to be in Ithaca."

Cammy clasped her hands and bent her head in mock thanks. "Glenda will make up for it, I'm sure. I'm worried she might want to conjure up Donovan's spirit. Funny that there's no mention of him on the news. I keep checking my apps whenever I can. Are you sure Deputy Hickman said the name was released to the media?"

"Uh-huh. He mentioned something about formalities. Hmm, think something went wrong and they backtracked?"

"I always thought once the next of kin were notified, it was good to go."

"Maybe that's the formality. Although I'm not sure that's the word I'd use."

"Huh?"

"Earlier today Franz told me Donovan took a call from his lawyer during their interview. Franz overheard him say he wasn't going to pay the shrew that much. I think it was the wife. You know—d-i-v-o-r-c-e. So I called Ronny to get her take since she seemed to have a hand in everything. Ronny said the wife, whose name is Felicity, is a real you-know-what and made mention of wanting to throw Donovan off the railing at the Guggenheim Museum. Of course, Felicity was pretty well snockered at the time, but still . . ."

Cammy put her palm to her cheek and took a breath. "You think the wife killed him and everything's on hold until the sheriff's office can piece it all together?"

"One way or another, yeah. Rats. I wish we could find out if she's holding a mega insurance policy. It's really tricky since she lives in Valhalla, where the magazine office is located. That means Grizzly Gary will have to play nice with the Mt. Pleasant Police Department. They're the ones who have jurisdiction in that area. And before you ask, I looked it up."

"She's got motive, that's for sure. But everything else is really sketchy."

"Like Adrienne's whereabouts. Deputy Hickman was going to— Oh my gosh. It's Sunday. And it's after three. Ada Mae's working at the Belhurst. Hang on."

I selected the Belhurst's number from my contacts, pushed speaker phone, and looked up at Cammy. "Ada Mae might know something. Boy, will I be glad when Gladys Pipp gets back to work at the sheriff's office tomorrow. Meanwhile I'm keeping my fingers crossed with this call."

Sure enough, Ada Mae was on duty and just as puzzled as I was. "Was there another murder?" she asked.

"What makes you ask?"

"It's been a regular traffic jam in here. A deputy from Ontario County came in a bit ago and spoke with the manager. Then another deputy arrived. This time from Yates County. Oh dear. I hope it's not that brunette who reminded me of Audrey Hepburn. The one you asked about the last time we spoke—Miss Stafine."

"What makes you think that?"

"The manager asked to see a copy of her car registration. It was for a rental. Then he walked outside and returned, shaking his head at the deputies. I figured the car was gone. And earlier today, Housekeeping asked if she had checked out because her bed was still made up from the day before. I told them no and asked if they bothered to look in the closet for a suitcase. Sure enough, her luggage was still there. Odd, though, that her toiletries weren't in the bathroom. Then again, some guests don't like leaving those items around, even though everything is sanitized."

"If she shows up, would you please call me or leave a message at Two Witches?"

"Certainly. I'll be here until nine. Let's hope she's safe and sound somewhere."

Six feet under or hiding out. I'm going with the latter choice.

"She could've gotten spooked and taken off somewhere," Cammy said when I got off the phone with Ada Mae.

"Then how do you explain Whitney's pashmina that went from Adrienne's car to our woods?"

"I can't. Still, that doesn't mean there isn't a logical explanation. Uh, other than an abduction. And before you say another word, if Adrienne had been abducted, there would have been other clues. Viable clues."

"I may know more tomorrow when I call that bartender from the Belhurst: Marsha Whitman. According to Ada Mae, she was on duty and Donovan may have returned to the bar following his not-so-pleasant conversation with our wavy-haired mystery man."

"And in the meantime?"

"I honestly wish I could go traipsing through the woods to see if there are any indications Adrienne was there."

"Good thing it's an event weekend and you're needed here."

"I did scout out one thing, though. Really early this morning. It didn't pan out so I let it go. But that was before I realized there's another way a vehicle can get up close to our woods."

"Whoa. You lost me. One thing at a time."

"I walked over to where our driveway leads into the woods in order to see if any tire tracks had flattened down the leaves and brush. Absolutely nothing. Charlie was with me but he was useless as far as tracking anything. But a few seconds ago, I remembered something. Stephanie's driveway also skirts around to those woods. Same with the old logging road on the back of our property. But that road is blocked off with stacks of wood. Too many concerns about poachers. Anyway, it's not too late for me to dart out of here and see if there are any recent tire tracks on Stephanie's end. Do me a favor and let her know I'll be scoping it out. I'd better leave right now before I get caught up in something and it gets too late."

Cammy's eyes widened and she put her palm to her neck.

"Relax, all I'm going to do is get out of my car and see if there are any recent tire tracks going into those woods. I know for a fact Stephanie and Derek don't drive in there."

"And I know for a fact that once you get an idea in your head, you don't stop. Whatever you do, don't go further than where that driveway meets the woods."

"I won't. After all, if I'm not back, the poor audience at our bonfire tonight will be stuck with Roger and the French and Indian War."

"Or start their own war. Hurry back."

Chapter 21

I interrupted Sam from his tasting before I charged out the door. Thankfully, the five guests at his table had just begun to try our semidry Riesling and were otherwise occupied.

"Psst, I need to ask you a quick question," I said. Sam stepped away from the table and we moved toward a corner of the room. "When your friends found that pashmina last night, how far into the woods was it?"

"Maybe eight or ten yards in. Sorry if it got all wadded up. I was in a hurry so I stuck it under my coat."

"Did you guys find it on the ground?"

Sam shook his head. "That's the odd thing. It was hanging over a tree branch. But like I said before, the wind picks up everything. It didn't get ripped or anything, did it?"

"No, just dusty. I was curious, that's all. Thanks. You'd better get back to your table. Looks like your guests are ready to try the next wine."

I asked myself what the odds were of a long pashmina found draped over a branch and not on the ground. Wind, my foot! That pashmina would have needed a hurricane. Besides, we haven't had any wind here in days. Cold air, maybe, but no wind.

Flashing a quick wave at Lizzie, I flew down the steps and pretty much power-walked my way up the hill to the side of the house where I'd parked the Subaru. A few minutes later I was headed north on Route 14 and over to Gable Hill. Less than six minutes according to the screen by the steering wheel.

Not sure of what I'd see, I took my time studying the ground where Stephanie's road ended at the woods. No tire tracks whatsoever, but I really didn't expect to see any. Not with what I thought happened. And now I knew I was on to something. Had Adrienne been abducted and forced into the woods, it wasn't by car. And while it was quite possible she had Whitney's pashmina with her on Saturday, I doubted she was the victim in this game.

Given the short distance into the woods, anyone could have spotted that pashmina on a branch. The thing is long. Not some measly neck scarf. That pashmina was planted. Adrienne knew about the bonfire Saturday night and knew Whitney would tell someone she left her silver wrap in Adrienne's rental. So why did Adrienne want everyone to believe something happened to her? Unless she was the one who planted it in order to cast off any suspicion she was responsible for her boss's death.

Too bad none of this explained why she hadn't been seen since Friday night. My gut feeling was that she was laying low until the right moment, when she'd appear and claim she was kidnapped. Yep, I've read enough of those novels, not to mention the TV crime shows I watched.

I got back in the car and took off for the winery with one quick stop—home. It was approaching four and I was famished. Rather than bother Emma and Fred, who had enough on their plates, I took a bagel out of the freezer, nuked it, toasted it, and smeared it with enough cream cheese to meet the daily requirement for calcium.

Since our entire crew was going to attend the bonfire, I had asked Emma and Fred to make cold-cut sandwiches so we'd have something to munch on between closing time and twilight when the bonfire began. "Nothing fancy," I told Fred earlier in the day. "Grab the leftover breads and slap on whatever extra cold cuts you've got."

"And ruin my reputation for gourmet sandwiches?" The color left his face momentarily.

"Trust me. Everyone will be so tired and hungry, they won't notice."

He winced and bit his lower lip before returning to the grill.

When I finished my bagel, I refilled Charlie's kibble and refreshed his water dish before walking back to the tasting room. The college student must have needed a break from playing photographer because Cammy was at the helm when I walked inside.

"Good," she said. "We don't have to send for a search crew. Tell me, did you find anything earthshattering?"

"It's what I didn't find that matters." I told her about my hunch Adrienne played us and Cammy thought it might have some validity.

"It still doesn't answer two of the big three—means and opportunity. And in this case, I'd put an extra emphasis on means. If she did poison Donovan, how'd she manage to drag his body over to the cauldron? Which brings me to yet another question. Did the sheriff's office actually come out and say he was poisoned?"

"In a manner of speaking. Deputy Hickman said there were no external wounds. Poisoning is a logical conclusion. If the guy died of natural causes, why go through all the drama?"

Cammy motioned for a woman dressed like Cher to step into the alcove for her photo. "I'll have to get back to you later on this. After this photo, I'm going to announce five more minutes until the contest ends. I'll let them know the winner will be posted on our website by the end of the day tomorrow. I figure you and I will need all that time to review the entries."

"At least Henry Speltmore will have it easy. All he has to do is get the names of the winners and put them on the Seneca Lake Wine Trail website before Christmas."

Cammy choked back a laugh. I was relieved this part of the weekend event was drawing to a close, but anxious about tonight's final bonfire. Something didn't feel right but I couldn't put my finger on it.

As far as planning was concerned, we were all set. Sam and his buddies were more than psyched to come hollering out the woods as planned, and we had more than enough marshmallows and toasting sticks for the crowd. Emma and Fred offered to hand out the treats this time so Cammy could enjoy the program.

Word must have gotten out about last night's tales from the beyond because a number of guests wanted to know if they needed reservations to attend tonight's bonfire. We told them there was no need for reservations and that we had enough benches for thirty or so people. We were also quick to add that if the benches were full, guests could still bring their own blankets or fold-up camp chairs and stools.

At quarter past five, Godfrey texted me. *See you at the bonfire. Too bad it's October. The Lampyridae would have been fascinating.*

I wasn't sure what the Lampyridae were, but I imagined they were horrible flying insects that came out to suck blood like mosquitos. Only Godfrey could appreciate them.

At five thirty on the nose, we locked the doors and began the cleanup. Most of the guests indicated they'd see us in another hour and a half and were looking forward to getting goose bumps. As for me, I was looking forward to getting it over with.

Bradley called, too. He'd stopped by Wegmans and bought enough munchies to keep us chomping and slurping well into the night. I told him I'd see him at my house at six thirty, and from there it was off to the bonfire. The only one I hadn't heard from was Whitney. True, I kind of brushed her off earlier in the day, insisting she visit other wineries, but I was certain she'd be back at ours. Not so much for the wine but to see if we learned anything more about Adrienne. I reminded myself Seneca Lake had over thirty wineries and for an energetic podcaster like Whitney, it was an invitation waiting to happen. And one I planned on extending for us as well as Don, Theo, and Stephanie.

For the next forty minutes, the crew loaded the dishwasher, cleaned the tables, filled the mini-fridges with wine for tomorrow, and swept up the place. In between, they snacked on Fred's sandwiches. Lizzie was the only one who remained at her post, reconciling the day's accounts.

I excused myself in order to meet Bradley but promised to be at the bonfire by twilight. As I started for the door, Glenda rushed over.

She was out of breath and kept tossing her hair every which way. "Zenora called. A recently departed spirit will reach out to you tonight."

Wonderful. I need this like a hole in the head.

"They may be better off with Verizon. Or T-Mobile."

"It's not funny, Norrie. Zenora said the spirit is not to be trusted. You don't think it could be the man from our cauldron, do you? Donovan, right? I thought we'd know for sure by now."

"Uh, yeah. Me, too. Listen, tell Zenora not to worry. I rarely converse with strangers."

"Seriously, this spirit may try to do you harm. I'll be certain to add more sage sticks to the bonfire but it won't be enough. You'll need to create a protective shield around you. You must swallow a teaspoon of turmeric in a glass of milk. It's the only way."

"I have vitamin C and D-three in the house. And I'm pretty sure Francine doesn't have any turmeric." *Unless it's something she uses for those healthy salads of hers.*

"No worries. I carry turmeric capsules with me for situations like this. Naturally sourced. Five hundred mgs. That's probably a teaspoon."

"I, um, er . . ."

"There must be some milk in the bistro. I can wait while you look."

"No milk. No turmeric. I'm sure the sage sticks will be plenty. Tell Zenora to recite a chant or something. I'll be fine."

"These are porous days, you know. All Saints' Day tomorrow and All Souls' Day on November second. Souls can move closer to our world at this time. If Zenora didn't have to work on Tuesday, she'd offer to set out food and drink for the soul whose body was found in our Hallow Wine Weekend display."

"Just as well. I think Deputy Hickman would consider it interfering with a crime scene. Apparently, we can't remove the display until he gives us the okay."

"That has to be the restless spirit. The news did say it was a suspicious death. Not the most pleasant welcome to our winery."

And when word gets out it's Donovan Brin, we'll be lucky if any other culinary and wine magazine writers set foot on our premises.

Chapter 22

Like the night before, the bonfire glowed in shades of orange, yellow, and red with hints of blue at the base. Its whitish smoke was pungent with the scent of sage and the heat it gave off assured me we'd be plenty warm for the next two hours. Bradley gave me a hug and told me to "break a leg" with tonight's show. He sat next to Don and Theo, who waved him over the minute they spotted us.

Godfrey was already seated on one of the front benches next to Cammy, and from the expression on her face, I figured he was either describing the lecture on cockroaches he gave at the Kiwanis dinner last night or some new and equally horrific insect. I wondered if Cammy was sorry she relinquished her marshmallow duty to Emma and Fred, but then again, she probably had some equally disturbing tales to tell him.

The sky was cloudier than the night before and it seemed to get darker earlier. As I looked around, the crowd appeared larger than last night's. A row of lawn chairs and camp chairs circled the perimeter of the mini-amphitheater John had set up. Travis and Robbie were off to the side of the bonfire, ready to grab the buckets of water if anything went south.

I introduced myself, thanked everyone for coming and began my first ghost story of the evening. No sooner had I uttered the words "in a white gown, the woman wails through the night, looking for—" when someone else completed my sentence with the words "Donovan Brin."

It was Ronny and she charged toward the bonfire, her camera sliding every which way across her chest. "Donovan's dead. I was about to turn my car engine off in the parking lot when I caught the news on the radio. They just announced it. 'Donovan Brin, a writer for *Wine Enthusiast*, was found dead at Two Witches Winery Friday morning under suspicious circumstances.' Donovan! I ran up here as fast as I could."

By now Ronny was inches away from me, her reddish hair taking on an odd glow from the fire.

Move over, Academy Award winners. Here goes nothing.

I flung my hand to my neck and stood absolutely still for a few seconds, ensuring that whatever I did, I wouldn't make eye contact with Cammy. "Donovan Brin! *That's* whose body was in our cauldron? Donovan Brin? That can't be. I spoke with him on Wednesday. Oh my gosh! What else did the news say?"

Ronny shook her head. "That was it. News at eleven." Then, she looked out at the thirty or so attendees and gasped. "Oh my gosh. I'm sorry. I didn't mean to ruin your program, but the news was so sudden. So shocking."

"Who's Donovan Brin?" someone shouted.

"Are we supposed to know him?" someone else yelled.

Then a few "Ews" followed by "I thought the witches were papier-mâché."

I didn't even try to explain. Words like *murder*, *killer*, and *maniac* echoed all over the place and more cell phones were whipped out of pockets and purses than dollar bills at the state fair.

I doubted I'd be able to rein in the crowd for at least another five or six minutes. But worst of all was when Ronny realized she'd only gotten half the equation.

"Adrienne!" she shrieked. "The news didn't say anything about Adrienne. She could be dead, too, for all any of us know."

I tried to have a private conversation with Ronny but it was impossible with all the bellowing from the crowd.

A heavyset man in a black parka waved his arms in the air. "How many dead bodies are on this property anyway?"

"Relax, buddy, it's part of the program," someone else yelled back. "Adrienne's probably the woman wailing in white. Let her finish the ghost story or we'll be here all night."

Thankfully Bradley got up and motioned Ronny away from the front of the bonfire. He, along with Don and Theo, moved toward the road side of the gathering, and from where I stood, it looked like a huddle of sorts. I imagined they told her what I'd been trying to keep under wraps all day—that Adrienne was AWOL and Donovan was indeed the corpse in the cauldron.

The only one missing from tonight's debacle was Whitney, and that changed in a matter of seconds. Unfortunately I didn't spot her until it was too late. I returned to the spot where I stood to tell the ghost story and picked up where I'd left off. Unbeknownst to me, Whitney thundered toward the crowd like the harried rabbit in *Alice in Wonderland.* At least that's how Cammy described her afterward.

In addition to the all-weather jacket and cream-colored scarf she wore into the winery, Whitney had donned one of those winter hats with the pom-pom on the top. No bag. I imagined her wallet and cell phone were tucked in one of her pockets.

"Her wails sounded as if they came from an unearthly realm," I said, "as the woman in white searched for her children's lost souls. Her voice, once soft and soothing, was now guttural and deep, as she—"

"Waaaaah!" The crowd heard the sound simultaneously as Sam and his buddies made their appearance, in dark cloaks with lantern-lit faces. Whitney was only two or three yards away, having edged her way through the crowd and close to the bonfire. She let out a high-pitched shriek followed by a series of nonstop screams. That resulted in more screams, this time from Sam and his friends.

Having written numerous screenplays, I was more than familiar with the term *mixed reaction,* only I'd never seen it applied quite the way it was during the bonfire. A number of people stood and applauded while others laughed themselves silly. But at least a third of the crowd was genuinely spooked and added their shrieks to the melee.

If it was difficult to settle the crowd down when Ronny made her appearance, it was virtually impossible with Whitney's unexpected entrance. Uncertain of what to do next, I shrugged my shoulders at Cammy, Godfrey, Glenda, and Roger.

Suddenly Godfrey stood and announced, "Who's interested in

hearing about blood-sucking insects in the Finger Lakes?"

"And ghostly sightings in the Ohio River Valley," Roger added.

An enthusiastic applause followed, and next thing I knew, the two of them had taken my place. I heard the words "Culicidae family" coming out of Godfrey's mouth and took off without even introducing them. I hurried over to Whitney and put a finger to my lips. "We need to talk in private. Well, semi-private. Donovan's photographer is over there conferring with Don and Theo from the Grey Egret, along with my boyfriend, Bradley. Our butts will freeze the farther we get from the bonfire so we need to make it quick."

She nodded and pulled her hat below her ears. "I took your advice and meandered down the wine trail. Time got away from me and I was starving. Next thing I knew, I was in Watkins Glen at a neat Italian Restaurant. I resigned myself to tasting your wines tomorrow and attending your bonfire tonight. It wasn't until I was a few miles from your winery when the news came on about Donovan Brin's less-than-natural death. I got here as fast as I could. Any word on Adrienne?"

I shook my head.

"This isn't looking good."

"I know. Come on, I'm getting cold standing here."

I realized it was ridiculous to remain outside in the cold when we could easily go back to my house and piece together what we knew about Donovan and Adrienne. "Wait here a sec. I'll tell Ronny and my friends they can continue talking at my house. It's not that far up the hill. And it's a heck of a lot warmer."

Whitney rubbed her arms together. "Good idea."

"Time to break up your huddle," I announced as I approached the close-knit group. "I need to get back to the bonfire in forty minutes or so to wrap things up, but there's no sense getting frostbite out here. We can try to figure things out at my house. Come on, what are you waiting for?"

No one needed to be convinced. In seconds, the small cluster broke up and walked up the hill.

Charlie wiggled around from person to person when we got inside the house. Fortunately, I had two boxes of hot chocolate K-cups on hand and immediately set to work preparing them. Since Francine had purchased the latest Keurig model, the K-Supreme Plus, I had two machines going at once: old faithful and the new Plus. The Plus was supposed to eke out more flavor but I doubted anyone noticed the difference. I know I didn't.

"Make yourselves comfortable," I said. "If you hurry, you can beat Charlie to the couch."

Even though we had a fireplace, I seldom used it and much preferred cranking up the natural gas heat to a point where it was comfortable but not extravagant. I could still remember my dad saying, "That's why they make sweaters."

"Sorry, guys," I said. "All of the marshmallows are at the bonfire so you'll have to make do with plain old hot chocolate."

"I'd make do with plain old hot water," Don said and chuckled. "That's how cold I am." He moved closer to Theo on the couch, giving Cammy enough room to share it with them. Ronny and Whitney sat in our oversize armchairs while Bradley and Glenda had to suffice with chairs from the dining room.

The kitchen chair I grabbed made a sharp noise as I slid it across the room and positioned it between the couch and Ronny. I winced. "We don't have much time so let's try to square our thoughts together and figure out what's going on. For those of you who don't know each other, I'll make it quick."

I introduced everyone at lightning speed and proceeded to recap what I knew, beginning with the grim discovery of a body in our cauldron display on Friday and culminating with Adrienne's disappearance. I made it a point to include the bizarre pashmina find in our woods as well as the troubling encounter Adrienne had with a wavy-haired man at our winery entrance.

"Obviously, we have Donovan's suspicious death hanging over us and I believe all of the other events are related." Then I looked at

Whitney and Ronny. "I think both of you may have pieces of this puzzle, but until we can link them, we're operating in the dark."

Then it dawned on me. Quite possibly Donovan's killer was seated a few feet from me. And if they worked in tandem, then it wasn't one killer, it was two.

Chapter 23

Neophyte sleuth or not, it didn't take a brain trust to figure out that one person couldn't have dragged Donovan's body into the cauldron alone. Or kidnapped Adrienne, for that matter. But looking at Whitney's and Ronny's faces, I seriously doubted they were the responsible parties. Then again, I'd been wrong before.

"What are we missing?" I asked the two of them. Then I focused on Whitney. "You met Adrienne at Belhurst Castle and later had dinner together at Port of Call. Did you get a sense she harbored enough of a grudge against her boss that she'd plot to kill him?"

Whitney pressed her hands against the hot chocolate mug and breathed in its steam. "I only met her that day. She's not exactly what one would call open and gregarious."

No. She puts Charles Dickens's Estella to shame.

I wasn't quite sure what to ask her next but thankfully Whitney kept talking. "It's funny but I sensed she was more concerned about her own safety than her boss's whereabouts."

"What do you mean?"

"The entire time we were at Port of Call, Adrienne either turned her head or sat up straight to get a better view of who was in the crowd. And it wasn't curiosity. I think she was afraid. And when she drove us back to the Belhurst, she circled the parking lot until she found just the right spot. I thought she was being picky at the time, but now that I think of it, the spot she selected was underneath one of the parking lot light posts. Whatever was going on, she wanted a clear view of who was around."

"Could be someone was in cahoots with her but now she was worried she'd be next on their hit list," Cammy said. "People who do things like that aren't very trustworthy when it comes to allegiances."

I knew Deputy Hickman brought her in to identify the body and most likely swore her to silence. As far as everyone else knew at the time, Donovan was missing, not dead. And I couldn't say a word about it.

Ronny stood and walked her hot chocolate mug to the sink. "I don't think there was any love lost between Adrienne and Donovan. But that doesn't mean she had something to do with his death. Not like Raisa James. Donovan stiffed her on stories all the time. She played by the rules. He didn't."

I wiped a bit of chocolate foam from my lip and looked around. Everyone had the same reaction I did—shock. "Raisa." I spoke her name slowly and deliberately. "She's the lady covering another wine-related story in Pennsylvania, right?"

"A cluster of boutique wineries in the central part of the state," Ronny said when she returned to her seat. "No events, just a general human interest wine story."

"No events meant Raisa could have easily been in our neck of the woods on Thursday before driving south to Pennsylvania. Who would have known?"

"Donovan," Don and Theo said at once.

Bradley turned to me and crinkled his nose. "I know it's only been two days since the body was discovered, but were you able to talk Eugene into telling you if any forensic evidence was found in that display?"

"Eugene wouldn't tell me if it was snowing, even if he was standing knee deep in the stuff. I'm banking on Gladys Pipp at the sheriff's office tomorrow. I even took out one of Francine's fancier jellies for her—strawberry and lemon."

Cammy took the small wooden tray that sat on an ottoman in the corner of the room and held it in front of our guests for their empty mugs. "If you ask me, Raisa might be our lead suspect. *Provided* she had some help. That brings us back to Adrienne."

I rubbed my hands together and glanced at everyone. "Here's a thought. If Adrienne isn't holed up somewhere scared out of her wits, then it's quite possible she and Raisa were the ones responsible for killing Donovan. Deputy Hickman did imply it was a poisoning. That's more in line with what women tend to do. And before everyone jumps down my throat, I'm not being sexist. I happened to have looked up the statistics on it."

"Way to go, Nancy Drew." Theo laughed.

"There's one more name we've left out of the mix," Ronny said. "Felicity. It won't be the first time a wife did her husband in. And don't forget, it's really easy to hop a flight from the Westchester airport to any of the big cities in the Finger Lakes."

"I'll confound us even more," I added. "There's a wavy-haired man with a stocky build out there whose photo Cammy took. He was at our entrance and it looked like he blocked the door as Adrienne was leaving on Friday. Coincidence? I think not."

"Well, coincidence or not," Theo said, "if we don't get back to that bonfire, Roger will have put the audience to sleep by now."

I flinched. "Unless Godfrey's still yammering about insects. Once he gets started, there's no stopping him. Come on, folks, we'd better head back down the hill. If you haven't given Cammy your mug, just leave it in the sink when you leave."

Ronny tapped my shoulder as we got to door and whispered, "Do you think I need to be worried? What if some deranged loco killed Donovan and got ahold of Adrienne? Am I next because I work for the same magazine?"

"I doubt it. This seems, well, more personal."

"It's Sunday night and no one's at the office." Ronny adjusted one of her earrings and gave her ear a tug. "First thing in the morning, I'm calling our editor to let her know about Donovan, unless the authorities contacted her already. Hmm, I doubt it or she would have phoned me. I suppose it doesn't really matter because it will be all over the news tomorrow anyway. Phooey. One way or another, I'm going to have a conversation with her. Geez, what do I tell her about Adrienne?"

"Nothing. Tell her what you know about Donovan and see what she says."

"I know what she's going to say: 'Stay put, Ronny. I'm going to call Adrienne and see if she can put that interview together from

Donovan's notes.'"

"In that case, mention plan B."

"What plan B?"

"Raisa. Tell your editor that maybe Raisa should do the story. Let her call Raisa and see what turns up. She's bound to have Raisa's cell number. By the way, our local deputy knows that you're here from the same magazine as Donovan and he'll track you down and tell you not to leave town yet."

"How do you know?"

"Trust me. Past experience. By the way, where are you staying?"

"At the Ramada Inn in Geneva. Donovan and Adrienne got the last two rooms at the Belhurst. I'll definitely hang on for at least another day or so."

"Did I hear you say you're staying a few more days?" Whitney was right behind us and overheard Ronny. "I plan to stick around as well. Lots of fodder for my podcasts." Then she looked at me. "You don't think that deputy's going to insist I stay longer, do you? I mean, a day or so is fine, but I've got other stories lined up in the city."

"I'm not sure. You were one of the last people to have a conversation with Adrienne, but then again, you'd only just met her."

I definitely needed a way to maintain my contact with them so I asked them to drop by tomorrow afternoon around three, when it's usually a lull time. "Whitney can finally get her wine tasting in," I said to Ronny, "and I'm sure there'll be lots of photo ops for you." *Even if I have to showcase Alvin and risk getting spit at.*

The women agreed, leaving me with one less thing to worry about. I stood off to the side as everyone exited the house and made sure I locked the door behind me. It wasn't something I normally did, at least not here in Penn Yan, but given the circumstances, it seemed prudent. Charlie was insistent on joining us so I made sure to leash him up again.

"John must have really gone overboard with those sage sticks," Glenda said as we walked back to the bonfire, "because I can catch the scent all the way over here. Let's hope it was enough protection."

Bradley elbowed me but neither of us said a word for fear we'd break out laughing. As our crew approached the bonfire, I heard Godfrey say, "Snow fleas aren't really fleas but they sure look like them. Next time there's a fresh snowfall, go outside and see if you can spot the springtails or collembolans. They eat things like fungal spores that get deposited in the snow and they can jump around just like fleas, but they don't bite."

"Ew!" someone exclaimed. "That's worse than ghost stories."

I rushed to the bonfire and thanked Godfrey and Roger for their enlightening tales as well as the audience for joining Two Witches and the Grey Egret. "Don't forget," I said, "our contest winners will be announced on our websites tomorrow. And don't wait for an event to visit us. Our wines taste wonderful no matter the season."

Again, the vincyard crew held out flashlights and lanterns so the crowd could find their way back to our parking lot in the dark. Only Cammy, Glenda, Theo, and Don remained with Bradley and me after the program was over.

"Hey, you left this on the bench in the front row," Godfrey said to me. He handed me my canvas bag, where I kept my ghost story notes in case I got stage fright and had to resort to a "readers theater" approach.

"Thanks. Hopefully I won't have to use this again any time soon." I opened it up to make sure everything was in there and noticed something silvery off to the side. I reached in and pulled out an unopened 3Musketeers bar. Room temperature thanks to the bag's proximity to the bonfire.

"What's the matter, Norrie?" Cammy asked. "It's a chocolate bar, not one of your sister's fiber ones."

Normally I would have laughed, but not this time. I turned to Glenda. "What was it Zenora said about that restless spirit?"

"She wasn't specific but said the spirit would reach out to you, why?"

"Because I don't eat 3Musketeer bars as a rule. I prefer whole chocolate, like Hershey bars."

Cammy shrugged. "Big deal. Chocolate's chocolate. Maybe someone gave you a gift."

"I hope so. I really do. Because the alternative's way too creepy for me."

A chorus of "huhs" and "whats" followed.

"The last time I saw a 3Musketeers bar was when I googled Donovan Brin. He held one of them in his hand and it looked like he had just taken a bite."

Glenda immediately opened her bag and took out a handful of salt, which she tossed in the air. Really pricey Himalayan pink salt, as I later found out. "That's Donovan. He reached out to you from the beyond."

"Or someone left me a gift," I muttered.

"He wants you to catch his killer, Norrie," she said. "I don't think he has any faith in our local deputies."

I tossed her the chocolate bar. "Who does?"

Chapter 24

"When I come over tomorrow after work, I'll bring a few changes of clothes," Bradley said when the two of us returned to my house with Charlie. "Not that I believe in all that hogwash from the netherworld, but someone may be messing around with you. Hold on a second."

He took out his phone and got on the internet. "Aha. I profiled the guy and guess what? Favorite snack foods include Tostitos, beef jerky, and 3Musketeers. Interesting selection. Whoever's behind this has obviously figured out you'd be googling Donovan, too. Of course, they had no way of knowing about Zenora, but it's still unnerving to plant an insidious link like that. Who knows what else they're thinking?"

"It's really too bad there was no way we could have gotten a good look at the audience around our bonfire tonight."

"I looked. All I saw were people with their hats pulled below their ears and scarves draped around their necks. Impossible to recognize anyone. Especially a match for the description you gave me of the mystery guy with the wavy hair. The one who intimidated Adrienne."

"Right now the only person I want to find *is* Adrienne. I think she knows more than she let on and now she's on the run. Remember the old saying, guilty by association? That could be the case with her."

"If that's the case, then you'd have to figure out what Donovan was into. And I don't mean writing articles about wine."

"Ronny mentioned their last big assignment in Napa. Maybe he found out something he shouldn't have. Come to think of it, Adrienne mentioned he became obsessed with an app on his phone when they got back."

Bradley put his hands on my shoulders and massaged them. "That could've been anything—his bank account, his safe driver app, video games . . . No way of knowing."

"Maybe it wasn't an app. Maybe he met another woman and they were messaging each other. Yikes. The wife could have found out and put an end to it. When Ronny told me the wife's name was Felicity, I tried googling her to see what she looked like. I came up empty. The only thing her Facebook profile showed was a photo of a butterfly."

"I know you won't let this go, but maybe it's time to switch tactics. When you deal with motive, it lends itself to all sorts of speculation. Figuring out the means gives you a tighter focus. Maybe Gladys will be able to fill in some blanks when you see her tomorrow. Strawberry jam and all."

I turned and nuzzled his neck. "It had to be poison. But how? Aargh. I'll be thinking about this all night."

"Hopefully with your eyes closed. I, for one, can't keep mine open. What do you say we hit the sack?"

"Looks like Charlie beat us to it. He's halfway up the stairs. By the way, I have another idea floating around in my head. After I see Gladys, I'll email the WOW wineries with that mystery guy's photo. Maybe one of their employees remembered seeing him. Or better yet, maybe they have a crowd photo."

"It can't hurt."

As it turned out, I didn't need to email the wineries. All I had to do was turn on the morning news. True, Ronny heard it on the radio last night but there's nothing like a full-screen snapshot of one Donovan Brin chatting it up with a huge crowd at what appeared to be a mega wine event somewhere. It must have been a file photo the news channel secured from *Wine Enthusiast* at some ungodly hour of the morning.

"Bradley!" I called out from the kitchen. He was still upstairs getting dressed. "Turn on the TV in the bedroom. Channel 13 WHAM."

I walked closer to the TV in the living room and stood there openmouthed. The commentator babbled on and on about Donovan and how Two Witches Winery was once again the scene of a suspicious death. But that wasn't what took my breath away. It was the two men in the background. Both stocky. Both with wavy hair. Only one with black rectangular glasses but both wearing golf shirts with that same wine logo with the *LV*.

"Do you spot it? The two men on the left-hand side? Rats. It's hard to see on that small TV in the bedroom, but from down here I can make it out. Check out the logo if you can."

Seconds later, the image disappeared and was replaced with one that showed wind damage suffered in Western New York between Rochester and Buffalo last night. I lowered the sound and walked back to the kitchen.

"I caught it for an instant." Bradley stood at the base of the stairs and glanced at the larger TV in the living room. "I couldn't make out any design or logo on the shirts but I did see the men for a second. Think it's our mystery guy?"

"And how. I'll see if I can contact someone at *Wine Enthusiast* today who can tell me where and when that photo was taken. Channel 13 won't know. By the way, yesterday afternoon I tried a google search for wineries with the initials *LV* and it was impossible."

"If Ronny saw that TV file photo, she might know."

"True. And she and Whitney will be at the winery this afternoon. Looks like a busy day ahead."

"Want me to pick up something for dinner or do you feel like going out?"

"I can't believe this is actually coming out of my mouth, but I'd rather stay home and make something. And before you get your hopes up, it'll be a plain old Crock-Pot roast with potatoes. I'll defrost the chuck roast I got last week and get it in the Crock-Pot before I leave the house."

"You're amazing."

"No, I just need time to figure this Donovan thing out before something worse happens."

• • •

At a little past eight, with only a cup of coffee for breakfast, I pulled into the Yates County Public Safety Building and found a spot close to the entrance. The weather had managed to turn even colder from yesterday, with November winds making their grand entrance. Good thing I opted for my fleece-lined jacket.

The receptionist on duty motioned me ahead to Gladys's office and even whispered that Deputy Hickman wasn't expected back for an hour when I asked her.

"Good morning, Norrie," Gladys said the minute she saw me. She was seated in front of a computer in her small workstation adjacent to Deputy Hickman's office. "I had a feeling you'd be in."

I smiled and handed her the strawberry-lemon jelly. "Francine's getting fancier these days with her jellies."

"That's so sweet of you. Thank you. I imagine you're here regarding the unfortunate incident at your winery on Friday."

I looked around before I spoke. "I wanted to know if a preliminary tox screen pulled up anything. I know the lab works weekends when it comes to suspicious deaths."

Gladys typed a few keys and moved her mouse around before shifting the monitor my way. "You know I can't divulge that kind of information." Then she patted her chest. "Oh, dear. I seem to have a bit of indigestion. I need to excuse myself and get a glass of water. The Tums works better with water." Then she winked and stepped away from her desk.

Thank you, Gladys.

I leaned over and eyeballed the monitor before scrolling down. The report was three pages long but all I needed was the pertinent information. Under *Testing Requested*, it said "postmortem toxicology." It listed Donovan's name, the date the report was issued and his gender. Under *Age*, it said "not given." I skipped ahead to a box in the middle of the first page. It was titled *Positive Findings*, and I knew I'd hit pay dirt. The box had four columns that cited the compound, the result, the number of units, and the matrix source.

Whatever that was. It didn't matter, I just needed to know what did him in.

The words *botulinum toxin* jumped out at me, followed by the more common word *Botox*. Whoever killed Donovan didn't do it with a tainted can of soup. Nope, they had to have injected him with enough of the stuff. True, those facial fillers like Juvéderm and Botox require prescriptions, but these days anyone can order stuff online and on the black market. Welcome to the twenty-first century.

"I'm back," Gladys announced from the corridor. I moved away from the monitor and pretended to look at something on my iPhone. "Sorry I couldn't be of more help, Norrie." Then she winked again. "Was there anything else you needed?"

"As a matter of fact, yes. And this can't possibly be top secret. In fact, it'll probably be on the noonday news."

"What's that?"

"A missing person report for Adrienne Stafine. It's been over forty-eight hours. Adrienne is Donovan Brin's assistant and she hasn't been seen since Friday night. I told Deputy Hickman about it yesterday and he said he'd take it under advisement."

"That seems to be his favorite expression these days. To answer your question, a report was issued at seven fifteen this morning from Ontario County and faxed over here for Deputy Hickman. It arrived before I came in to work."

"It was? Who did? I mean, who reported her missing?"

"The manager from Belhurst Castle in Geneva. Give me a moment, I have some notes on this."

She shuffled some papers around on her desk and cleared her throat. "Here it is. The manager noted Miss Stafine had not been in her room for two days. Guests must register their vehicles with the front desk so he had that information and called the rental agency to see if Miss Stafine had returned her car."

"I take it she didn't."

"Correct. Not only that, but the GPS was disabled. At that point, the manager filed a missing person report with the Ontario County Sheriff's Office. Oh, dear. First Mr. Brin and now his assistant. This is very concerning."

"I know."

"My understanding is that Mr. Brin was here to write a piece about your Merlot. It wasn't as if he was one of those investigative reporters covering something risky."

Just then the phone rang and Gladys took the call. I stood and mouthed "Thank you" as I walked toward the corridor. She put a hand over the receiver and replied, "Any time."

I hustled out of there for fear I'd run into Grizzly Gary and that was the last thing I needed. Instead, I ran into someone else and there was nothing I could do about it.

Chapter 25

It was after nine and I was famished. The Penn Yan Diner on East Elm Street, a refurbished 1925 railcar, had a breakfast menu that couldn't be beat and I wasted no time driving over there.

I was met by a blast of warm steam heat as I walked inside and took a seat at one of the empty four-person tables. I tossed my jacket over a chair and picked up the menu. It was a relief to get out of the early November wind and rub my hands together.

A twentysomething waitress with purple streaks in her pigtails walked over and plunked a coffee mug on top of the paper place mat. "Regular or decaf?" she asked.

"Regular."

I didn't need to specify cream, sugar, or otherwise because it was all on the table. Little creamers, little pourers, little packets. You name it, it was there. It was difficult to make a selection from their menu because all of the breakfasts sounded wonderful. I asked for a half order of their sausage gravy biscuits because I knew the full order would feed an entire army. It wasn't every diner that served their biscuits from scratch, but thankfully, this one did.

As I took the first sip of my coffee while waiting for my meal, I heard a voice from behind me that sent a chill down my back. It was Marilyn Ansley, Rosalee's sister, and the unofficial town crier for Seneca Lake. She was taller than Rosalee by at least a few inches but they both had the same sturdy country girl physique. Marilyn was younger by at least a decade, putting her somewhere between late sixties or early seventies.

I couldn't very well duck under the table so I had no choice but to say hello as she passed my table. In retrospect, I should have buried myself in the paper menu.

"Norrie!" she exclaimed. "Imagine running into you here." She zipped open her parka, revealing a brown and green sweatshirt with three kittens drinking from a bowl of milk. The words *Lap up all the joy you can* were scrawled across the shirt.

"It's nice to see you again. Rosalee said you were the MC at her bonfire this weekend."

"Those winery events never seem to end. And just because I own the land, my sister insists I take part in everything. Not that I minded this event. I love telling stories. In fact—" She stopped and looked around. "Say, why don't I join you? I'm a good half hour early for my women's chitchat breakfast. No sense standing in the aisle gabbing when I can get comfortable."

"I, um—"

"Thanks." She pulled out the chair across from mine and put her coat on the one next to it. Then she waved to the waitress. "Coffee, Aimee. And bring me a cinnamon bun please while I wait to order my real breakfast with the chitchat ladies."

When Rosalee told our WOW group that Marilyn could chew your ears off and start on your nose, I thought she was exaggerating. Apparently not. Even with a giant cinnamon bun in her mouth, the woman kept on talking. At one point I was afraid she'd run out of breath and I'd have to call the paramedics.

She finished the last bite of her pre-breakfast and washed it down with coffee before continuing where she had left off. Frankly, the words glazed over me until she said, "Hooligans. That's who messed with our Hallow Wine Weekend display. And to think we worked so hard on making those enormous papier-mâché candy corn pieces."

"Huh? What? I think I missed something."

Marilyn put her coffee mug down and wiped her lip with a frayed napkin that she had used to polish the silverware at the table. "Rosalee and I, along with her tasting room staff, made this adorable display that featured giant candy corn pieces and a sign that read *Have a Corny Hallow Wine Weekend*. Some delinquent, most likely from one of the local colleges, switched out the giant *C* in *Corny* and replaced it with a giant *H*. I thought my sister would blow a gasket. If that wasn't bad enough, they stuck a cardboard goose on one of the candy corns as if it was laying an egg."

I choked back a laugh and nearly spat out my coffee. "When did you notice this?"

"Friday morning. We took the goose out of the display and made another *C*. Later on, we found out from some wine tasters that the goose had come from Glenrosa Winery down the road. Rosalee called them and found out some miscreants put one of our candy corn pieces in their display under a resin goose so it looked like the goose pooped out the candy."

This time I burst out laughing. "Guess this gives new meaning to the expression trick or treat." Then it hit me. Marilyn had inadvertently solved part of the murder puzzle. All those mismatched pieces we were dealing with had nothing whatsoever to do with Donovan's murder. Secret message my patootie. It was a prank. A Halloween prank. Heck, those college kids were notorious for that kind of stuff.

"I wish Rosalee had your sense of humor," Marilyn said. "You should have heard her rant."

"I can imagine. I only wish I knew what time those pranksters did their trick on our display. It had to be before Donovan's body, dagger and all, was shoved in there. Better yet, I wish I knew who those kids were."

At that exact second, Aimee arrived with my biscuits and gravy and I all but inhaled them.

"Those look wonderful," Marilyn said. She glanced at her wristwatch and then looked at the waitress. "Can you bring me a half order of those while I wait. I'll order my real meal when the ladies arrive."

Good grief! How many meals can this lady consume?

"Sure thing," Aimee replied. Then she leaned over and whispered over my shoulder, "My brother would kill me if he knew I told you this, so whatever you do, don't mention where you heard it. He and his frat brothers were the ones who wreaked havoc on the Hallow Wine

Weekend displays. Then when they found out a body was dumped in one of them, they totally freaked out. My brother said they didn't come across anything like that at all. Listen, last thing he needs is to get on probation or worse. He's a good kid. On the Dean's List, too. If I give you his name, it'll start a family war."

"I understand. But can you tell me the name of his fraternity?"

"It's Alpha Tau on St. Clair Street in Geneva. Right off the Hobart-William Smith quad."

"Thanks. I really appreciate it. And if you do any wine tasting, come to Two Witches. I'm one of the owners and we'll comp the tasting."

"Sounds great." Then she looked at Marilyn. "I'll be right back with your order."

I devoured my biscuits and was done eating just as Marilyn's breakfast order, and her friends, arrived. "If you don't mind, Norrie, I might as well have Aimee put my order at the chitchat ladies table."

Mind? I'll walk it there myself.

"No problem. It was really nice running into you like this. Enjoy your breakfast."

I left Aimee a generous tip, grabbed my jacket and headed out the door. Once inside my car, I phoned Stephanie.

"When was the last time you were at a frat house?" I asked when she picked up the phone. She was in their tasting room and most likely running things since it was an early Monday morning.

"Is this some kind of trick question?"

"No, more like a sleuthing expedition." I told her everything I'd found out over the weekend as well as what I learned during my encounter with Marilyn at the Penn Yan Diner. Stephanie burst out laughing about the *C* and *H* switch at Rosalee's as well as the Glenrosa's goose pooping out a giant candy corn.

"Boy, talk about a Halloween prank. That's classic."

"Prank or not, once we talk to those guys we can narrow down the time line and find out if they saw anything suspicious. You know what this means, Stephanie. We might be able to finger our killer. Or killers."

"Can't you take Theo like you always do? Or Bradley? What time does he get off work? Those frat brothers are up until all hours of the night."

"It has to be you. No one else."

"Me? Why?"

"One look at you and those guys will spill the beans like nobody's business."

I wasn't kidding either. Stephanie had always reminded me of Christy Brinkley in her supermodel days, only taller and curvier. With her long blond hair, which she flipped like an artform, Stephanie could beguile any male in her vicinity. It was too bad she wasn't around during the Cold War because she would have made one hell of a secret weapon for the government.

"Honestly, Norrie. That's really sweet of you to say so, but I'm no investigator."

"You don't have to be. I'll ask the questions and you can bat your eyes and flip your hair. They'll be so distracted, they'll cough up everything they know."

"When?"

"How about tomorrow night after eight? I'd go tonight but I put a roast in the Crock-Pot for Bradley and me."

"Sounds like you two are getting serious."

"I don't know what to call it, but it works. So, tomorrow night? I'll swing by and pick you up at eight."

"Okay. Derek shouldn't have a problem getting the boys to bed. Face it, if Donovan's killer is still lurking around, we need to know sooner than later. I read somewhere that killers tend to hang around after they've done the deed. Creepy, huh?"

"And how."

Chapter 26

The only thing I accomplished between Monday morning and Tuesday evening, other than a bizarre conversation with Zenora, a go-nowhere meeting with Ronny and Whitney, and a less-than-fruitful chat with Marsha Whitman from the Belhurst, was the pot roast I prepared in the Crock-Pot Monday morning. Easy peasy. Three pounds of chuck roast, packet of Lipton's onion soup mix, packet of Hidden Valley ranch dressing, quarter stick of butter and ta-da! Well, maybe that wasn't all I did. I called the editorial department at *Wine Enthusiast* later that afternoon to see if anyone could tell me when or where that TV photo was taken.

Lamentably, no one could. I was on hold for over ten minutes while the clerk who answered my call tried to track down who sent the news media that photo. When she returned to the phone all she could tell me was that it was taken at a winery sometime in the past two years.

Very helpful.

I asked if anyone recognized the two men but that was a big fat no as well.

"We were in a rush for time," she explained, "so we grabbed the first file photo that came up. Since then, we sent the media a professional headshot of Mr. Brin for their use."

I thanked her for her time and told her how sorry we were for their loss. There was no sense asking her if she knew whether or not the feature story would be assigned to someone else since Ronny already gave me her take on the matter. No doubt about it, I had to track down Adrienne and do it quickly, but I also needed to tie up the little loose end regarding the fraternity pranksters. It didn't give me a whole lot of time.

And then there was the elusive Raisa James. Ronny did call her editor, who indicated she was on the verge of scrapping the entire feature since Raisa was stuck in the middle-of-nowhere Pennsylvania working on a fascinating piece that featured a burgeoning winery. Aargh! Too bad that wasn't the worst part. Ronny placed the call at a little past nine in the morning on Monday. Talk about timing. It was minutes after the editor received a call from the Ontario County Sheriff's Office regarding the missing person report issued for Adrienne Stafine.

According to the editor, "the whole piece just went up in smoke," and unless Adrienne made an appearance and/or Raisa could extricate herself from Pennsylvania's heartland, they'd have to move on.

When Ronny broke the news to me at three fifteen that Monday afternoon, I developed a tic in my eye. A sign of anxiety, no doubt. We were seated in our bistro sipping on hot cider while Whitney finally had the chance to taste a number of our wines.

"There's another solution, you know," Ronny said as I frantically swirled the cinnamon stick around in my drink so I'd forget about the tic.

"What's that?"

"*You* could write the article. You're a screenwriter. Who would know? We could send it in as if Donovan wrote it before he, well, you know."

"I think it may have lawsuit written all over it. Besides, Adrienne has the notes."

"But Donovan had his mini recorder. If someone didn't take it from his room, then it had to be on his body when the coroner removed it."

"Please don't tell me you're suggesting I sneak into the county morgue and go through their boxes of evidence."

"How badly do you want the article written?"

I rubbed my eye hoping it would stop the tic and quoted Deputy Hickman's favorite response—"I'll take it under advisement."

Much as I hated to admit it, I was no stranger to taking chances. But the county morgue? Then again, Ronny's words were hard to ignore—*"How badly do you want the article written?"* It's not every day that Merlots from small upstate New York wineries are featured in renowned magazines. An opportunity like this doesn't come along every decade. Aargh.

If nothing else, the mere thought of breaking into the Yates County Morgue gave me all the impetus I needed to focus on finding Adrienne and figuring out exactly who was responsible for knocking off Donovan. At least Whitney and Ronny would be in town since they got the official word from not one but two county sheriff's offices—"Don't leave town."

Ronny's idea was so over-the-top, even for me, that I didn't dare mention it to Bradley Monday night. Then Tuesday morning rolled around, and Ronny's idea didn't sound so crazy after the conversation I had with Zenora.

She called me at the winery shortly before eleven when she took her break. As usual, Zenora sounded short of breath and frantic. "Norrie—you haven't taken down that cauldron display, have you?"

"Sadly, no. Deputy Hickman thinks the juxtaposition of objects may be a clue. I know for a fact it was a fraternity prank but I'll have to get a confession from the culprits. Why?"

"Today is the Day of the Dead."

Oh, no. Please don't tell me she has some wackadoodle thing in mind.

"I know. My Spanish classes celebrated it every year with overcooked dead bread."

"Then you understand why it's important for you to share a meal with the spirit that last inhabited the cauldron: Donovan Brin. His soul is lingering around the display. It won't move on."

"Can't he linger without a full meal?"

"I'm serious, Norrie. Bring him something to drink and something to eat. It doesn't have to be fancy. Too bad you don't know what he likes to eat."

"Uh, actually, I do. Tostitos, beef jerky and 3Musketeers."

"That's wonderful. Bring those foods to the cauldron, say a few words to him, and sit down so you can enjoy eating together."

"It's freezing outside. I wouldn't be surprised if we get an inch of snow. If I sit on the ground, I'm liable to get stuck there."

"Take a blanket. Or a towel. You need to do this. The last thing Two Witches needs is a restless spirit hovering around."

"How long do I have to stay there?"

"Until he's done eating and drinking."

"And how would I know that? Is the food supposed to vanish?"

"Don't be ridiculous. It will have lost its taste. Try a Tostito or a bite of the beef jerky. Even the chocolate. If it seems tasteless, then he's done."

I pressed three fingers to my forehead and rubbed. "That means I'll have to drive to the convenience store down the road. We don't sell those foods here."

"Good, good. You've got it all planned. Oh, before I forget—don't try to pry information out of him. It might be misconstrued. Just share the food."

"I, um, er—"

And like that, Zenora ended the call. I wanted to ignore the entire conversation altogether but I knew better. Zenora and Glenda would plague me nonstop if I didn't dine with the late Donovan. And frankly, that would be worse than his restless spirit shuffling about. I grabbed my jacket, muttered something to Lizzie and drove the half mile down the road to the convenience store. I returned with all three items plus Cheetos, and pretzel rods.

The tricky part was pulling it off without looking as if I'd lost my marbles. The only saving grace, if one could call it that, was Alvin. His pen was only a few feet from the cauldron. If I could make it appear as if I was talking to the goat and munching food, our customers would be less likely to think I'd lost my mind.

I moseyed over to Alvin, muttered a few words, and walked over to the cauldron. "Think of this as a cocktail party, Donovan," I said, "I'm not sitting down on the cold damp ground." With that, I opened the bag of Tostitos, popped one in my mouth, and tossed another into the cauldron. With any luck, a bird would get it before nightfall. As for sampling to see if the flavor was there, forget it!

Looking over my shoulder, I made sure no one was entering or exiting the winery. Then, I did it again. Tostito for me. Tostito for Donovan. That's when Alvin lost it. In retrospect, I should have offered the goat a Tostito, but how was I supposed to know he'd like it?

Alvin stood at the edge of his pen, leaned over and spat a wad of hay and grain right at me. That was before he stood on his hind legs and threatened to knock over the fence. But that wasn't the worst of it. To make it really clear how ticked off he was, he lifted his head in the air and peed in my direction.

Frantic to put as much distance as possible between Alvin and me, I spun around and sprinted toward the winery entrance. Unfortunately, I stumbled over a rock and landed on the ground, inches from Donovan's last known resting place.

"Oh, what the hell!" I shouted to his spirit. "Have yourself a field day." I threw a 3Muskeeters bar into the cauldron along with a package of Slim Jim Originals. Then, for good measure, I tossed a few more Tostitos into Alvin's pen before wiping most of the slime off my forehead with my arm and walking back to my office. I left the Cheetos and the pretzels in the car for fear I'd binge eat both bags. Thankfully everyone was busy, especially Lizzie, who had customers at the cash register. I ducked into the restroom, tidied up, and returned to my desk as if nothing had happened.

Now, at a little past seven that evening, I paced around the kitchen practicing the interrogation tactics I was about to use on whoever answered the door at Alpha Tau. I paused every now and then to munch on the leftover pot roast, along with Charlie. The dog refused to eat his kibble and instead eyeballed the plate of meat that I set on the table. Sucker that I was, I gave in to him.

Bradley, meanwhile, was dining in Geneva with his boss, Marvin, and a new client of theirs who had recently moved to the area. When we spoke the night before, he said he expected to be back at my house before ten the next evening and was sorry we wouldn't be eating together that night. "Please tell me if I'm being intrusive. I don't want you to feel as if I've planted myself here, but I'm really concerned about Donovan's killer. Or killers. They must know by now you're looking into it."

It was impossible to resist those cobalt blue eyes of his, especially when he leaned in to plant a kiss on my lips.

"Are you kidding? I love having you here. Even if it's only for a few weeks. Seeing each other sporadically when you came to the city was tough on both of us. Charlie and I will devour the leftovers and you and I can go out or do takeout tomorrow. Besides, I happen to have plans tomorrow night myself."

I explained about the little visit Stephanie and I planned to make at the frat house and he didn't know what to think. "Got to admit," he said, "it was a stroke of luck finding out about those pranksters from one of their sisters. I'm surprised you didn't coerce Theo into joining you. Or Godfrey."

"They don't have Stephanie's skill set."

"Huh?"

"Eyelash batting, hair flipping, leg crossing, lip moistening—"

"I get the idea. Frankly, you never cease to amaze me. Just be careful and keep your cell phone close."

"Don't worry. I think those guys are going to be harmless enough. I only hope they spill out everything they saw and heard that Thursday night when Donovan met his demise. Funny, but it seems as if I'm pulling pieces and parts of fabric together, hoping to make a quilt."

"I suppose that's how it is with investigations. Relax, I have faith in you."

"Good. Because once I'm done here, it's on to Adrienne and Raisa."

Chapter 27

At ten to eight, I pulled up in front of Stephanie's house. Their porch lighting accented the green gables and highlighted the pumpkins that clung to every corner on their wraparound porch. I imagined the pumpkins would soon be replaced by whatever turkey-themed decorations their twin boys came up with.

The front light flickered on and off, signaling Stephanie had seen me and was on her way. I glanced at myself in the rearview mirror and shrugged. I wasn't the one who had to mesmerize those college boys.

"Brr, it's chilly," Stephanie announced as she got into the passenger seat. "One minute I'm applying sunblock and the next I'm looking around for my gloves."

"I know. In a few weeks I'll have to dig out Francine's snow boots."

"Hey, I got your text about the Botox. Don't worry. I didn't say anything to Derek. I know it's hush-hush for now. Boy, what would we do without Gladys, huh?"

"No kidding. But Botox? That came out of the blue. Not that I'm an expert on home poisonings, but usually it's antifreeze or rat poison."

"Are you thinking what I am? That the killer or killers are women? Lots of women I know order those fillers online. Ugh. I hate to think it, but it's only a matter of time before I'll be dipping into that well. Only I'm not dumb enough to do it myself. Heck, that's why they have medical offices and salons. The worst are the lip fillers. One wrong move and there's no going back."

"I don't think you'll need to worry about that for a long, long time."

"You think?"

"Oh, yeah. Listen, about the Botox . . . I suppose two women could have pulled it off. It's feasible. But which two women? Adrienne, Ronny, or Raisa? I'm not putting Whitney on the list unless she's got a motive I'm not aware of. She has nothing to do with the magazine and only met Adrienne a few days ago at the Belhurst."

"Maybe we'll luck out and one of those frat guys will have seen our perpetrators."

"That's what I'm banking on."

Less than fifteen minutes later, I turned onto St. Clair and parked across the street from Alpha Tau. Apparently no one worried about the electric bill because the lights were on in every window. The house was an old Victorian that must have belonged to one of Geneva's gentry back in the day. Now, it had a banner that hung above the porch that read *Alpha Tau—It doesn't get any better*. Yeesh.

I turned to Stephanie and shut off the engine. "All set to work your magic?"

"I suppose. Here goes nothing."

We got out of the car and walked directly across the street and onto their porch. A skeleton wearing a Hobart sweatshirt and Hanes boxers leaned against the front window. Two shriveled pumpkins clung on to life next to the skeleton.

A sign on the door read *Enter at your own risk*, and I rolled my eyes. "Oh, brother. Talk about clichés." Since I couldn't spot a doorbell, I knocked on the frame and noticed it was in dire need of a paint job. I imagined the rest of the exterior was as well, but it was too dark to tell.

Seconds later, someone yelled, "It's open. You don't need an invitation."

I stepped inside with Stephanie at my heels. And while the front room didn't resemble anything I'd seen in *Animal House*, it certainly wasn't going to win any awards for tidiness. A few pop bottles on the floor, trash baskets overflowing with paper and candy wrappers, and an open pizza box on a side table that may have been there since Labor Day.

A dark-haired kid with day-old stubble was curled up in a faded brown recliner typing something on his laptop and another kid, who was seated on the equally faded brown couch, was talking on his cell phone. All I could make out was, "Gimme a break, Gloria."

The room off to the side of the front room seemed to be where all the action was—a large wall TV, now showing a commercial, and at least four or five guys who were watching the show.

I cleared my throat and used my best presentation voice. "Hi! We need to speak with someone regarding the vandalism at our wineries. It's that or we go to the police."

Suddenly the dark-haired kid closed his laptop and the kid who was on the phone ended the call. *No breaks now from Gloria.* Then they noticed Stephanie and nearly tripped over the runner on the floor to approach her. I attributed that to Stephanie unbuttoning her deep teal stadium coat, revealing a V-neck knit that clung ever so tightly to her skin.

The dark-haired kid spoke first. "Uh, sorry. What's this about vandalism?" Then he stepped closer to Stephanie. "Whatever it is, we'll pay for it."

"Take a good look," I said, cutting in between the two of them. I held up a photo of the Gable Hill Grim Reaper choking the daylights out of Don and Theo's poor felted egret.

"It was meant to be a joke," he said. "We didn't destroy anything."

"Only our business. Oh, and did I mention the dead body in our cauldron? Was that a joke, too'?"

Funny, but even as I mentioned a dead body, the dark-haired kid never took his eyes off Stephanie. It was the other kid who spoke and he all but choked on his words. "You have to believe us, we had nothing to do with that. Evan flipped out when he heard the news because he and Mack were the ones who pranked that winery and the two right next to it."

I put the cell phone back in my pocket and took a breath. Normally I would have asked if there was someplace we could sit and talk but thoughts of bedbugs and roaches crossed my mind so I decided to remain standing. "Where can we find Evan and Mack?"

"Mack's at the library but Evan's upstairs. Hang on, I'll get him. Did you, um, want to sit down or something?"

I shook my head. Adamantly, too. "No, this is fine."

While the kid went to get Evan, I introduced myself and Stephanie to his friend.

The guy couldn't be more apologetic. And nervous. "How did you know it was our fraternity?"

"I'm one of the owners of Two Witches and our tasting room gets lots of traffic. People talk. Especially when they're tasting wine."

"Look, I didn't prank your winery. I did Glenrosa and Terrace Wineries on the lakeside. But I've known Evan for three years and if he saw a dead body, he would have passed out right on the spot."

Just then, Evan approached us. He was tall and lanky with the same facial features as Aimee, the waitress with the purple streaks in her pigtails. He had to be her brother. Judging from his demeanor, his friend gave him the heads-up about our visit.

Evan ran a hand through his light brown hair and then balled it up into his other one. "Please don't rat us out with the police. We didn't have anything to do with that dead guy. Honest. All we did was put the scythe from the Grim Reaper display into the cauldron display, remove one of the egrets from the big pumpkin and tape the recipe card from Two Witches to the pumpkin. Oh, yeah, after that we put the bird in the hands of the Grim Reaper. We thought it was pretty funny. Um, well, until we heard the news the next day."

Then Stephanie flipped her hair and moistened her lips. "We won't report this to the police but only if you help us out."

As soon as she said that, all three guys responded with a chorus of "sure," "anything," "whatever you need," and "no problem."

"Okay, fine," I said. "Here's the deal. We need to establish a time line for that murder in order to track down the killer. Or killers."

"Uh, shouldn't the police be doing that?" the red-haired kid asked.

"Actually, it's the sheriff's office in Penn Yan. They're the lead agency on the case and they're assisted by the Ontario County Sheriff's Office and the Geneva Police Department."

The guys looked at each other before Evan spoke. "Sounds like nothing will get done. Only paperwork."

Give that kid an A+.

I nodded. "That's why we're looking into it. Unofficially, of course. We don't want our wineries to carry the stigma of murder on them."

"What do you need from us?" he asked.

"A detailed description of anything you might have seen, heard, or even smelled the night you decided to have some fun with our cauldron display. Also, the time you got there and the time you left. More or less."

"Okay. Mack and I went in his car. An old Nissan. All of us left the frat house around the same time but we went to different wineries on the west side of the lake."

"Geez, how many was that?" I was incredulous.

"Ten or eleven," the dark-haired kid said. "We had a good night because it wasn't raining, snowing, or blowing. Not like other years."

"And the time?"

"Mack and I left here at seven. I know because an *NCIS* repeat just came on. Our first stop was Gable Hill. Real quick. We grabbed the scythe and got out of there. Went to your winery next and stuck the scythe in the cauldron. Then we drove back down your road and grabbed one of the egrets from that display. We stuck the recipe card on the back of their pumpkin for good measure before driving back to Gable Hill to give the Reaper an egret to choke."

And these guys will be running the country in another few years.

"Did you see any other cars in our parking lots? Or anything out of the ordinary?"

Evan shook his head. "No cars in the parking lots but a car turned into your driveway right after we turned north onto Route 14 to go to Gable Hill. The car that pulled into your drive was headed south."

Suddenly, I was on overdrive. "What kind of a car? Sedan? SUV? Color? Make?"

Stephanie tapped my arm. "It's not a quiz show. Let him think."

"An SUV for sure. Maybe dark blue or black."

Plenty of room for a corpse in an SUV. Easy to load into the hatchback, too.

I took a breath and tried to calculate the time. "Okay, so if you left here at seven and drove to our wineries, that would have taken you about twenty minutes. Twenty-five tops if there was traffic. Factor in the three stops you made before looping back to Gable Hill with the egret. I'm guessing maybe five minutes a stop, right? I mean, how long does it take to remove a scythe and stash it elsewhere. Same deal with the egret."

"Removing the egret took longer. It was attached to the pumpkin with wire and we had to unravel it. It's not like we came prepared with a wire cutter. The only thing we brought was tape for the recipe card."

"You must have planned this way ahead of time if you thought to bring tape."

"Only two days before," the dark-haired kid said. "During breaks from our classes, we drove to the west side wineries to check out their displays. All the way from Geneva to Himrod. Then we picked the wineries we wanted to mess with."

Lucky us.

"Wait a sec. You said you checked out all the west side winery displays, right?" I asked.

"Uh-huh."

"In any of the displays, did you happen to see a dagger?"

"I didn't," the red-haired kid answered. "What about you guys?"

"Nope," they replied in unison. Then the dark-haired kid crinkled his nose. "The only time I've seen a dagger up close and personal was on the wall behind the bar at Stonecutters Tavern at Belhurst Castle. I had dinner there with my folks during Homecoming and Parents Weekend in September. Why?"

"Because it was another gift we found in our cauldron. The thing is, whoever delivered it plunged it into the back of the corpse."

"Holy hell," one of them muttered. "That wasn't on the news."

I put a finger to my lips. "Keep it that way."

"We better not go down for this," Evan said to his buddies. "My parents will yank me out of here so fast, my feet won't even be in my shoes."

I handed them the Two Witches business card and recited the law enforcement motto before we left. "If you think of anything else, call me."

Then the dark-haired kid looked at Stephanie. "Do you have a business card, too?"

I did at least three mental eye rolls.

Chapter 28

"I don't know about you," I said to Stephanie as I put the key in the ignition, "but it's early and I could go for a drink at Stonecutters Tavern. It's on the way home."

"A drink or a look at the wall behind their bar?"

"Both. Isn't it a bit coincidental that our suspects, with the exception of Ronny, are staying at the Belhurst? And it wouldn't be all that difficult to remove a dagger from the wall and slip it into a bag if the killer worked in tandem with someone to create a distraction."

"That's called speculation."

"Ugh. You're sounding like Grizzly Gary."

"That's because he lectures us enough. It's seeping in. And yeah, a drink sounds good."

I snagged a decent parking spot close to the main entrance and pulled my scarf tight around my neck. "I nearly froze to death leaving the frat house. I swear the temperature must have dropped at least ten degrees in the time we were there."

"It sure feels that way. You know what I dread most? It's digging out my heavy parka and wearing it for the next five months. No wonder bears hibernate. And that's not the worst of it. The boys are totally impervious to the cold. When I'm forced to be outside with them, I pretty much bribe them with hot chocolate and cookies to go back inside. Thank goodness Derek enjoys all that outdoor stuff. Building snow forts and tobogganing look great in the movies, but the reality is waterlogged boots and wet clothes."

"Too bad there aren't many wineries in the Caribbean."

We both laughed and walked inside the building.

The Stonecutters Tavern, situated inside Belhurst Castle, was one of those casual pubs that combined elegance and down-home comfort. Oversize chairs coupled with tables that could seat two to twenty encompassed the large area. In warmer weather, patio doors opened up to a fabulous deck and view of Seneca Lake.

The décor was autumn in all its glory—mums, pumpkins, gourds, and corn stalks tastefully wrapped in orange and yellow ribbons. The bar and large fireplace were the focal points and I was relived that it was a Tuesday and not the weekend or we'd never get seats at the horseshoe-shaped bar that overlooked the lake. As soon as we entered the room, I charged toward the bar to see if the dagger was still hanging there. Drat! It was.

"Well, this is a wasted trip," I said to Stephanie. "The dagger that kid mentioned is still there."

"It's not wasted for me. I never get out of the house. And since you're driving, I'm ordering a mixed drink." With that, she took a seat at the bar and helped herself to the bowl of assorted nuts and crackers.

I ordered a tonic water with lime and resigned myself to the fact we may never figure out where that dagger came from. When the bartender, a man in his late fifties or early sixties with salt-and-pepper hair, served our drinks, I asked about the dagger. "Um, has that dagger always been on the wall next to the picture window?"

"As far as I know. And I've been working here for over five years. Same deal with the sword on the other side of the window. My understanding is that the hotel owner brought them back from Toledo, Spain, during his travels in the 1980s. Of course, nowadays you can get that stuff off of eBay and probably even Amazon."

Stephanie held the glass mug that contained her hot toddy against her chest and inhaled. "Now this is what I call an autumn drink." She took a small sip and closed her eyes.

The bartender turned his head and looked at the dagger. "Funny, but daggers must be a hot topic this week."

"What do you mean?"

"I overheard two ladies mention it when I went to refill some ice Saturday afternoon. They were seated adjacent to the bar at one of the round tables. Couldn't see their faces. One of them said, 'Doesn't that dagger look just like—' but I didn't hear the rest. Then, later that same afternoon, two clean-cut gentlemen stopped in. Young guys, thirties maybe. They noticed the dagger and one of them said he was surprised the media didn't mention it. Then the other one said there was a reason for that. I had no idea what they were talking about. Maybe something on Netflix. It's always something on Netflix."

"Do you remember what they looked like?" I asked.

"One was tall and thin. Light hair. Round face. The other was stockier but with a baby face."

I turned to Stephanie when the bartender walked to the other end of the bar. "Eugene and Clarence for sure. They know about the dagger in Donovan's back but the news media never revealed it. It wasn't the cause of death. The report I saw on Gladys's computer said Botox. No word about a dagger. That means my original conjecture must have been right. It was an afterthought. And most likely by someone other than the killer. It wouldn't make sense for Donovan's killer to dump the body and then decide to stick a dagger in his back. Most killers want to get it over with. But spurned lovers like to leave messages."

"What spurned lover?"

"I'm not sure. Maybe one who arranged for his murder and then decided to stick it to him. Literally."

"And you think Eugene's going to talk?"

"Forget Eugene. The guy's got a permanent case of lockjaw but I might be able to eke out some information from Clarence. Then again, I may be able to kill two birds with one stone."

"Now you've lost me."

"What I'm about to suggest isn't ethical. Heck, it may even be criminal. But not a felony. Maybe a misdemeanor."

"That's not sounding too good. What is it?"

"Ronny told me her editor may axe our feature story if Adrienne doesn't show up or if Raisa doesn't finish up fast enough in Pennsylvania. Those are the only two who could write it. Unless I ghostwrite it on the sly and pass it off as Donovan's."

Stephanie shot me a look as if I was about to launch a nuclear bomb on a colony of penguins.

"The trouble is, I'd need Donovan's mini-recorder for his notes and that may be with his stuff in the morgue."

At the mention of the word *morgue*, Stephanie stopped coddling her hot toddy and took a long stiff drink. "That's the most insane idea I've ever heard. What kind of a nutcase sneaks into a morgue?"

"Not the morgue exactly. The evidence file in the morgue."

"Oh, that sounds a *whole* lot better. Are you nuts?"

"I may be able to find out if any prints were retrieved from the dagger and if I'm lucky, I might be able to borrow Donovan's mini-recorder for the article."

"Borrow? It's stealing evidence from a murder. That may actually be a felony. I don't suppose you ran it by Bradley?"

"Of course not. *That* would be crazy. Besides, I'm only toying with the idea at this point."

"Don't! Maybe we should concentrate on what we do know. According to the frat guys, the dagger didn't come from anyone's Halloween display and we ruled out the one from here. Where does that leave us?"

"Nowhere. Same deal with the Botox. From what you told me, anyone could purchase it online. But think about it for a minute. Botox isn't a typical poison. Whoever used it must have been familiar with it and with its properties. That means they had to be using it on themselves. In nonlethal doses. It was a poison of convenience."

"Hmm, I seem to remember reading something like that in one of my mysteries, only they used eyedrops. The detective was able to figure out who did it from a prescription one of his suspects had for the eyedrops."

"Okay. That brings us back to the only suspects we have: Adrienne, Ronny, possibly Whitney, and Raisa, who we never met and who may never have set foot in Penn Yan."

"You forgot about the mystery man. The one who was in the photo with Donovan and who blocked Adrienne at your winery's door."

"That's a long shot."

"He's still a suspect. And by the way, men can be pretty vain when it comes to laugh lines and wrinkles. You'd be surprised to learn how many men use dermal fillers. Forget what I said earlier about the culprit being a woman. Guess it's an open playing field, huh?"

I took another sip of my drink and tried to get the image out of my head. "What do you suggest we do now?"

"Put everything on hold and get home before Derek sends out the militia. If either of us has an epiphany, we can text each other."

• • •

Bradley and Charlie were snuggled together on the couch watching the news when I came in. Neither of them stirred, although Bradley called out he was glad to see I got home safe and sound. "How'd your sleuthing go at the frat house?"

"Aimee from the diner was right. It was an idiotic prank those guys pulled and no secret codes or messages. Grizzly Gary's been watching too many episodes of *FBI*." I took off my jacket and hung it in the closet, along with my scarf. Then I nudged Charlie to the edge of the couch so I could skootch in closer to Bradley. "Alpha Tau divvied up the wineries and the two guys who messed with ours arrived to do their damage before Donovan was dropped into the cauldron. We did get a time line of sorts, though. And something else. They saw a car pull into our driveway around seventy forty-five that Thursday night as they pulled out onto Route 14. A dark SUV. Some help, huh?"

"One thing for sure. Whoever did this must have planned ahead. They had to have parked their car below the building so they could walk up and cover your security cameras. Hey, did the sheriff's office ever find out what it was? Whipped cream? Shaving cream?"

"Shaving cream. And those things come in travel sizes, unlike whipped cream. Real easy to stash it in a pocket. Anyway, I'll let Deputy Hickman's office know that I heard through the grapevine it was a fraternity prank. I really don't want to get Evan, that's the kid's name, in trouble. Or go back on my word to his sister."

"If nothing else, you might be able to get the okay to take down the display. I imagine they've garnered as much forensic evidence as they needed, and since the displacement of objects was intended as a joke, there's no reason to have it remain standing."

"Three more days and it'll be an eyesore. Worse than Christmas decorations that stay up until Valentine's Day. Besides, Cammy is itching to put up the Thanksgiving cutout of a turkey she and Glenda made last August. It reads *Gobble Up the Fun at Two Witches*. You know, that Hallow Wine Weekend display might just meet with a mishap if Alvin gets loose. Then again, I might put a bug in Gladys's ear."

"Go with the bug."

Chapter 29

I called Gladys after Bradley had left for his office the next morning. It was a little past eight and I knew she'd be settled in at her desk. What I didn't know was that Eugene was a few feet away when she took my call.

"Norrie! I'll be right with you. I'm finishing up with something. Can you hold for just a min—"

And then I heard Eugene's tight voice because Gladys hadn't put me on hold. It was choppy, shrill, and fast. "Is that Norrie Ellington? Is she on her way over? She's not in the outer room, is she?"

A brilliant, albeit reckless, thought sprung to mind and I shouted, "Please tell Eugene in the forensic lab I'm on my way over to see him."

"I've got to be in Dundee." His voice was louder and registered even more alarm. "No sense wasting time. Here's the report Deputy Hickman wanted. He really should learn how to access his email."

Now Gladys's voice. "Oh, he can access it, all right. He simply prefers his notes on paper and doesn't want to print them out himself. Have a nice day, Eugene."

Gladys was apologetic when she got back on the line with me. "I'm sorry, Norrie. That poor young man was as flustered as I've ever seen. He raced straight out the main door without going back to his office. I don't even think he went back for his jacket. Must be he needs to be in Dundee in a hurry. How can I help you?"

I gave her the thirty-second rundown on the pranks those frat boys pulled off on the night Donovan's body was dumped in our cauldron and asked if she could pass it along to Deputy Hickman as chitchat she heard recently, rather than gospel from my mouth. "We really need to take down that Hallow Wine Weekend display," I said. "It's bad for business and face it, there are no secret messages or codes. Those college kids had a lark, that's all."

"I'll see what I can do. No promises, but I'll try."

"Um, I imagine those folks in the lab are up to their elbows with the murder. And Adrienne Stafine's disappearance."

"Two of them are conferring in Ontario County this morning. They're expected back by eleven." Next, she lowered her voice. "I shouldn't be telling you this, but they searched her room for any evidence of foul play."

"And Eugene?"

"He was directed to gather some evidence for a robbery that took place last night in Dundee. I imagine he'll be back around that time as well."

"Thanks, Gladys. I'll try to stop by before the end of the week. You've got to try Francine's blueberry jam."

"I'll look forward to it."

The second I put the receiver down, I grabbed my fleece-lined jacket and scarf. I'd already fed Charlie and changed his water. So what if my attire consisted of worn jeans and an old Penn Yan Mustangs sweatshirt? With any amount of luck, no one would see me where I was going.

I shot off a text to Cammy telling her I'd be in the tasting room before noon and left it at that. Then I started up the Subaru and drove south on Route 14 until I hit Route 54. From there, it was a straight shot into the village of Penn Yan and Main Street, where the public safety building was located. At that hour, most of the traffic was headed north to Geneva, a boon as far as I was concerned.

I knew the forensic lab and the morgue were down the corridor from the sheriff's office but I couldn't risk going past whoever had security duty that day. I also knew, from prior experience, it had its own entrance in between the county lockup and the larger sheriff's complex. However, the chances of that door being open were slim to none. Aargh.

It was time to put my acting skills to use once again. As long as it didn't become a thing. I googled recent arrests in Yates County and held my breath as I phoned the county jail. "Good morning," I said.

"Can you please tell me if Brian Wormley is still being held? He called our family yesterday regarding bail."

"Hold on a moment. Yes. His bail hearing is not until tomorrow. If you wish to visit with him, you'll need to show identification at the door."

"Thank you." I hung up immediately and let out a long sigh. Then, with a quick tug, I tightened my scarf, got out of the car and made a beeline for the county lock-up side of the building.

Once inside, I went through the metal detector and told the deputy I'd like to visit with Brian Wormley. He directed me to a glass-enclosed window off to the left, but when he turned his attention away from me to speak with an elderly couple, I literally spun on my heels and raced down the corridor to the forensic lab. Banking on the fact Eugene didn't bother to lock the door, I opened it a hair and peered inside. Empty.

Rather than knock on the doorjamb and call attention to myself, I pulled out a pair of food handler's gloves I'd taken from our winery, slipped them on and stepped inside. I closed the door behind me and called out, "Is Eugene here?" No answer. The only sound was the hum of a computer on a desk I presumed was his. To be sure, I tiptoed over and moseyed through some benign correspondence. Yep, it was Eugene's desk, all right. Across from it were two other desks with computers that weren't booted up. *Must be the techs who are conferring in Ontario County.*

Behind Eugene's desk was a door with a sign that read *File Storage. Authorized Entry Only*. To make matters worse, it had one of those number-sequence locks on it rather than one that required a key. The annoying tic I'd developed during my conversation with Ronny returned with a vengeance. I told myself it could have been worse. Like those irritable stomach issues people have. Seems every night there's a new commercial for products to deal with them.

Tic or no tic, I took a breath and tried to remember a phone conversation I overheard last December between Gladys and one of the techs. Something about the code to the evidence storage getting updated to the new year. "Just tap 0 and the year. Deputy Hickman likes to keep things simple." I crossed my fingers this was what she referred to. I tapped 0 and the current year before turning the knob. Hallelujah! The door opened and I walked inside. Someone, most likely Eugene, had left the overhead florescent lights on. Good. No need to monkey around finding a wall switch.

The room was narrow and long with floor-to-ceiling shelves on both sides. A stepladder rested against the wall straight ahead. *Fantastic. How am I ever going to find what I'm looking for?*

Had this been a TV drama, I would have walked directly to the evidence box I needed. But this wasn't TV and the shelves contained manila envelopes as well as cardboard boxes and a few misshaped boxes that had obviously been cobbled together. I took a step toward the closest shelf and held my breath. *Please don't tell me they use the Dewey Decimal System or something worse to catalogue this stuff.*

Then, as I eyeballed one of the boxes, I realized I had nothing to worry about. Everything was labeled with the date first, followed by the name of the victim. Now, the only thing I needed to do was to find the recent dates since the box in front of me read "1978, Morton Dubrowski."

Without wasting a second, I turned to the shelving behind me and immediately saw that the dates were more current. Late 1990s to the present. Like a kid lunging for something at a buffet table, I pulled out the box with the date of Donovan's murder written in bold black marker, followed by the words *Donovan Brin.*

No sense dragging it out of the office where I could accidently tip something over on one of the desks. There was plenty of room on the floor between the shelving, and if the tile was as polished as it was in Eugene's office, dirt would be my last concern.

I crisscrossed my legs, campfire style, with the box in front of me and lifted the lid. A lined piece of paper was taped to the underside and listed the contents. The mini-recorder was one of them, along with the dagger, but in order to locate them, I had to remove the clear plastic bag that held Donovan's clothing and another smaller bag that contained his wallet. I expected to see a cell phone but it wasn't there. Either the killers got rid of it or the lab guys were sifting through it for evidence.

The mini-recorder resembled a flash drive and I stared at it as if it was the Holy Grail. Ronny was right about me being able to take Donovan's interviews and spin them into a comprehensive feature article about our Merlots, but she was wrong about my ethics.

If it meant our three wineries would lose this golden opportunity for publicity, then so be it. I had to live with myself and absconding with that mini-recorder was out of the question. I snuck into the evidence closet to take a closer look at the dagger and that's exactly what I did. More or less.

If it was dusted for fingerprints, that information would be sitting on Eugene's computer, and for some reason, I didn't have any ethical or otherwise problems downloading his files onto the flash drive I brought along. After all, I wasn't about to use that information for personal gain, like the mini-recorder. I was anxious to find out why our winery wound up being the dumping ground for a corpse, not to mention one of the places where a feature writer's assistant was last seen.

The dagger was heavier than I realized, and I had to study it through the plastic bag. Even with the food handler's gloves on, I wasn't about to risk anything. It looked like the typical dagger readers like me had come to expect in novels like *Ivanhoe* and *The Once and Future King*. Lots of scrollwork on the cross-guard and some intricate design on the grip but no set-in jewels.

I took out my phone and snapped a quick photo before flipping the bag over to see the other side. The second I did that, I froze. A faded piece of paper, about the size of a postage stamp, was affixed to the top of the blade. It was yellowish with jagged edges but the writing was crystal clear—New York Renaissance Faire, Tuxedo, NY.

Stunned didn't come close to describing my reaction. Whoever plunged that dagger into Donovan got it from the Ren-fest in Tuxedo, New York. The Ren-fest! That was less than an hour's drive on the New York State Thruway from Valhalla. With phone in hand, I texted Cammy. *The dagger is from the Ren-fest. Only an hour from Tuxedo. Mum's the word.*

She texted back a few seconds later. *R U with U Gene?*

I texted back *More or less.*

Chapter 30

Careful to put everything back in the evidence box the way I found it, I took my time. Satisfied no one would notice anything different, I returned the box to its place on the shelf and walked to Eugene's desk. That's when I heard footsteps in the hallway. Heavy, thumping footsteps. The kind Grizzly Gary makes. With no time for a quick exit, I did the only thing possible, I raced to the evidence closet, tapped the sequence numbers again and let myself back inside. This time wedged behind a narrow opening where the first shelving unit met the door.

"Eugene? Are you in here?" It was definitely Grizzly Gary's voice. "If you can hear me from the evidence closet, forget about deciphering a code on those Hallow-whatever displays. Gladys will email you. Thought I'd tell you firsthand since I was on this side of the building on another matter. Call me."

The door slammed and, in that instant, I thought it was the most welcome sound I'd ever heard. I let myself out of the closet and scurried over to Eugene's desktop computer. Since he'd left it on, I selected the icon for his Word files and searched under "Fingerprint files." Nothing. Then I tried "Prints." Still nothing. Upon closer inspection, I saw the files were sorted by date and three initials. Ignoring the numbers, I let my eyes scroll down until I located *Bri*. Then, I removed the flash drive from my pocket, inserted it into the computer and copied the file.

Don't let Grizzly Gary return. Too tempting to throw me in the county lock-up.

The instant I downloaded the file, I shoved the flash drive back in my pocket and opened the door a crack to make sure the corridor was vacant. And while I had the all clear on that end, the security detail was still fast at work by the entrance.

"Oops," I said as I passed the deputy on duty, "I thought the restrooms were down that hallway."

"They're on the other side. Past the water fountain."

"Thanks."

A quick detour followed by a mad dash to my car and I was home free. The tic was gone but my pulse raced. I waited until I had exited the parking lot and was halfway down Main Street before I pulled into an open parking space and texted Stephanie, Theo, and Bradley. *Dagger is from Tuxedo Ren-fest.* I added a "wow" emoji for good measure before sending it off.

When I got back to the winery, a sullen-faced Cammy greeted me. "Do you know there's a warrant out for Adrienne's arrest?"

"What? When did that happen? Gladys didn't say anything when I spoke with her a little while ago."

"That's because the warrant was just issued by Ontario County. *Their* sheriff's office, not Yates County. It came over my news app a few seconds ago. Adrienne jumped from missing person to possible murderess. Although they didn't quite phrase it that way. I read the statement and it seems like the forensic techs from both counties discovered syringes in her hotel room that contained Botox. And since that was the murder weapon used on Donovan, well, you can fill in the rest."

"Holy cow. Adrienne." *We'll never appear in* Wine Enthusiast. "Do they have any idea where she could be?"

Cammy shook her head. "There's a BOLO out for her."

"Okay. Even if it was Adrienne's Botox, that doesn't mean she was the one who killed him. Although, she did have a pretty good motive. I still think she's running scared. Hey, at least I managed to find out where that dagger came from."

"Yeah. I read your text. Don't tell me Gladys spilled the beans? She'll lose her job one of these days."

I shook my head. "Not Gladys. Come on, I need a cup of coffee. Let's talk in the bistro for a few minutes and I'll fill you in."

With a large mocha latte in my hand and a marzipan croissant on a plate, I detailed all of my morning escapades to Cammy. She gripped the handle of her coffee mug until the whites of her knuckles showed as I told her how I snuck into Eugene's lab, found the dagger, and copied the file on the fingerprints from his computer.

"I haven't had a chance to see what's on the file yet, but as soon as I get into my office, I will. I don't think it's at all coincidental that the Ren-fest and Valhalla are a stone's throw away. It had to be someone who worked for the magazine, or Felicity. Not a secret her marriage was on the rocks. In fact, that was Ronny's take, too."

"Ever consider the killer or the dagger handler could have been Ronny? Murderers always deflect to another person to throw everyone off."

I chugged the rest of my latte and licked the foam off of my lips. "Let's go find out."

Cammy stood and walked, coffee mug in hand, to my office. "I'm googling local bail bond companies and putting them on speed dial."

I laughed but Cammy just shook her head.

"Seriously? You broke into Eugene's office. What next? The Pentagon?"

"I didn't break in, but I did catch a break. He left the door open."

"Oh, brother."

As we approached my office, Lizzie called out, "You're quite popular this morning, Norrie. Sorry I didn't see you come in. Busy with customers. Theo called and so did Stephanie. Both of them wanted you to call back as soon as you got here. And they both said your voicemail is full."

"Thanks, Lizzie. I'll call them."

"You know, Nancy Drew would never let her voicemail box fill up, if indeed they had such a thing back in the 1930s. She was very fastidious that way."

"Uh, yeah. I'll keep that in mind."

Cammy tried not to chuckle as we skirted across the foyer and walked into my office.

"Here goes nothing. It'll take a few seconds for the computer to boot up. Grab a chair."

Once the image of a vineyard popped up on the monitor, I put in the flash drive and pulled up the file. "Oh, no. I forgot something. Unless there are fingerprints on the dagger that belong to someone who's in the state or federal database, we're up the proverbial creek."

"Don't give up so fast. You haven't even looked. Lots of people are in those databases: teachers, hospital employees, certain business employees . . . not just criminals."

"This doesn't look good. The report is only one and a half pages. Hold on, I'll print us copies."

Two seconds later, Cammy and I read the report. Very professional. Very concise. And absolutely useless. The latent prints found on the dagger were so inconclusive that no discernible arches, loops, or whorls could be found. I had hit a big, fat dead end.

I was about to end my search when I realized there was a second part to the file. It was documented as miscellaneous evidence. Obviously Eugene was quite the busy bee when he nitpicked at the cauldron.

"A strand of hair!" I shouted. "Um, make that two."

"I can hear you. I'm right next to you. What strands of hair?"

"Read farther down the page."

"How can you read so fast?"

"Believe it or not, I took a speedreading class when I was in ninth grade. It was one of those summer school options. I was too young to work, too old for camp, and too bored to be home."

"Just give me the highlights."

"Two strands of brown hair were discovered on Donovan's person, but get this, they're not from the same person. One was long and straight and the other, shorter and wavy. Both free of hair dyes and treatments. Rats. It says inconclusive pending DNA testing. Hah! A whole lot of good that's going to do. It's like fingerprints. Unless there's a comparison, all they've got is hair."

"Guess we're back to our original lineup of suspects, although it seems the sheriff's offices have already made their selection—Adrienne."

"Sure, the one person who's gone AWOL," I groaned.

"And who happens to be a brunette."

"Two strands of hair found on a body aren't enough for a conviction. Adrienne worked closely with Donovan. All she needed to do was lean over his shoulder. You know how flyaway strands of hair can get."

"And the other strand?"

"Maybe someone else leaned over him."

"Sounds like lots of leaning if you ask me. So now what's your plan?"

"Mention Renaissance Faire to Ronny and she how she reacts."

"I take it Whitney's off the short list for now."

"Yeah. No motive."

"And Raisa?"

"You can't commit a murder without opportunity. And she's in Pennsylvania."

Cammy folded Eugene's fingerprint report in half. "We don't know that for sure. It's secondhand information from Ronny. And I'm not sure we can trust Ronny. It seems she's a little too familiar with everyone's goings-on. And as far as her being a redhead, just because one of her red-spiked tips weren't found on Donovan doesn't exactly give her a free pass."

"True, but her motive's weak. So what if she loathed Donovan? Lots of people abhor other people but they don't shoot them up with botulism toxin. Much as I hate to concur with Grizzly Gary, Adrienne's still coming out the winner in this race. Look, I'm not exactly a card-carrying member of her fan club, but deep down, I don't think she's our killer. The evidence is circumstantial and for all we know, she may be a victim."

"Go back a step. You said there were two strands of hair. One that quite possibly belonged to Adrienne. We know she has long dark hair. That leaves the other strand. Who has *wavy* dark hair?"

"I can't think of any— Oh my gosh—the stocky man with the

black glasses who blocked Adrienne at our entrance. He has dark wavy hair. *Wine Enthusiast* has a file photo of him. Well, of him in the background of a photo that featured Donovan. Of course they have no idea who the guy is either. All they know is that the photo came from some event."

"There's someone else who might have dark wavy hair—the wife."

"Felicity?"

"Uh-huh."

"I didn't get very far when I tried to find her on social media."

"Try Ronny media. Like I said before, that girl is a wealth of information when it comes to knowing other people's business. I'm sure she can give you a description of Felicity right down to the color of her fingernail polish."

"I wrote down her cell number. Give me a second."

As I fumbled around my desk, moving piles of paper, Cammy stood. "I need to return this mug to the bistro and get back to the tasting room. Keep me posted."

"I'll drop your mug off. I'm famished and my stomach is calling the shots. My conversation with Ronny will have to wait a few minutes."

"It's not as if that strand of hair is going anywhere."

"But it is. Both strands are. The report said inconclusive pending DNA evidence. That means they're being tested in a lab."

"Then you can relax. With any luck, Deputy Hickman may connect one of those strands to Donovan's killer."

"Unless he links it to the wrong suspect."

Chapter 31

The aroma of freshly baked rolls wafted in the air as I approached the bistro. It was a little before noon and the only thing I'd put in my stomach that morning was coffee. Usually, I'd be ravenous, but I was so engrossed in finding evidence that pointed to Donovan's killer, I hadn't realized how hungry I was. Not until I stood in front of the glass-enclosed counter that showcased Emma and Fred's cold sandwiches, rolls, and pastries.

"Hi, guys!" I said. "Can I get two paninis with bacon, egg, and avocado? Oh, and a Coke. Large."

Emma stepped back. "Two paninis? You must really be hungry."

I told her about my morning venture and when I got to the part about sneaking into Eugene's office, she looked stricken. "They don't have security cameras in the forensic office, do they?"

Suddenly, I was no longer in the mood for a panini. Let alone two of them. Security cameras were the last thing I thought of when I snuck down the corridor and into Eugene's office.

"Are you all right, Norrie? Forget about what I asked. I'm sure the sheriff's office is way too busy to look at security footage each night."

Unless some deputy gets bored at his or her desk during night duty.

"I hope you're right. Listen, make that one panini. I don't want to overdo it."

"Sounds good. It'll be right out."

As if I didn't have enough on my mind, I now had to come up with a believable excuse for wandering down the hall in the public safety building and walking into Eugene's office. Then again, what were the odds Deputy Hickman would confront me? I could always say I needed to speak with Eugene and the door was open. The second half was true.

The corner table near the window was vacant and I plunked myself down. Seconds later, Emma handed me the Coke. "I take it Adrienne is still missing, huh?"

"Missing, hiding, abducted. She's not here. That's for sure."

"Maybe there'll be a break in the case. It hasn't been that long. Not even a week." She turned to the grill where Fred stood and started back. "Your panini's ready. Hang on."

She returned a second later but had to rush back. I must have caught her at a lull because four customers now stood in front of the showcase. "Thanks, Emma!" I shouted and she gave me a quick thumbs-up.

The savory apple-smoked bacon hit my taste buds first, followed by the more subtle avocado and egg. I was on my last bite when a slender black woman in jeans approached me. She had thick, dense hair with tight auburn curls that framed her oval face. Her dark blue stadium coat was open, revealing a mock turtleneck top and colorful scarf. I judged her to be in her early thirties.

"Excuse me. Are you Norrie Ellington? An older gentleman at one of the tasting tables said he saw you walk back here."

Roger, no doubt.

"I'm Norrie. Can I help you?"

She smiled and reached out her hand. "Raisa James from *Wine Enthusiast*. I got bombarded with phone calls and text messages from Ronny Morgan and the feature editor at our magazine. Awful thing about Donovan. Not to mention the circumstances. What kind of weirdo kills someone and stashes the body in a Halloween display?"

Oh, you'd be surprised.

"I know. We're all in shock. Donovan had interviewed our winemaker and the two neighboring ones regarding our Merlot only a few days before. We were ecstatic to be selected to appear in your magazine. Everything seemed to be running smoothly until Friday morning. Now there's a full-blown murder investigation going on."

"I read the BOLO alert on my phone. Adrienne Stafine. I couldn't believe my eyes. They think *she* murdered her boss?"

"Sit down. Please. Can I offer you anything to eat or drink?"

"Anything hot. Coffee, tea, hot chocolate. It's freezing outside.

And I thought it was finger-numbing in Pennsylvania. It's got to be at least fifteen degrees colder up here."

"Hold on. I've got just the thing." I waved to Fred from the edge of the display and asked for a large mocha latte. He winked and held up his hand, indicating it would only be a second. "Thanks," I said when he handed it to me. "Another writer from *Wine Enthusiast* showed up. Maybe she'll do the story."

He grinned. "I'll keep my fingers crossed."

"This is my ultimate favorite latte," I said as I handed the cup to Raisa. "Enjoy."

She took a sip, careful not to get her lips too foamy. "Ronny was insistent I get my butt up here and pick up where Donovan left off but it isn't that easy. That's what I told my editor when she said the same thing. Unless Donovan recorded the interviews, or actually took notes, which I doubt, I'd have to re-interview everyone. Too bad the one person who holds all the answers is missing."

"Yeah. It's a mess. To answer your question, Donovan did record the interviews but his recording device is in an evidence file at the county's public safety building. As far as notes go, Adrienne told me she was the one who pieced it together. That was days ago, before she disappeared."

Raisa sighed and took another sip of the latte. "You're right. This is wonderful. Tell me, do you think your winemaker would find it an imposition to do another interview? It would have to be in the next day or so. I'd also need to contact the other wineries, but Ronny was adamant I see you first. She's a real card, isn't she?"

"She's, uh, certainly something. Funny, but I was about to call her this afternoon."

"She's down the lake near Watkins Glen. Taking snapshots she can stockpile. I got a room at the same hotel she's staying at, the Ramada Inn on Seneca Lake. I like staying at places where I can walk to all the action."

"I don't think you'll find much action in downtown Geneva, but if you're looking for a neat Italian bar and restaurant, try Rosinetti's. It's a short walk from the hotel and an even shorter drive. Our tasting room manager's family owns it. You'll get plenty of local ambience in addition to great food."

"Sounds good. I'll make it a point to drag Ronny along. Anyway, I'd better pay a visit to the Grey Egret and Gable Hill. Thanks for the latte. Do you mind giving me your number? That way I can call or text you later."

"Sure." I rattled it off as she tapped it into her phone. "It was nice meeting you. Bizarre circumstances and all."

She nodded. "It's a first for me, too. One minute I'm chitchatting about homemade wines with a boutique winery and the next thing I know, I get a call telling me to wrap things up and head north."

"Wow. I guess those Merlots are even more special than I thought."

"Oh, they're special, all right, but I think it's the element of murder that's got my editor jazzed. She's sent me two texts in the past hour with possible titles: *A Merlot for the Killing* and *A Merlot Worthy of Murder.* It's a tad macabre for me, but hey, I'm on payroll. What can I say?"

I was stunned. Nothing like murder and wine to increase readership. Raisa must have noticed the look on my face because she quickly added, "Don't worry. All I intend to ask about is the wine."

"Thanks. Because that's all we're allowed to talk about."

"Let me know if you hear anything regarding Adrienne, will you?"

"Tell me, you're familiar with her. Is she prone to taking a hike when things get dicey?"

"Not that I'm aware. She always struck me as one of those gals who'd tough it out even if they were seething inside. That's why it's preposterous to even consider she'd kill someone. Let alone Donovan. Not to say the thought might not have crossed her mind. Between you and me, it crossed everyone's mind. Donovan was the quintessential SOB and I don't use those initials lightly. Still, murder? Even he didn't deserve that."

"No one does." *And yet the bodies keep cropping up down here on the farm.*

I walked her back to the entrance and thanked her for stopping by.

"Don't forget, call me if you hear anything. You have my number and you know where I'm staying."

"Definitely."

I watched as she walked down the steps toward her car. It was a dark-colored rental like all of the others and for a brief second, I wondered if she was really in Pennsylvania all that time.

"Is everything all right, Norrie?" Lizzie asked from her usual spot at the computer/cash register. "You've been fixated on the parking lot for over a minute."

"Huh?" I walked toward her and leaned on the counter. "That was Raisa James. The other feature writer at the magazine. With any luck, she'll be able to salvage the Merlot article for us, although her editor might want it to take a darker tone."

"Mr. Brin's unfortunate demise?"

"Unsolved murders attract readers. They also bring the lookie-loos and crazies to the winery."

"I might have a bit of good news for you in that regard. An email from the sheriff's office was sent to us as well as the Grey Egret and Gable Hill. It arrived as you escorted Ms. James to the door. According to the secretary, Gladys Pipp, Deputy Hickman has given us the all clear to remove the Hallow Wine Weekend display and throw away the crime scene tape."

"Hallelujah! I'm on it!"

Before Lizzie could respond, I shouted to Cammy, who was on her way from the kitchen with a tray of wineglasses. "If anyone can break away, tell them to meet me outside. We need to dismantle the cauldron and load it into Sam's car so he can return it to the prop department. We might be able to store the papier-mâché witches in our barn unless Sam wants to lend them to his college. Anyway, it's time to kiss this nightmare goodbye."

Cries of "Grizzly Gary gave the all clear" filled the room as Cammy, Sam, Roger, Glenda and I assisted with the teardown in between tastings. With the five of us flexing our muscles, the job wasn't as noxious as I thought it would be. What *was* noxious was the bitter cold air we had to contend with.

"You think that means they've got solid evidence on Adrienne?" Sam asked as he lifted the hatchback to his 2017 Kia Sportage once he backed it up near Alvin's pen. He rubbed his hands together and glanced at the goat. "Good, he's eating hay. I make it a point not to disturb him."

"I make it a point not to go near him. And I wouldn't call it *solid evidence*, but coupled with Adrienne's disappearance, it doesn't look good."

In that instant, my cell phone vibrated and it was a text from Bradley. *Flip-flop on divorce. Donovan's lawyer served wife papers. XOXO*

"What's the matter?" Cammy asked. She pulled her waffle-knit beanie over her ears and stepped toward me. "You look like hell froze over."

"It might have. I asked Bradley to see if Marvin might have an inkling about Donovan's wife divorcing him, since Marvin has legal connections in Valhalla."

"And?"

"It was the other way around. This changes everything. There's nothing worse than a jilted lover. Unless it was a jilted wife."

"Terrific, Miss Marple. Now all you have to do is prove Felicity was the one who injected him with Botox, shoved him into the cauldron, and stuck a dagger in his back for good measure."

"The woman was highly motivated."

"So are home sellers but that doesn't mean they go out and lasso their buyers."

"I'm serious, Cammy. She could be our killer."

"Okay, but who was her accomplice?"

"That's what we need to find out."

Chapter 32

Like a fourteen-year-old who acquired a juicy piece of gossip, I immediately texted Don, Theo, and Stephanie as soon as I got back to my office. Well, almost immediately. I texted Bradley back with a series of emojis hoping one would fit.

A few seconds later Theo called. "I can't text to save my life. I started but my message was longer than the preamble to the Constitution. Way to go, Bradley! Or should I say, Marvin. Nothing pushes a motive up the Richter scale like rejection. It morphs into revenge and that's one heck of a reason for murder. Now all you need to convict Felicity is means and opportunity."

"You sound like Cammy. In fact, the two of you could have rehearsed."

Theo laughed. "Tell her great minds think alike. Say, that's good news about Raisa stepping in, huh? But honestly, I'm not sure I'm thrilled with customers equating our Merlot with murder."

"I take it she told you what the feature editor thought."

"Odd, but Raisa had a very different take when we spoke. She wondered if Donovan was knocked off in order to block the article. Seems things like that happen in the food industry."

"We mulled that over a while back. It wouldn't happen on our wine trail. All of us support each other."

"Our Merlots are in competition across the U.S. Who knows how ruthless some of those people are. Especially if they're trying to make a big-time name for themselves."

"I still think it was personal. And if Raisa thought that about Donovan, why isn't she worried?"

"Maybe no one knows she got duped into writing the article. Hold on a second. Don's waving his hands in the air like a madman. I need to see what he wants. Don't hang up. He probably misplaced a corkscrew for our Blanc de Blanc."

I could hear Theo in the background and it was no corkscrew. Not with the words *No way, under everyone's nose*, and *egg on their face*.

"Did you get all of that?" he asked.

"Not really. What's going on?"

"Don just found out from one of our customers that Donovan's rental car was located smack downtown in Penn Yan. Parked on North Main Street behind the hospital. No one gave it a second thought. Place is swarming with deputies."

Good. That means they're not looking at security footage.

I pictured Eugene up to his elbows dusting for prints and checking for fibers. In the back of my mind, I thought I remembered something about cars involved in criminal cases being towed to a county lab, but only after cursory evidence was taken.

"How'd your customer know?"

"Her sister, who lives on that street, called her. Hey, you know what this means, don't you? The forensic crew may find adequate evidence to nail down the killer. And I mean more than a strand of hair and an empty Botox syringe."

"I don't know. Those are pretty compelling, even if they are circumstantial. They'd have to find a recording or something. One that really incriminates the murderer."

"Let's see if we can get together later this week and bandy our theories around. Maybe a potluck dish-to-pass dinner at our place. I'll call you and the Ipswiches."

"Sounds good. As long as Wegmans is doing the cooking."

• • •

Bradley looked as if he'd been working on overload when he plunked two hot meatball subs on the kitchen table and a plastic container of Caesar salad. "I didn't forget," he said. "In fact, I even remembered the extra croutons to go with the salad."

"Hmm, maybe I'm not in such a hurry to have Donovan's killer caught if it means Uncle Joe's dinners instead of peanut butter and jelly."

I gave him a hug and opened the fridge. "O'Doul's near beer or Coke?"

"The near-enough-to-beer the better. What a bizarre day."

"Ditto that."

We spent the next half hour trading work stories before settling in on the couch. Charlie must have sensed how tired we were because he didn't try to cajole us into giving him extra kibble or people food. Instead, he opted for his usual spot on the kitchen rug.

I told Bradley about the potluck dinner later in the week and he blurted out the word *Wegmans* before I could. Then he quickly added, "A regular potluck dinner, right? Not a loony Zenora séance? I've come to expect that sort of thing whenever there's an unsolved murder."

"Shh. Bite your tongue. She's way too inundated with student research projects this time of year."

I stretched out my legs and reached for the remote, when the landline rang. "Lucky you, have fun picking a decent channel." As I approached the phone, a disturbing thought crossed my mind. What if one of those deputies *did* review the security footage? With fingers crossed, I took the call, not bothering to look at the caller ID.

"Norrie? It's Belinda! I hope I'm not disturbing you but a package arrived for you today from L.L. Bean. Do you want me to have it forwarded?"

"Yikes. I forgot all about it. I ordered a pair of those wicked warm slippers for winter. Just put the box in the hall closet. How's everything going?"

"Do you have any idea how much dust accumulates on lightbulbs? It decreases the illumination. I took out all of your lightbulbs and gave them a good dusting. Especially the ones in the bathroom over the sink."

"Uh, gee, thanks."

"By the way, I read about Donovan Brin's murder. It's classified as a murder now, isn't it?" She kept talking before I could respond. "His wife, or should I say *widow*, has a huge account with us. I'm not sure if she's one of those trust-fund babies, but she's certainly more than well-to-do. The scuttlebutt in our branch was that he filed for divorce and refused to give her half of his assets. Not that she needed them, but money has a way of taking the sting out of things."

My gosh. Who doesn't know about Felicity?

"Really? You don't suppose—"

"That she killed him? Funny you should ask because that rumor's been circulating around here as well. Even the tellers are yakking when they're in the break room."

"Donovan was found dead in Penn Yan. That's hours from the city."

"Only if you drive. Lots of puddle-jumper flights from Westchester, where she lives."

"Belinda, this may sound like a really strange question, but do you know if she used fillers to look younger?"

"Like Botox?"

"Yeah."

"That *is* a strange question, but offhand, no. But there's an easy way to find out. Check old photos of her and compare them."

"All her social media accounts show butterfly pictures for the profile."

Belinda laughed. "My aunt's profile is a toucan. Go figure. Try newsclips for art openings. She's a heavy donor from what I hear."

"Thanks, Belinda. I will. Oh, and thanks about the lightbulbs."

"No problem. Next week I plan to disinfect the framework under the windows. Talk about dust accumulating. Anyway, I'll put your package in the front closet."

"Great. Thanks again."

I squeezed Bradley's shoulder when I returned to the couch. "Tell Marvin he's got some competition. That was my tenant, Belinda Kuentz, and you won't believe what she knows about Felicity." *And dusting lightbulbs.*

"Let me guess. She thinks Felicity is the Merry Widow?"

"Only if I can prove she dabbled in Botox."

With my head nestled comfortably on Bradley's shoulder, I watched the contestants on *Crime Show Kitchen* try to figure out the mystery recipe they had to duplicate. "Some sort of vanilla cake with vanilla frosting," Bradley said. "I don't see any chocolate."

"I think it needs to be more specific. A King's cake? Princess cake? Queen Victoria cake?"

"How do you know all those cakes? You hardly cook and I know you don't bake."

I bumped his shoulder with my arm. "I binge watch this show along with British mysteries."

"That explains it."

Once again, I nestled my head against his upper torso. Too bad it was short-lived. A minute or two later, my cell phone rang. Apparently I'd forgotten to keep it on vibrate.

Please don't let this be about the security footage.

The caller's voice was familiar but it took me a second to place it. "Norrie. I hope I'm not interrupting your dinner, or worse yet, your sleep."

Whitney. It was Whitney. And my sleep? I'm in my twenties, not my dotage.

"No, not at all. What's up?" I walked to the kitchen so as not to disturb Bradley's focus on *Crime Scene Kitchen.*

Whitney's voice had an element of alarm in it. "Adrienne's not Donovan's killer. Even if there *is* a warrant for her arrest. She's been kidnapped. I know it."

"Did you call one of the sheriff's offices?"

"No, because they'd tell me to go packing. Remember the night when you stopped by our table at Port of Call?"

"Uh-huh. Why?"

"Adrienne made a comment I didn't think much of at the time. She said she couldn't *read* Donovan. Said he was elated when he finished up with his article on those California organic wineries but seemed to be looking over his shoulder once they got to Seneca Lake. Almost as if he was being followed or something. But that's not why I called. When I went to Port of Call, I took a small bag, not my usual one. You know, fancy places and all that."

I mumbled some sort of acknowledgment and she kept talking. "Anyway, after I removed my wallet and phone, I stashed that bag in the armoire in my room. I didn't open it until tonight. That's when I saw the note."

"The note. What note?"

"Adrienne must have written it and put it in my bag sometime that evening. Easy to do when someone's not looking. And I made more than one trek to the bar."

"Okay. A note. What did it say?"

"It was on a Port of Call cocktail napkin and it said, 'If Donovan goes down, so do I. It's guilt by association. And he's guilty.'"

"Of what? What is, I mean *was*, he guilty of? Did she say? Did you read both sides? Open it up?"

"All of the above and it was only on the front side. Below the cute logo with the wineglass inside a nautical steering wheel. Now do you see what I mean about not going to a sheriff's office? You don't think *I* have anything to worry about, do you? I'd only just met Adrienne when she and her boss arrived at the Belhurst. If someone stalked Donovan and thought she was mixed up in, well, who knows what, and then they saw me having dinner with her, then I'd be implicated, too."

"Uh, that's taking it to the extreme, but honestly, if I were you, I'd stay in after dark and order room service. At least until Adrienne is found."

"This is really scary. I thought some jilted lover did him in with a little help, but now, I'm convinced it's something much more sinister. That note cinched it for me. Adrienne's been abducted but those deputies would only tell me it's speculation on my part."

The woman learns fast.

"Maybe now would be a good time to stockpile some podcasts for your show. And the closer to the Belhurst, the better. Just to stay on the safe side."

I can't believe I'm being this mercenary.

"That's a good idea. Do you think your tasting room manager would be up for talking?"

"And then some. Same deal at the Grey Egret and Gable Hill. Plus, we're in a tight little group with three other nearby wineries. I'll text you their info as well."

"Sounds good. Anything to get my mind off of murder."

"What was that all about?" Bradley cocked his head as I walked toward the couch.

"Whitney found a cryptic note from Adrienne. Written when they were at Port of Call the Friday night before Hallow Wine Weekend. Adrienne must have slipped it in her bag."

"Cryptic how?" Bradley picked up the remote and lowered the sound.

"Adrienne intimated Donovan was into something nefarious and that she'd be implicated as well. Or worse."

"I hate to say it, but I think we're past the 'or worse' point as far as Adrienne is concerned. Maybe those forensic techs will sort it out if they find anything in Donovan's car."

"Forget forensics. We need an old-fashioned gumshoe break in the case, but I'm not holding my breath."

As it turned out, I didn't have to. My break came an hour later thanks to a lousy TV lineup.

Chapter 33

"A chiffon cake. I thought chiffon was a fabric." Bradley put the remote on the coffee table and shook his head.

"It is. It's both." I sank into the couch and leaned back. "Francine liked making them when we were in middle school. Frankly, they were too airy for me. I needed at least three forkfuls to get the taste."

He picked up the remote again and pushed Guide. "Ugh. Miserable night. Nothing on."

"Keep scrolling. Maybe something will catch our eyes. I need to get my mind off of Donovan and Adrienne. At least for one night."

"Hey, here's an oldie. *Laverne and Shirley.* We weren't even born when it aired. And the name's old, too. Not many Lavernes around."

"Laverne. Laverne. Why does that name sound familiar? And I don't mean the show. I heard it recently. Give me a minute or it will plague me all night."

Bradley laughed. "Take as much time as you need. Want to watch it?"

"Sure."

A few minutes in and we were both in stiches. Laverne and Shirley tried to get positions as beer tasters for the brewery where they worked and I thought about the similarities between brewing and winemaking when something hit me hard and fast—the name.

"It's that organic vineyard. The one in Napa. Oh my gosh! Adrienne mentioned Frontanac, Clear Meadows, and LaVerna. LaVerna. *LV. LV.* The letters, the logo. Oh my gosh. That mystery man with the *LV* wine logo shirt had to be from LaVerna. And Adrienne also mentioned the change in Donovan's mood when they left California. Bradley, I think I'm looking at the proverbial smoking gun. Hang on."

I bolted from the couch and grabbed my iPhone. A quick search got me to LaVerna Vineyards and a full-blown photo of the mystery man—Larry Marchese. He stood, wineglass in hand, next to his partner and brother, Vern Marchese. Duh! LaVerna!

"That's the man who had the unpleasant conversation, according to Ada Mae, with Donovan. The same man who accosted Adrienne. This is no coincidence. And he has a brother. A brother."

I kept repeating words and couldn't seem to slow down.

"Take it easy. Before you go off the rails on this, do what you always do."

"Panic first and work backward?"

"Only the second half of that equation. Come on, let's ditch the TV and see what we can find on LaVerna Vineyards."

"Let me boot up my laptop. Bigger screen. We can still stay on the couch."

In the hour and a half that followed, not only did we become experts on the history and philosophy of LaVerna Vineyards, but we were totally baffled over a possible motive for one or both brothers to have done Donovan in. Still, what the heck was one of them doing in the Finger Lakes? And could he have abducted Adrienne?

Bradley rubbed the back of my neck for a quick second. "You mentioned Ronny was in Napa with Donovan, right?"

I nodded.

"Did she mention anything out of the ordinary?"

"Both Ronny and Adrienne said Donovan was in a foul mood when they went to California and alluded it had something to do with Felicity. Then, when he left, he was in better spirits. Much better spirits. Until he got to the Finger Lakes."

"Usually, people's moods don't change that fast. Something had to have happened."

"Or something Donovan *made* happen. And maybe that's what killed him. Phooey. It's late or I'd call Ronny. I've got her cell."

"Sounds like you've got a whole lot more than that. You've got another lead. And one you can substantiate. Larry Marchese was actually here. Not like Felicity."

"Thank you for channel surfing." I ran my fingers through his sandy blond hair and gave him a kiss that signaled our TV watching was over for the night.

• • •

"Two wills and a codicil," Bradley said as we munched on toast laden with Francine's strawberry jam the next morning.

"Sounds like the title of a movie."

"Nope. Only my fun-filled workday, give or take a few appointments. Unfortunately, one of them is for five and I won't get finished until seven. Want to meet for a quick soup and sandwich at Tim Hortons?"

"Sounds good. It's better than defrosting anything Francine left and I'm too distracted to rig up dinner. Thank goodness we're joining Don and Theo tomorrow. They must have gotten up at some ungodly hour because Theo sent me a text. Dinner at eight."

"Now that sounds like a movie."

"Ha. We could turn this into one of those board games if we had the time and inclination. Too bad we're up to our necks chasing down clues." I walked to the Keurig and plopped in a second pod of McCafé. "I think we hit the jackpot with LaVerna. All we need now is for Ronny to fill in the blanks. Once I get to the winery, I'll call her and ask her to join me for lunch today."

"That's what I adore about you. Once you set your sights on something, you don't stop."

"Yeah, I think Deputy Hickman thinks the same thing, only not in the endearing way you do."

Bradley laughed before clearing the table. "Got to run. See you at Tim Hortons. Seven thirty?"

"Perfect."

• • •

"Good morning, everyone!" I announced as I bounded into the winery and headed straight for my office. "I know. I know. I'm really early but that's because I may have a new clue on Donovan's death. I'll catch you up in a bit."

My proclamation was followed by a few "huhs?" and "whats?" as I hurried past the crew and made a beeline for the phone. Ronny had just returned from the Ramada's fitness room when she answered my call. "Great timing, Norrie. A minute later and I would have been in the shower. What's up? Any news on Donovan or Adrienne?"

"That's why I called. No news but a possible lead. Any chance you can have lunch with me today? I can meet you at your hotel and we can eat at the Pier House. It's the Ramada's restaurant and the food's really good. Especially their burgers."

"Um, sure. Is it a solid lead?"

Her voice sounded anxious but maybe I read too much into it. "Possibly. How about noon?"

"Works for me."

The frenetic pace of the weekend was long gone and upon a quick inspection, I saw the tasting room was under control. No sense dawdling. The computer and I were going to be tight friends for the next hour or so. I picked up where Bradley and I had left off last night on our internet search of LaVerna Vineyards.

An hour in and my mind had turned to mush. The vineyard was classified as a certified sustainable winery, which meant it adhered to certain practices like using compost, and natural or biological sprays, as opposed to commercial sprays, to deal with vineyard pests. I knew from prior conversations with Godfrey and John that natural predators, like owls, were sometimes used to eradicate certain grape-eating pests.

Then my mind snapped back into full gear. Had Donovan discovered LaVerna was not as sustainable as it claimed? And if so, then what? I moved on to the actual number of acres and average number of bottles produced in a year. One acre usually produces 600 cases. *Usually. Not necessarily.* Mind-numbing. Until I remembered something Bradley and I read last night: The past year was a banner year for LaVerna and they produced 106,000 cases of wine.

Terrific for them, only LaVerna had 100 acres, which should have translated into 60,000. Did that mean their yield was spectacular enough to have produced the extra 46,000? And if not, then how could they explain it?

I was all but out of my chair when I ran the numbers. Heck, I was no mathematician, but if it sounded fishy to me, it must have really smelled to Donovan.

Chapter 34

To be on the safe side, I ran it by John. He was on the south side of the vineyard when I called, checking the past season's shoots to see if they had matured. Much easier to do once the leaves go through the color wheel and start to fall.

"You think there was some hanky-panky going on with the yield numbers for that winery?" he asked.

"Maybe. That's why I'm asking you. My math skills don't go much beyond fifth grade."

"It's multiplication and subtrac—oh, never mind. Run it by me again."

I did. Twice.

"Frankly, I'm not sure, Norrie, but it would be challenging to prove. It's not an exact science, even if we're talking numbers. An acre can yield four to five tons and each ton produces about a hundred and seventy gallons of wine. But here's the caveat. A one-ton difference for an acre is a big deal. And, if the vineyard had a bad season, it may only yield two tons an acre."

"Oh, they had a spectacular season." *Even if it was only on paper.*

"You said they wound up with 46,000 extra cases of wine, given their number of acres?"

"Uh-huh."

"Hmm, that *is* questionable. Then again, they might have had a truly banner year. It happens. Tell me, why all the interest in this particular winery?"

I gave him the background about Donovan's visit to the organic wineries in Napa and the feature articles he had written about them. Add that to the unwelcome dealings Donovan and Adrienne had with one of LaVerna's owners. Right here in our winery and at Belhurst Castle. John was still perplexed until I spelled it out in no uncertain terms—"I think Donovan figured out something about LaVerna he shouldn't have, and it got him killed."

"That's going to be virtually impossible to prove. You know that, don't you?"

"I don't have to prove it. I only have to introduce a theory of such magnitude that it can't be ignored."

"Listen. One man is dead and his assistant is missing. Even if you *are* right, the person or persons behind it won't think twice about adding a third person to their list. Let the sheriff's office deal with it."

Yeesh. How many more people can say that?

"I'm trying, John. But it's not easy."

"Well, keep trying."

I thanked him and looked at the numbers again. No doubt in my mind. LaVerna was up to something sneaky and wanted to keep it that way. With any luck, Ronny might be able to help me figure out what it was.

While waiting for noon to roll around, I relieved people from the tasting tables and shared what little I'd discerned about Donovan's murder and Adrienne's disappearance. Everyone put in his or her two cents and it was clearly a divided camp. Half the employees were convinced Adrienne was abducted and the other half were adamant she was behind her boss's murder and therefore on the run.

When I offered up the mystery man, aka Larry, as the possible killer, it, too, was met with a mixed reaction. And advice from Glenda.

She adjusted one of her half-moon earrings and motioned me closer to her. "There are too many suspects, and when that happens, the latest one rises to the top, like seltzer bubbles. Zenora and I are embracing certain herbs as a means to clear our heads and improve our focus."

"Sounds like a commercial for one of those vitamin supplements."

"Posh! Those are so watered down or dried out, you might as well chew on paper. Zenora grows her own lemon balm ingredients and wanted to do the same with ashwagandha, but that shrub requires so much heat and humidity, it would be impossible here. Anyway, the lemon balm would be perfect for you."

"For me to what?" And I was still struggling to get a grip on the ashwagandha.

"To drink it in tea. So you can focus without distraction. Zenora would be happy to provide you with some."

"Uh, thank her for me, but I'm narrowing things down. Really. In fact, I'm meeting with Ronny for lunch today at the Ramada. If anyone knows what happened at LaVerna Vineyards, she would."

"If you change your mind, let me know."

I nodded, smiled, and got the heck out of the tasting room before I agreed to eating one of Zenora's herbs.

When I stepped out of the winery, a cutting wind hit me in the face and I wondered if I shouldn't have purchased one of those snoods after all. At least it wasn't snowing. Not yet, anyway. It was, after all, November, and the Finger Lakes were known to be fickle when it came to weather. Not willing to take any risks, I called Hank Walden, told him I was babysitting the winery again, and asked if his garage could get snow tires on the Subaru in the next day or so.

"Bring her in tomorrow morning around nine," Hank said. "We got a cancellation. Say, I read about that body in your Halloween display. Did they ever figure out who killed the guy?"

"Not yet."

"Heck of a thing, huh?"

"Oh, yeah."

• • •

Ronny wasn't in the Ramada's restaurant when I arrived, but I was a good fifteen minutes early. I got us a table adjacent to their massive picture window that overlooked Seneca Lake. In spite of the fact I'd driven with the heat on, I was still cold. Enough so as to order hot coffee from their bar instead of my usual Coke or tonic water. I'd been so preoccupied all morning, I hadn't even bothered to check my text messages. While I waited for my coffee, I clicked the green-cloud icon on my phone and all but retched.

It was from Godfrey and it read: *Startling news. Jason spotted a variation of the Melicodes tenebrosa. Not the normal spur-throated grasshopper. Call me when U can. Fun bonfire. Thx.*

I didn't need to call. I knew what was coming. I would need to call in the United States Marines to extract my sister and brother-in-law from some jungle in the Philippines. I texted back: *They better not stay any longer.* Then I added a cute emoji and wrote: *Thx for the bonfire rescue. Will call.*

The spur-throated grasshopper. Can't my sister and brother-in-law be content with the stinging, biting, yucky insects we have here? I walked to the bar, got my coffee and sank down in the comfy captain's chair and gazed at the lake. A few minutes later, Ronny sauntered into the room, saw me, and walked over.

"Am I late?" she asked as she sat.

"No, I'm early for once. Usually I'm the one who's late. I haven't ordered yet. Only coffee."

"Funny how cold weather always seems to take us by surprise. You'd think us New Yorkers would be used to it by now."

I shook my head. "I'll never get used to it."

"I've got to admit, California was awfully inviting, but my work's cut out for me here. At least for the time being."

A tall, lanky waiter, most likely a college student, greeted us and handed us the lunch menu. I gave it a quick glance and ordered the ground steak burger with Swiss. Ronny was as decisive as I was when it came to ordering and she followed suit, only with cheddar cheese instead of Swiss.

When the waiter left, she propped an elbow on the table and leaned her head on it. "This lead you mentioned, is it a finger-pointer or something entirely different?"

"I think a little bit of both. But if I'm ever going to figure this out, I'll need you to put yourself back in Napa for a while."

"I'd love to do that, but I'm sure you mean figuratively. So, how can I help?"

"You were at LaVerna Vineyards the same time Donovan and Adrienne were. Backing up that feature article with photos. You must have witnessed Donovan's interaction with Larry Marchese, one of the owners."

"With Larry and Vern. I remember being introduced to both of the brothers, although, after that, I hardly saw Vern."

"Did you notice anything off-kilter with Donovan and Larry?"

"Not off-kilter, but peculiar. I can't put my finger on it. But I noticed it shortly after Donovan interviewed Larry. It was sometime the following day and the men were face-to-face in LaVerna's tasting room. An intense conversation for sure. I pretended not to notice and took shots of customers enjoying the wines."

"Could you overhear anything?"

Ronny shook her head. "No, but here's the freaky thing. Donovan was in a rotten mood when we flew out of New York and spent most of the time on his phone with his lawyer. The wife thing. You know. Anyway, after that conversation, or whatever you call it with Larry, Donovan's mood flipped a hundred and eighty degrees. All of a sudden, it was like he won the lottery. Only not exuberant and jovial. More like the Cheshire cat with a tasty secret or treat he didn't want to share. Go figure."

"Was Adrienne aware of this change, too?"

"I'm sure she was, but Adrienne plays her cards close to her chest, if you know what I mean. She didn't say much."

"What about Larry Marchese? Was he the happy camper, too?"

"Ha! Now that's the million-dollar question. If it was a horror movie, or even sci-fi, I'd say the signals got crossed. Larry was in a fairly good mood when I said hi to him earlier. After his conversation with Donovan, he brushed past everyone in his tasting room and looked as if he'd snap any second."

Forget about Larry snapping. My mind clicked, snapped, and somersaulted. The bit of information on LaVerna that I had uncovered, coupled with Ronny's recollections, pointed to the one thing I couldn't let go of—not only did Donovan figure out something about the Marchese operation, but he must have used it for blackmail.

Chapter 35

I was fifteen steps ahead of myself with no chance of slowing down. The note Adrienne left for Whitney pretty much cinched it. "Guilt by association."

"Ronny, I really need you to think hard and fast on this one. Are the Marchese brothers running any other wineries in this area? Maybe under a different name. Adrienne and Donovan had encounters with Larry. Adrienne at our winery and Donovan at the Belhurst. Both of them unpleasant if not intimidating."

"Yikes."

"It took me a while to figure out who the guy was, but it's Larry. And he's here on Seneca Lake. Either Donovan told Larry he'd be covering our wineries for Hallow Wine Weekend and that's what brought the guy here, or there's a connection between Larry, Vern, and someone else in the Finger Lakes."

"Gee, our magazine wasn't aware of the Marchese brothers running another winery up here. And no one mentioned it during our stay in Napa. Are you insinuating Adrienne's in worse trouble than anyone thought?"

"And then some."

When our burgers arrived, I was happy for the distraction. Mine was moist, juicy, and flavorful but it was no compensation for the horrible thoughts that continued to cross my mind. Ronny, too, seemed worried. She wiped the edges of her mouth with a napkin before crinkling its corners in her hand. "Are the sheriffs' offices making any headway finding her?"

"Not that I know of. I really think she's been kidnapped. And I think it has something to do with LaVerna. I believe Donovan was blackmailing the owners. Not that I have any proof, mind you, but the clues are all there. And as for *what* he held over their heads, I'm not sure either. It could be any number of things."

"Good grief. Maybe that explains why Donovan and Larry's

moods shifted so dramatically. But I can't believe Adrienne would get caught up in anything like that."

"Not caught up. Only associated with Donovan, and that's all it took. *If* I'm right. I tend to go full steam ahead and then fill in the blanks. There's not enough evidence or information to toss this to the sheriff's office in Penn Yan, but that's my next step."

"Like I said before, if there's anything I can do to help, call me, text me, or find me at the Ramada. I'm not leaving town anytime soon."

I thanked Ronny for meeting with me and promised to keep her posted. She said she'd track me down if she remembered anything at all that might bring me closer to finding out what really happened. With that, I took off for the winery with a new determination to back up my latest theory.

• • •

With Thanksgiving only three weeks away, the enthusiasm of the holidays was evident in our tasting room. Lots of visitors and a full line at the cash register. The jack-o'-lantern pumpkins were flipped around to resemble ordinary fall pumpkins, and a few handmade turkeys, compliments of Emma and Fred, completed the décor. I slipped in, waved to Lizzie, and retreated to my office. My conversation with Ronny left me no choice. Well, I *did* have a choice, I simply chose to take a risk that would make everything else I've ever done seem benign.

Positive that Adrienne was being kept somewhere against her will, and convinced Donovan was responsible for his own demise by blackmailing LaVerna Vineyards, I called the only person I knew who could give me the answer I needed—Belinda Kuentz.

Belinda had already told me Felicity had an account at her bank and it was more than substantial. If that was the case, then Donovan had to have one, too, in addition to any shared bank account or accounts they most likely set up. I picked up the phone and placed the call before I lost my nerve.

"Good afternoon, this is Norrie Ellington from Two Witches Winery and I'd like to speak with your client manager Belinda Kuentz." *So far so good.*

"One moment, please."

"Norrie!" Belinda's voice was as animated as usual. "Is everything all right?"

"I need your help to track down Donovan's killer."

"Me? I'm a client specialist manager, not an investigator."

"You work for a bank. That's all I need. Belinda, are you in your office? Can we speak privately? Hmm, come to think of it, many of those bank phone lines are monitored. Used for training purposes, blah-blah. I'll call you on your cell phone tonight."

"Uh, sure. I get home around six. This doesn't involve anything dangerous, does it?"

"Nah. It's more of a desk job. I'll talk to you later. Thanks, Belinda."

The hamburger bounced around in my stomach the more I thought about what I was going to do. Words like *illegal*, *felony*, and *incarceration* came to mind and they were only a sampling. I didn't dare run this one by Cammy, Don, Theo, Godfrey, or heaven forbid Bradley. They'd have words like *treacherous*, *risky*, and *insane*.

I repeated to myself "Without taking chances, no progress would have been made in the world," but I wasn't writing a dialogue for one of my screenplays. I was teetering on a precipice without a safety harness.

I didn't have to meet Bradley until seven thirty at Tim Hortons so that gave me plenty of time to speak with Belinda and nail down my convincing argument. Too bad Glenda and Zenora couldn't conjure up the recently departed F. Lee Bailey. I'd need him.

Rather than phone from the winery, I waited until we closed up for the day to call Belinda from the house. It was nearing six thirty and I'd rehearsed my end of the conversation at least half a dozen times.

"Hey, Belinda, it's Norrie again."

"I polished three door handles waiting for your call. This is so alarming. Tracking down a killer. I've never even taken one of those self-defense classes."

"Uh, as I mentioned before, it doesn't involve anything physical. Okay. I'll just spit it out. Donovan and Felicity have bank accounts with you. Or at least I think Donovan does."

"He does."

"Uh, good. Look, I think Donovan blackmailed a vintner in California and was getting paid off. Until he got knocked off."

"Please don't ask me—"

"I need to find out if my hunch is right and the only way I can do it is to see if Donovan received payoff money via direct deposits to his account. You know. Like Chime for Bankcorp or online direct pay for Wells Fargo."

"I know what they are."

"All I'm asking you to do is take a look at his accounts and see if any large-sum monies got deposited."

"That's illegal. Or at the very least, unethical."

"I'll stick with unethical. Lots of wiggle room. Listen, it's not as if you're really doing anything wrong. All you're doing is checking his account. It's not as if you're taking money from it. Think of it as a client service. To make sure everything looks good."

"Some client service. The man is dead."

"But the bank account isn't." *Until Felicity gets her hot little fingers on it.*

"I could lose my job. And shouldn't the police or the sheriff's deputies or whoever be doing this?"

"They will. Once I can prove to them it's where they should be looking. And I can't do that unless you look first. Client managers always peruse their customers' accounts to make sure no unauthorized transactions have taken place."

"Yeah, but with the client's permission."

"In this case, Belinda, the client won't object."

Belinda let out a slow, tortuous sigh. "I have a feeling there's more to it, isn't there?"

"Donovan was the receiving end. You'd have to see where those transfers into his account originated. And I seriously doubt they used PayPal. Then again, we're talking deposits. There's nothing illegal about depositing money in someone else's account. Services rendered and all that. Hey, the only entity who'd really care is the IRS if Donovan evaded taxes, but it's a moot point now."

"I don't know, Norrie. I haven't done a thing and I'm nervous. Can I think it over and let you know tomorrow?"

Oh, no. Those are the worst words ever when it comes to making a decision. It's a polite way of saying No way!

My stomach tightened and I had to think fast. No time to rationalize. I had to dangle whatever carrot I could. The stress factor was now in control. My brain went haywire and what followed couldn't be taken back. The words erupted from my mouth like molten lava from Kilauea. "I'll extend your lease until February if you do this."

Belinda wheezed and I wasn't sure if she was about to sneeze or gasp.

"Are you all right?"

"I'm stunned but I still can't—"

"Make it March. I'll extend the lease until March."

Silence for all of ten seconds and then, "Holy cow, Norrie. It's as if I'd be making a deal with the devil."

Oh, great. I'm now Lucifer in wedge heels.

"It's an unconventional request, I'll grant you that, but it's certainly within your scope as a client manager. Think about Donovan's poor assistant. She may be bound and gagged somewhere. You get to do the heroic thing."

"Can I repaint your bathroom? The blue tones make me woozy. I was thinking of a creamy whitish yellow."

J. C. Eaton

"Fine. Fine. Repaint the bathroom." *Heck, repaint the entire condo apartment while you're at it.*

"I'll try to get this information to you tomorrow. I'll work it into my schedule and call you when I have an answer."

"That's wonderful. Uh, your computer keyboard moves aren't tracked, are they?"

"Not the keyboard, no, but my searches are. In this case, if anyone asks, I'll tell them I was checking Donovan's accounts to make sure they weren't tampered with, given his unfortunate death."

"See, you're a pro at this already." *And I'm going to be stuck here living in vineyard hell for the next four months.*

When I got off the phone with Belinda, I called Godfrey.

The alarm in Godfrey's voice when he took the call was pretty evident. "I take it you're fuming over my text. Don't shoot the messenger, okay? I wanted to give you the heads-up about the Melicodes tenebrosa and the possibility that Jason and Francine may ask you to stay on a bit longer."

"It's fine. I can stay until March first. Call them on the satellite phone and tell them I'll stay for a few more months."

"Whoa. What brought that on? Is it your relationship with Bradley?"

"Bradley? What? No. Not that. Okay, promise you won't go berserk when I tell you why I have to stay here."

"*Have* to stay here?"

"Yeah. I sort of made a deal with someone in order to get some private information about Donovan's bank accounts."

"Private as in *illegal*?"

"Nah, more like *unsanctioned*."

"You're right. You may be staying here longer—in the county jail!"

Chapter 36

Godfrey listened without as much as a sigh or cough as I told him about my arrangement with Belinda. "Promise me you won't breathe a word of this to Bradley," I said. "Don't get me wrong, I plan to tell him. Once Belinda finds the evidence. And I'm positive she will."

"You should know me by now. I'm not about to blab anything to anyone. But I know you. Your conscience won't leave you alone until you let Bradley in on your plan. Aargh. I have to admit, you may be on the right track. Blackmail and murder often go hand in hand."

"At least my sister and Jason will be happy I'm staying longer."

"They won't be the only ones. You can add me to the list."

I wasn't sure how to take his comment. That's what happens when you kiss someone out of nowhere like I impulsively did with Godfrey a while back. Now I have to live with it. I muttered something pleasant and inconsequential and told him I'd let him know what Belinda finds out. Then, I changed into form-fitting jeans and a striking V-neck top before hustling off to meet Bradley at Tim Hortons.

Belinda was right. I was Lucifer in wedges.

• • •

The second I opened the door to the Tim Hortons on Hamilton Street, I inhaled a combination of seasonal scents that somehow worked: cinnamon coffee, creamed soups, and donuts. Bradley was seated by the window and gave me a huge smile the second I approached the small two-person table.

"Great timing. I ordered your favorite hot latte. I figured you'd be freezing. Grab a seat and I'll get it."

I took off my jacket and threw it over the back of the chair. When Bradley returned with the latte and placed it in front of me, he tilted his head. "You look pretty snazzy for a fast-food meal. Might as well spit it out. What nefarious plan did you come up with?"

"Am I that transparent?"

"Like Saran Wrap."

"Let me begin by saying it's not illegal." *At least I don't think it's illegal.*

"Oh, brother. I haven't heard it and already I'm worried."

"Relax. Take a sip of your coffee before we put in our orders."

It was hard to read Bradley's expressions between his coffee drinking and my need to go full speed ahead with the explanation. I backtracked to my conversation with Ronny and went on to detail my subsequent chat with John. Then, on to the jugular—the undeniable possibility of blackmail and my deal with Belinda.

Bradley rubbed his right temple and gulped the remainder of his coffee. "You're right. It's not exactly illegal in the pure sense of the word, but it sure crosses every ethical boundary. Not that bankers don't do that all the time, but they do it at the request of their customers."

"That's what Belinda said."

"Tell me"—Bradley reached across the table and held my wrist—"how'd you convince her to take that chance?"

"By extending her sublet an extra three months."

"I don't know who's more diabolical—you or Donovan."

"Hey, I'm one of the good guys. And you should be overjoyed I'm staying here longer."

"I'm overjoyed, all right, but I'm stunned. Have you thought of what you'd do next if Belinda does manage to find out if money had been funneled in? You can't tell those deputies or it will cost your tenant her job. And her reputation."

"I suppose it would depend on where Donovan's payoff money originated. I could always nag Grizzly Gary and make him think looking into bank accounts was his idea. I've done that sort of thing before."

"Norrie, you've done that *exact* thing in the past. And by the way, you really should let Don and Theo in on your plan when we see them tomorrow. Stephanie and her husband, too."

"Absolutely. And for all we know, they might have a better idea of what to do if Belinda uncovers the truth. I'm glad Don and Theo decided on tomorrow night for the potluck. Perfect timing. I'll pick up one of Wegmans entrées and a dozen mini-rolls."

"Speaking of food, I'm starving. What are you up for? I'll go place the order."

• • •

The next day I was a veritable jack-in-the-box as I waited for Belinda to call. Every time I heard the winery phone ring—and believe me, it rang a lot—I jumped. By midmorning, Lizzie was most likely sick of me asking her if anyone called for me. I finally broke down and told her I was expecting to hear from someone about information regarding Donovan. I left it at that.

Six and a half hours went by and no call from Belinda. Either she hadn't had any luck, or she had been escorted out of the bank, possessions and all, by security. Then, at twenty of five, I got a text from her: *$ in. Will call U 2 nite.*

Money in! Money in! She found something. The annoying tic in my eye came back with a vengeance and it was accompanied by one on my upper lip. I raced to the restroom and leaned into the mirror. Not discernible to the naked eye. Still, I knew the stress had taken its toll. Once back at my desk, I texted Bradley: *She found deposits. XOXO*

• • •

"Belinda Kuentz may call me any second," I announced to Don and Theo when Bradley and I arrived at their place a little past seven.

Don looked at Theo. "Do we know her?"

"It's Norrie's tenant."

"Oh, okay."

I handed Don the carefully wrapped entrée from Wegmans and

walked toward their living room. "I've been dying to tell you this all day but wanted to wait until Stephanie and Derek got here."

"Stephanie's running late. Can't you tell us and repeat it for them?"

"I'll wait until you stash the food in the kitchen. I don't want you to miss a single word."

Don shot Bradley a look and he shrugged. "Better brace yourselves."

With the food safely out of reach from Isolde, and all of us seated in the living room, I spewed out the blackmail theory, my conversation with Ronny, and the reason I'd be gracing Seneca Lake with my presence for an additional few months.

"If you don't hear from that woman in the next hour," Theo said, "you better make sure she wasn't arrested. And by the way, the bank account search was a pretty good move on your part. Not exactly *principled*, but effective."

"See?" I glanced at Bradley. "Theo thinks it was effective."

"I didn't say it wasn't effective, I said it wasn't ethical, and Theo said the same thing."

Don pointed to a cheese and cracker platter on their coffee table. "Forget about who said what, it's like watching an old Abbott and Costello movie."

Just then, their bell rang and the Ipswiches came inside. Each of them toting a pie.

"You've got to hear this," I could hear Don tell them, "Norrie's taken the sleuthing to a whole new level. And by the way, I'd stick to credit unions when it comes to banking."

Everybody spoke at once as they tried to tell Stephanie and Derek what I'd done. As more and more details unfolded, the couple looked my way with an occasional "Is that true, Norrie?" or "You didn't really ask her to do that, did you?"

I topped a cracker with salami and reached for the mustard knife. "It's not as if the sheriffs' offices could get a subpoena. Evidence and all that. I had to use the resources I had."

Stephanie perused the cheese platter before selecting a slice of cheddar with an olive. "Have you figured out what you're going to do next if those bank accounts point to blackmail payoffs?"

Just then, Don stood as if the place was on fire. "Good grief. We've been so busy with Norrie's news I forgot to ask what everyone wants to drink. Wine, soda, coffee, tea, you name it."

Wine was the overall winner and Theo immediately got up and walked to the kitchen, followed by Don. Our dinner, a potpourri of dishes ranging from Don's fettucine with mushrooms to Wegmans' braised beef and broccoli, was topped off with strawberry rhubarb and apple pies, baked by Stephanie's mother-in-law and part-time babysitter. Derek mentioned she had also baked sugar cookies for the boys. A bribe for good behavior, no doubt.

With full stomachs, we lingered over coffee and did what we set out to do—bandy our theories around. I was now convinced someone at LaVerna Vineyards was responsible for Donovan's death, although the Botox seemed an odd weapon of choice. Like a game of Clue, we named our suspects, announced their murder weapons, and proceeded to support our theories. Then Belinda called and everything changed.

Chapter 37

"Do you mind if I put you on speaker?" I asked her as soon as I took the call. "I'm with the other winery owners and friends who have a vested interest in this."

"Okay. Sure. I'm back at your condo so no one can listen in at this end."

"Uh-huh. What did you find out? Your text said you saw money going into Donovan's account."

"You were right, Norrie. About payoffs and all. I checked the account he had in his name, as well as the joint account he had with his wife. Then, I checked hers for good measure. I kept telling myself it was a look-see."

"It was. There's no problem. Go on."

"Only Donovan's account showed the deposits. Four of them in the past month. None prior. They came slightly under the ten grand limit so our bank didn't have to report it to the IRS. Money laundering and all that."

"Do you have the dates?"

Belinda rattled off the dates while I shouted, "Will someone write these down?"

Theo waved a pen in the air and I asked Belinda to repeat the dates slowly.

I was certain the dates would jibe with the time Donovan left California to the day he wound up in our cauldron.

"I followed the routing numbers and found out who made the deposits."

"Who? Who?" Then I shouted to Theo, "Write this down, too."

I fully expected the money to come from either Larry or Vern Marchese, or from their business, so when Belinda said, "Mrs. Avinna Parkhurst," my jaw dropped.

"Avinna Parkhurst? Who on earth is that?"

"I knew you'd ask me, Norrie, but all I can give you is her address, and I shouldn't even do that. It's 121 Glencoe Avenue in Penn Yan. That's the city where you live, isn't it?"

"Um, the village. Yes. But our winery is off of Route 14 on Seneca Lake. Belinda, are you sure she's the one who deposited the monies into Donovan's account?"

"Yes. I checked the numbers three times and even did a backward search. Listen, let me know what you find out."

"I will, Belinda. I will. Thanks so much!"

"Avinna Parkhurst," I shouted again, in case anyone missed it the first time. "She has to be a Marchese relative, don't you think?"

Meanwhile, Don pulled up Zillow on his phone and looked at the address. "Whoever she is, she owns one hell of a Victorian house at the dead end of the street. The only thing past it, and you can't drive there from her block, is the cemetery."

The cemetery. That's fitting.

"I'm googling her," Stephanie said. "Maybe one of you can see if she's on Facebook."

As fingers flew over our handheld devices, I had an epiphany. "I'm speed dialing Rosalee."

"Rosalee Marbleton?" Derek pinched his shoulder blades together and stretched his arms. "What's Rosalee got to do with this?"

"Not Rosalee. Marilyn. Her nosy sister. If anyone knows who Avinna is, it's Marilyn. Give me a second."

After four rings, Rosalee picked up and rattled off Marilyn's phone number as soon as I explained the situation. "Well, it's finally come to that. My sister's penchant for snooping and gossiping has finally paid off. She's become the county expert."

"Uh, it's just that she's well-connected."

"Well-connected my derrière."

"I appreciate this, Rosalee, I really do. Catch you later."

Seconds later, I had Marilyn on the line. "I'm so sorry I had to leave your table to join the ladies chitchat group on Monday," she said, "but once they start talking, there's no stopping them and I didn't want to miss anything."

No kidding.

I kept the phone on speaker but motioned for everyone to keep still.

"That's fine. I understood. Um, Marilyn, the reason I'm calling is because I'm hoping you might know who Avinna Parkhurst is. It's a long story but—"

"Avinna Parkhurst on Glencoe? Mrs. 'I have more money than any of you' Parkhurst? *That* Avinna Parkhurst?"

"Uh, yeah. I mean, how many Avinna Parkhursts in Penn Yan can there be?"

"I suppose. Anyway, she's a California transplant. Comes from a family of vineyard owners. Is that why you're interested? She's a regular pa-toot! Don't do any business with her."

"You wouldn't happen to know what vineyards her family owned, would you?"

"Not the vineyards. But they must be just as snotty. Avinna once bragged her family started organic winemaking. Organic. That's the new thing, now."

I mouthed the word *organic* to everyone even though they could hear Marilyn loud and clear.

"She's also a black widow, according to the scuttlebutt. Avinna's in her sixties and married a wealthy retired railroad man, almost twice her age—Orson Parkhurst. That's how she wound up in Penn Yan. Rattling around in that dreadfully ostentatious house of hers. A few Christmases ago, she had the ladies league over for tea. Horrible design sense. What with all that medieval weaponry on the walls. Club, maces, swords, even a poleaxe. She said it was a passion of her late husband. He must have been a real beaut, too."

The dagger in Donovan's back. Did it originate on Avinna's wall?

"Now, you didn't hear this from me," Marilyn went on, "but I think Avinna's getting ready to trap another unsuspecting husband into her web. Less wrinkle lines on her face than when I last ran into her. Between you and me, you can always tell if a woman's using fillers by looking at the neck. It's a dead giveaway. Turkey jowls and all."

I instinctively placed a palm on my neck. "Thanks, Marilyn. That was very helpful."

"If you don't mind my asking, why the interest in that woman?"

"It's only a hunch but she may have something to do with Donovan Brin's murder. The writer from *Wine Enthusiast.* I really can't say much more."

"Harrumph. Just goes to show you, you never know your neighbors. Anyway, maybe we'll run into each other again at the diner."

"Could be. Thanks again."

Theo, Stephanie and Derek tripped over each other with their comments the instant I ended the call.

"California organic vineyards! Duh!"

"She could have a stockpile of Botox!"

"Medieval weapons on the wall. Bet a dagger is missing!"

Their commentary ended only when Don and Bradley insisted they slow down.

"I've got to admit," Bradley said, "this is way too coincidental. But it's coincidental, not definitive."

I took a sip of my coffee, now cold, and sighed. "Deputy Hickman will tell me it belongs in one of my screenplays. But when is a coincidence *not* a coincidence? If Avinna is a relative of the Marchese brothers, it's quite possible they're staying with her. Certainly enough room in that house, and only one way to find out."

A resounding *no* filled the room and I swallowed more cold coffee. "I'm not suggesting we break in."

"Since when?" Theo mumbled under his breath.

Suddenly the room got quiet and everyone looked at me.

"I'm not saying we break in. More like sneaking in with a ruse. Adrienne could be there against her will."

"I'm not sure I like where this is going," Bradley said.

Theo gave Bradley's shoulder a squeeze. "Get used to it, buddy. She can't help herself."

"Avinna's house sits at the dead end of the block, so if one of us drives by or parks there, someone will be bound to notice." Don stood and walked toward the sink. "I'm making another pot of coffee. Marilyn yakked so much, mine got cold. By the way, that woman missed her mark. She should be writing tell-all novels like *Peyton Place*. What doesn't she know about Penn Yan?"

Derek laughed. "Not much, apparently."

Isolde rubbed against my legs and I bent down to pet her. "Whoever is inside the house won't notice if we park in the cemetery and take a lovely little autumn hike to the back of the property."

Again the room got still. "I'm not suggesting *all* of us. It's Friday night and everyone has to work tomorrow. Everyone except—"

"Fine," Bradley said. "This can't be any worse than the last rendezvous you dragged me into."

Then Theo chimed in. "Not without me. We've got plenty of coverage for tomorrow, especially if we give it an early start. Catch them off guard. Like eight in the morning. Plenty of time to get back to our wineries."

Don rolled his eyes. "I'm putting the local bail bondsman on speed dial."

Stephanie gave Derek a poke. "Your mother's watching the boys tomorrow and we've got plenty of coverage as well. I'll join the crew. Besides, I'm up at the crack of dawn every day."

Derek shook his head. "Good grief. Why don't we cut to the chase and send in a marching band?"

"Nah," I said. "It'll ruin all the fun."

Chapter 38

Fortified by a second pot of coffee, the six of us sketched out a surveillance plan that we thought would work. Funny, but on paper it was logical and feasible. In reality, it was neither.

As planned, Bradley and I took Francine's Subaru and met up with Theo and Stephanie in front of the Grey Egret at seven forty-five the following morning.

"I bet no one thought to bring thermoses of coffee," Theo said as he got into the car, "but I did. It's downright freezing today. I even remembered insulated cups."

Thankfully I'd already had a cup for breakfast. "You guys enjoy it. I like both hands on the wheel."

Both hands on the wheel and my mind going all over the place.

Our plan was simple, really. We'd park in the cemetery and approach the house from the rear, pretending to look for a lost cat. Then we'd sneak around the windows and peer in. At the first sight of Larry or Vern Marchese, we'd use our phones to snap a photo.

I seriously doubted we'd spot Adrienne, but we had to establish a connection between the men and Avinna. If so, we'd come up with plan B. Whatever the heck *that* was.

Never before has the phrase "winging it" been as apparent as it was that morning. Once I turned into Lakeview Cemetery, I wound around until we were adjacent to Avinna's property. I pulled the car off the drive and the four of us got out.

Stephanie took one look at the surroundings and almost jumped ship. "Heck, Don didn't mention there were woods between Avinna's house and the cemetery. Doesn't Zillow show you all that stuff?"

I shrugged. "Plot maps and greenery. Hey, at least you're wearing hiking boots."

Bradley and Theo started for the woods. "Come on, let's get a move on."

A few minutes later, we were at the edge of the cemetery property staring at Avinna's lawn, now covered with leaves in all colors. "Hold on a minute, everyone," I said. "We need to agree on what the cat looks like if anyone asks."

"How about a tabby?" Stephanie answered. "They're pretty common."

Theo shook his head. "Then they'll want to know about the stripes. They're not the same."

"Then a black cat," she said. "With amber eyes. Real easy."

"Black cat it is. By the name of Midnight. All of us can remember that, right?"

A series of groans followed as we stepped onto the private property and called out the cat's name. Theo and Bradley moved left, leaving Stephanie and me to skirt around to the right and get closer to the windows.

"Did you hear that?" I asked her. "Someone slammed a car door shut. We've got to get around front. No sense trying to be inconspicuous. Let's move toward the house next door and call out 'Here kitty, kitty.' That way we can see who's there."

As Stephanie and I made our way across the lawn, I kept my fingers crossed Bradley and Theo would be able to get a peek inside the windows. Just then the front door opened and our mystery man, aka Larry Marchese, trotted down the steps, his hand pulling a suitcase. No mistaking him with his wavy hair and black rectangular glasses. He walked directly to a dark-colored car on the street and turned back to the house. "Hurry up, Vern. We'll miss our flight."

"That must be the brother," Stephanie whispered. "He's in the doorway."

"I guess that cinches the relationship, but now what do we do?" The tic in my eye returned. No surprise. "We can't confront them."

Just then, we heard a woman's voice. "You forgot your laptop, Larry, and Vern can't carry everything."

Larry traipsed back to the house, pausing to acknowledge Vern while I ducked under a row of juniper bushes. Thankfully, Avinna had let them grow tall, allowing me to crawl toward the front door. That's when Avinna stepped outside and handed Larry the laptop. I wanted to get a closer look at her but couldn't due to my vantage point.

"Don't drop the laptop." Her voice was rough and raspy. "Thanks for tying up that mess. No sense hanging around. We're off the hook now that they've fingered Donovan's assistant. Too bad they might not find her. Serves her right for colluding with that son of a gun."

"We had no choice or we'd be in the poorhouse. Getting milked dry by Donovan. What I don't understand is how he figured out we imported nonorganic grapes to beef up our production. At least we were smart enough to cover our tracks when it came to nonbiological sprays. Real easy to switch labels."

"Well, I wouldn't worry about it if I were you. It's something you and Vern can mull over on your flight home. Better get a move on."

"Hey, one more thing, sis—Whatever prompted you to go off script and stab Donovan with one of Orson's daggers? You know you'll never get that dagger back."

"Phooey on the dagger. He bought it at a Renaissance Festival sale. I can afford a new one with real gems."

I nudged Stephanie and mouthed, "Are you getting this?" She had her phone on and appeared to be recording the conversation. Same as me.

"Yes," she mouthed back. "Shh!"

Avinna continued, "That scoundrel nearly put us out of business. He stabbed all of us in the back when he wrote that article and then turned around and blackmailed us. I wanted to get even."

"Well, you did, sis. You did. All of us did."

Larry leaned forward and gave Avinna a peck on the cheek and made a beeline for the car.

"We've got to do something," Stephanie whispered.

"Keep your phone on record." With that, I charged out from the bushes and shouted, "Bradley, Theo! Call the sheriff's office. Those are the men who vandalized our Hallow Wine Weekend display. I recognize them from the footage. It wasn't that blurry after all."

Then, without pausing to catch my breath, I waved my hands in the air as I raced toward their car. "It took some work from our IT specialist at Two Witches Winery, but we got that video cleared up. Seems shaving cream can only distort surface images. The real images came through and I tracked down the culprits to you two gentlemen. Penn Yan's a small town, you know. And by the way, that display was very costly. I'm pressing charges."

By now the four of us were only feet away from Larry and Vern.

"How much is this going to cost me?" Larry asked. He reached into his pocket and pulled out a handful of hundreds.

I'm in the wrong business. I can't even pull out a handful of tens.

"What's going on?" Avinna shouted from the front door.

"Nothing," Vern shouted back. "Go back inside."

"Take it or leave it." Larry elbowed past us and opened the front door to the car. "Hurry up, Vern."

As Vern approached the passenger door, a woman in a teal jogging suit rushed toward us. "Is this your kitty? I heard you yelling for your cat. I found this guy during my jog." She held a small tuxedo cat in her arms and all of sudden, Vern sneezed uncontrollably.

"I'm allergic. Get that thing away from me." More sneezing. "Get it away, I say. I could go into anaphylactic shock." In seconds, his eyes watered and he reached into his pocket, retrieving a hanky. Then, more sneezing.

I took the cat from the woman and walked closer to Vern. "Make one move toward that car and there won't be enough Benadryl in the world to save you." Then to Bradley, "Did you get the sheriff's office?"

"Oh, yeah. Any minute now."

Larry let the driver's side door close and started to walk around the front of the vehicle. That's when Theo approached from behind, opened the door and stood between it and the driver's seat. "No one's going anywhere," he announced. "Not yet."

I pictured an all-out brawl but that never happened. Instead, the unmistakable sound of a siren pierced my ears and I knew the sheriff's office had responded. "Give it up," I said. Then Larry sneezed, and before I knew it, he and his brother were sneezing in tandem.

At that moment, an official Yates County Sheriff's Office vehicle pulled up alongside the rental car and my stomach turned. Deputy Hickman thundered out of his seat and tromped toward us, followed by his assistant, Deputy Eustis.

"Why does this *not* surprise me in the least, Miss Ellington? I should have suspected something when the distress call said 'citizen apprehending killers.'" Then he flashed a look at Theo and Bradley before turning to Stephanie and then back to me. "You just can't stop drawing more people into your amateur investigations, can you? When did you say your sister was returning?"

I shrugged. "Her sojourn has been extended."

Deputy Hickmann shuddered and approached the Marchese brothers.

"Those are the men who killed Donovan," I said. "Larry and Vern Marchese from California. And their sister, Avinna Parkhurst, was the one who put the dagger in Donovan's back. Stephanie has it all on her phone recorder."

"I do," she said. "Care to listen?" She tapped the phone and Avinna's voice could be heard. "Thanks for tying up that mess."

"That's quite enough, Mrs. Ipswich."

"It's not," I blurted out. "It's not. I think they've got Adrienne Stafine locked up in their house. I'm sure they were planning on killing her, too, since they thought she was in cahoots with Donovan."

"What?" Larry and Vern flashed each other looks and then continued to sneeze. I motioned for the woman in the teal jogging outfit to step back and she handed me the cat. "I need to get going. It looks as if you'll be occupied for a while. I'm glad I found your kitty." With that, she jogged down the block before I had the chance to tell her it wasn't my cat.

"We most certainly did not kidnap Miss Stafine," Larry told Grizzly Gary. "Feel free to search the house."

"I fully intend to do that. Warrant and all," was his response. Next, he motioned to Clarence, who in turn asked if he should take notes.

"Not now!" Grizzly Gary responded. "We need to bring them in for questioning." Then he gave the men one of his notoriously unfriendly looks. "Would that be all right with you gentlemen? Or should I arrest you on the spot for creating a disturbance on a city street?"

Neither brother said a word as Larry was escorted into the backseat of Deputy Hickman's car.

"I've notified my office and another sheriff's vehicle will be here to escort your brother to the public safety building. I recommend no one say another word until we reconvene there. Understood?"

Deputy Hickman and Clarence stood guard over Vern and I moseyed closer to Bradley, Stephanie and Theo as the cat nestled in my arms.

"I know that look of yours, Norrie," Stephanie said. "No cats. Derek and the boys are enough for now."

Theo reached for the cat. "He's a cute little guy."

"How do you know it's a he?"

For the first time since I met him, Theo blushed. "Trust me. I looked. It's a he. Until someone claims him, I suppose Don and I can hold on to him. Don's a sucker for kittens and Isolde might like a friend. In fact, I think I'll name the little guy Tristan."

Guess Don's not the only sucker for kittens.

In a flash, the second deputy car pulled up and Vern Marchese was escorted into it. Then Deputy Hickman walked to the front door of Avinna's house. Within seconds, I watched as a slender woman with a perfectly layered bob exited the house, her silver hair an identical match to the pashmina she had draped over her dark slacks. And not any pashmina. Like the one Whitney had worn when we first met, this one had intermittent gold tassels on the edges, too.

"I'll need statements from all of you," Grizzly Gary bellowed. He opened the door to his vehicle and motioned Avinna in. Then he turned to us. "And I'll need to have a copy made of the phone recording. Don't fiddle-diddle around. Drive to the public safety building pronto. Or walk. I don't see a car."

With that, he slammed the door before I could utter a word.

Chapter 39

"What are the chances of two identical silver pashminas showing up in Penn Yan?" I asked. "Especially with that signature gold tasseling."

"What are you getting at?" Theo asked. "I thought you had the pashmina at your house."

"I returned it to Whitney when Deputy Hickman blew me off. No sense having me hold on to it. Listen, I think we've been played. Big-time. We need to get into Avinna's huge coach-house garage and see if Adrienne's rental car is there, along with Whitney's rental and Avinna's car."

"Whitney?" Stephanie, Theo, and Bradley all asked at once.

"Yep. Whitney. Oh, heck. Forget the garage. We're wasting time. I think Whitney's not who she claims to be and Adrienne is in that house against her will. If Whitney watched Larry, Vern, and Avinna get carted off, she's likely to shut Adrienne up for good. Come on, we've got to get inside the house."

"Isn't Deputy Hickman coming back with a warrant?" Stephanie asked.

"That could take hours, knowing him."

"You and Stephanie stay here in front," Bradley said to me. "In case Whitney *is* in there and makes a run for it. She'll have to exit the house in order to get into the garage. Good thing it's two separate buildings. I'll see if there's a way inside the house from the rear."

"Right behind you, Bradley." Theo tucked the cat further inside his jacket before he and Bradley took off.

"You really think Whitney and Adrienne are in there?" Stephanie asked me.

"I'm banking on it. You need to stay here and keep watch. Don't do anything. Just call the sheriff's office if you see her. I'm going to try the front door. Avinna left in a hurry. With any luck, she didn't have time to lock it."

"What if she—"

Stephanie's words were lost as I turned the doorknob and let myself inside. The door creaked and I jumped, knocking into a side table.

"Is that you, Aunt Avinna?" a voice came from upstairs. "I was in the shower. Did I miss my dad and Uncle Vern? I wanted to say goodbye before they left. Aunt Avinna?"

I always thought the expression "my blood ran cold" was a bit overdone, but in this case, not only did it turn cold, it all but froze. I walked backward toward the door, refusing to take my eyes off of the ornate wooden staircase.

Thankfully the door was still open and I turned to Stephanie. "Whitney's inside," I whispered. "Get Bradley and Theo but don't make a sound when you come inside."

Stephanie nodded and I walked back inside the house.

Whitney's voice got louder. "Aunt Avinna? I'll be down in a second."

Marilyn wasn't kidding when she said the walls boasted medieval weaponry. Heck, they made the Tower of London's museum look like child's play. I tiptoed past a heavy oak credenza and reached for a club. It was the only thing I thought I could manage if Whitney came at me.

By now I was positive Adrienne was being held but I wasn't about to open doors and poke around. I'd seen enough horror movies as a teen. It was always the damp, dark basement or the creepy cobweb-laced attic. Instead, I did an equally stupid thing. I walked up the stairs and gripped the club until my knuckles turned white.

Five or six feet past the top of the stairs and a door flung open, all but knocking me on my keester. I jumped back, grasped the club as if it was a baseball bat and got ready to swing, when I found myself face-to-face with Adrienne.

"Adrienne?" I lowered the club and took a step back. "Are you all right?"

That's when I heard Whitney's voice and felt her breath on the back of my neck. The musty attic and dank basement were looking better and better. "You shouldn't have come, Norrie. You should have left things alone." The breath on my neck felt sharp and I realized it wasn't breath at all. It was the tip of a syringe.

I ducked down, spun on my heels and came back swinging. The club hit Whitney on her thigh, sending the syringe flying and causing Whitney to double over. "See me in another twenty years when I'll be ready for facial filler," I said.

"Norrie? Norrie?" Bradley and Theo's voices intensified.

"Up here!" I held the club in front of Whitney, who was still doubled over.

"If you wouldn't mind," Adrienne said, "I'd like to take that club and use it on her other thigh."

Whitney glared at Adrienne. "My uncle should've gotten rid of you when he had a chance. But no, he listened to my aunt, who said she wanted to deal with it at the opportune time. You had to be working in cahoots with Donovan."

"Sorry to disappoint you," Adrienne said, "but we've been through this before. And yes, I was the one who found out about the commercial use of pesticide at LaVerna and maybe I shouldn't have told Donovan, but I wasn't the one who used that information to extort money from your family."

Bradley and Theo thundered up the stairs just as Stephanie shouted from the doorway, "Where is everyone? I called the sheriff's office when no one came outside. Is everything okay?"

"It is now!" I yelled back.

"You won't get away with this," Whitney huffed at Adrienne.

I rolled my eyes, my hands still firmly gripped on the club. "I don't think you will, either," I said.

With Bradley and Theo blocking Whitney from any possible escape, and me hovering over her, I was almost euphoric. That's when Grizzly Gary's grating voice echoed up the stairs. "Miss Ellington!

Didn't I tell you to go directly to the public safety building?"

I leaned over the staircase, medieval club and all. "There was one more player and I caught her."

"Put down that baseball bat before you injure someone. We already know. We were on our way back here when Mrs. Ipswich phoned."

"Oh."

There were no other words that formed in my mouth. "Oh" seemed to have said it all.

"Do you want me to take notes, Deputy Hickman?" It was Clarence's voice directly below us.

Grizzly Gary bellowed back, "No!" He looked directly at Whitney and told her she was being charged with suspicion of kidnapping Adrienne Stafine and collusion in regard to Donovan's murder. I was about to ask if that shouldn't be *accomplice* to murder but I didn't need to ruffle his feathers any more than I already had.

With hands behind her back, Whitney was escorted down the stairs and out the door, but not before Deputy Hickman gave us the eye. "Report to the public safety building! All of you! I don't want to get another emergency call telling me you've been involved in something else. Understood?"

Stephanie and I nodded while Bradley and Theo responded with loud *okays*. Once Whitney and the deputies were out the door, the five of us retreated down the stairs.

"Guess I better hang this club back up, huh?" I said. More of a statement than a question.

Adrienne looked at the club, then at me. "I hoped you would have whacked her so hard she'd fly over the handrail, but getting her arrested was even better."

"Oh, she did that all by herself. Listen, I know we're supposed to hightail it over to the sheriff's office, but I really need to find out what happened. Half the world thinks you killed your boss."

"That's what Whitney intended, although she wasn't the brainchild behind this—Avinna was. I hadn't a clue. Not even an inkling. Boy, was I duped. I even confided in her. Turns out there *is* no *Wines in Our Lives* podcast. It was all a ruse."

"Tell me," I asked, "how did Whitney manage to abduct you? And when?"

"That's the million-dollar question. And to be honest, I can't say it *was* Whitney. No doubt she was in on it, though. The last thing I remember clearly was ordering room service the Saturday morning of Hallow Wine Weekend. I thought my coffee tasted a bit bitter but added an extra packet of sugar and more creamer. Next thing I knew, I was foggy-headed, and after that, I woke up in a locked bedroom at Avinna's house. No cell phone, no bag, no nothing. After a few days under house arrest, they finally let me use the bathroom without someone guarding the door. And forget about a window. My room had stained-glass windows that I couldn't open. It was awful."

Stephanie bit her lower lip and swallowed. "I can't believe Whitney tricked us like that."

I moved the club to my other hand. The thing seemed to have gotten heavier. "Yeah, great acting skills, too. Especially at the bonfire. Geez, she makes Amy from *Gone Girl* look like an amateur."

Adrienne chuckled. I think it was the first time I saw her display a positive emotion. "I might have been cooped up in my room," she said, "but the heating vent led directly to the living room so I was privy to their scheme. I'm lucky you showed up when you did because the Marchese family had a fatal plan for me, too. When Donovan uncovered a number of unscrupulous actions at LaVerna, he knew he'd found a way to survive his impending divorce without sacrificing his lifestyle. What he didn't count on was that the Marchese siblings wanted to keep their lifestyle as well. And they had no problem with eliminating him for good."

Theo elbowed me. "This could be your next screenplay. Just set it in a cutesy village."

I'd like to set it on the next planet.

"Oh my gosh. How long have we been here yakking? We'd better get a move on, although I'm not thrilled by walking all the way to the cemetery for my car. Then again, I don't want an official escort from you know who."

Adrienne smiled. "Maybe you won't have to. I overheard Avinna say she put my things in the drawer to the left of the sink. Maybe my car keys are there. I know for sure my car's in her garage because Whitney mentioned removing the GPS."

"What are we waiting for?" Bradley asked.

Wasting no time, Adrienne bolted for the kitchen and the rest of us followed.

"They're here!" She held up the keys and then paused. "Something else is here, too. Adrienne gingerly placed a thumb drive in my hand and winked. "It's the article for *Wine Enthusiast*. Donovan's article. About to be published posthumously."

"You mean *your article*, published in his name."

"I'll have other chances."

We exited the kitchen and I made a quick dash to the living room to return the club to its sacred spot on the wall. Next, it was a beeline for the garage. Since it was a coach-house garage, its doors were easily pried open, and without further ado we all crammed inside the rental. Five adults and one cat. Adrienne drove us back to my car.

"You better let Don know what's going on," I called out to Theo as Bradley and I got into the Subaru.

"I already did. He sent me three angry emojis."

"That's better than one angry sheriff's deputy!" *Or not.*

Chapter 40

When the five of us stepped inside the public safety building and explained our situation, the deputy on duty directed us to Deputy Hickman's office. Then he gave me a cockeyed look. "Are you Norrie Ellington?"

"Uh-huh. Why?"

He tried not to laugh but finally succumbed. "Sorry, but I pictured the Queen of Hearts."

"Eugene! What did he tell you about me?"

The deputy, who looked as if he'd turned twenty-one yesterday, cringed. "Keep a wide berth."

"Oh, brother."

By now, Bradley, Theo and Stephanie were in stitches while Adrienne was downright puzzled. I did the best I could to ignore them and looked directly at the deputy. "I don't see Avinna Parkhurst and her brothers or Whitney Fontana."

"They're being booked on the other side of the building. Deputy Hickman left a message for you to wait in the conference room for him. It's a few yards down the corridor on the left."

I thanked him and gave him my widest smile. *The Queen of Hearts. Honestly.*

Talk about a nondescript conference room. Not even antidrug posters on the beige walls. Only portraits of prior county sheriffs surrounding the large rectangular table. Wooden chairs, sans arms, completed the décor.

"This is our tax money, fast at work," Theo muttered. "Gives *style* and *function* a whole new meaning."

"Shh!" I pointed to the door. "I can hear footsteps."

Less than a second later, Grizzly Gary entered the room with Clarence at his heels. "Good. You're all seated." He snapped a finger at Clarence and directed him to hand us pens and blank sheets of paper. Then he cleared his throat. "No sense asking you to tell me what ensued. You'd be speaking all over each other and I'd wind up with a royal headache. Grab a pen and write down everything that happened this morning, beginning with your arrival at the Marchese residence. Miss Stafine, of course, should document the days preceding this morning."

I waved the paper in the air. "But—"

"It's not a screenplay, Miss Ellington. Only witness statements. Normally completed in separate areas but I trust this will not be a collaborative effort. Should any of you need to expound on anything, take another piece of paper. Now then, before you begin writing, I'll need the iPhones that captured the conversation between Avinna Parkhurst and her brother Larry."

Stephanie and I handed over our phones, but not before asking when we could expect them back. "Once the forensic office makes an audible copy." He then handed us an official Yates County property form to fill out.

"Terrific," I muttered when he left the room. "Now I've got to run into Walmart to buy one of those burner phones. This is a nightmare."

"Derek's going to pitch a fit," Stephanie added. "Better make that two burner phones."

"Mind if we make a stop on the way home?" I asked Theo and Bradley.

"No problem," was their response.

I used Bradley's phone to text Cammy and reassure her all was well, while Stephanie notified Gable Hill on Theo's phone. Adrienne, meanwhile, used her own phone to call the editor at *Wine Enthusiast*.

"I feel horrible for Raisa James," she said when she got off the phone. "She drove all the way here to re-interview the winemakers and pen the article."

"Maybe she can take advantage of the situation and write an entirely different article. One that involves some investigative journalism as well as suspense. Title it 'When Wine Turns to Murder' and explain how LaVerna Vineyards beguiled the public, only to be blackmailed.”

“That’s a fantastic idea, Norrie.” Adrienne contacted the editor again and beamed when their conversation ended. “She’s calling Raisa right now. Ronny Morgan, too.”

And while Adrienne had to remain longer at the sheriff’s office since she was a victim of foul play, and heaven knows that involved more paperwork, the rest of us were free to go.

By the time we completed our statements and drove to Walmart, we were totally wiped out, buoyed only by the euphoria of finding Donovan’s killers. Still, it would take another day before the actual plot would be made public.

• • •

“There you are!” Cammy announced when Bradley and I walked into the tasting room at a little past three. She was at the cash register conversing with Lizzie and rushed over to give me a hug. “We thought Grizzly Gary might have charged you with something.”

“No, but we should charge the sheriff’s office for solving their case.” I looked around and it was the usual three o’clock lull. “I’ll give you guys the condensed version and fill in the blanks later.”

Cammy and Lizzie darted their eyes back and forth at each other as Bradley and I told them about my conversation with Belinda and the deduction I made about Adrienne being held captive, before moving on to the arrest of the Marchese family.

“It was a carefully constructed murder,” I said. “We learned the Marchese brothers flew out here to get Donovan out of their lives for good and happened to notice our cauldron as they scoped out the wine trail. Convenient, huh? Along with their niece, Whitney, who had been staying with her aunt Avinna until she made her move to the Belhurst, they devised a way to drug Donovan and dump him into our cauldron the night before Travis discovered his body. The brains belonged to

Whitney and Avinna, but the brawn was certainly Larry and Vern."

"And the Botox?" Cammy asked.

"Avinna's. No wonder Marilyn said the woman was husband hunting."

"Holy cannoli!" Cammy put a palm against her cheek. "That's screenplay material."

"Actually, it may turn out to be Raisa James material if all goes well. Meanwhile, I'm without my iPhone thanks to Grizzly Gary. Well, at least temporarily, but it's a small price to pay."

"Is this murder scenario public knowledge?" Lizzie asked. "Nancy Drew was quite circumspect when it came to sharing information."

"It's winery knowledge, for now, but I can assure you, it'll be on the nightly news and replayed so often, all of us will be nauseated."

Sure enough, the news anchors on all of the Rochester and Syracuse stations "broke the story" in time for the nightly broadcast at nine.

"I can't believe it's finally over," I said to Bradley over a late-night cup of cocoa. "To be honest, I thought this was one murder that would go unsolved." I reached down and gave Charlie a shortbread cookie.

"Not with you at the helm. Still, it was surprising. Especially Avinna and that dagger. Who'd figure her late husband thought medieval weaponry made decorative sense."

"And those threatening notes? Boy, was Whitney clever. First writing threatening notes telling us to back off, because she knew we were looking into Donovan's murder, dropping hints about Stephanie needing to worry about her appearance, and then pretending to get a note from Adrienne. Not to mention planting Botox syringes in Adrienne's room. I wonder whose playbook Whitney had stashed away."

"What I don't get is the pashmina in the woods. It was Whitney's but she led us to believe Adrienne was in possession of it."

"That's easy. To throw us off. To have us fixate on Adrienne as either victim or perpetrator, thus taking the heat off Whitney."

"Got to hand it to her. It worked. At least the 3Musketeers bar mystery got solved. Lizzie bought a three-for-one special at CVS and thought she'd surprise me with a little gift. Geez. The poor woman felt awful when she found out how freaked out we were."

"Listen," Bradley said, reaching his hand across the table to grasp mine, "backtracking to things that work, that's exactly what I want for our relationship. The last thing I'd want to do is crowd you. I was nervous as hell thinking Donovan's killer would come after you so I planted myself here. That's not fair to you. We never even sat down to discuss the arrangement."

I squeezed his hand. "It has been and still is wonderful, but we both need breathing space from time to time. Maybe stay over three or four days a week?"

"As much or as little as you need, I'm not going anywhere."

We finished our chocolatey nightcaps and headed upstairs. Maybe my deal with Belinda wasn't so bad after all.

Epilogue

In the days and weeks that followed, it seemed the public and social media couldn't get enough of the Marchese family and LaVerna Vineyards. News of their clandestine operation, not to mention murder and kidnapping, was everywhere.

Raisa James had raced back to the city to work on not one but five serialized pieces for her magazine, detailing everything from Donovan's murder to deceit in the wine industry. Just what all of us needed. "Hey, even bad publicity is better than no publicity," Theo said at our Thursday WOW meeting. Ronny got in the action as well, since her photos would accompany Raisa's text.

The only saving grace was the article Adrienne had written about our Merlots. As a result, even more visitors poured—ouch—into our wineries to taste a wine with "layered hints of blackberries, chocolate, and cloves."

Not to be outdone, however, was Jason's article, "Prevalence Rates of the Melicodes Tenebrosa in the Philippine Islands." It was published by *Entomology Today* in time for the holiday season. Godfrey was beside himself and couldn't stop yammering about it. Yep, all was right with the world. Well, *almost all.*

A few days before Thanksgiving, Zenora stopped by the winery and handed me a lovely seasonal basket filled with dry herbs. It had a bright red ribbon on it as well as a sprig of pine.

"It's late in the season for fresh herbs," she said, "but the dry variety is equally effective."

"Effective as in tasty?"

"As in necessary to ward off evil spirits. I had a most compelling vision of snow, ice, and murder."

"A holiday murder mystery movie?" *Even the Hallmark Channel is getting bold.*

"No. Something on Two Witches Hill. I thought you should be prepared."

Oh, I'll be prepared, all right. To bolt the doors, turn off the lights and wait for spring.

About the Author

J. C. Eaton is the pen name of husband-and-wife writing team Ann I. Goldfarb and James E. Clapp.

A New York native, Ann spent most of her life in education, first as a classroom teacher and later as a middle school principal and professional staff developer. Writing as J. C. Eaton, she and James have authored the Sophie Kimball Mysteries, the first book of which, *Booked 4* Murder, took first place in the 2018 New Mexico-Arizona Book Awards in the Cozy Mystery category. They are also the authors of the Wine Trail Mysteries and the Marcie Rayner Mysteries. In addition, Ann has published nine YA time travel mysteries under her own name.

When James E. Clapp retired as the tasting room manager for a large upstate New York winery, he never imagined he'd be co-authoring cozy mysteries with his wife. Nonfiction in the form of informational brochures and workshop materials treating the winery industry were his forte, along with an extensive background and experience in construction that started with his service in the U.S. Navy and included vocational school classroom teaching.

You can visit Ann and James at www.jceatonmysteries.com, www.jceatonauthor.com, www.facebook.com/JCEatonauthor/, and www.timetravelmysteries.com.

9 781958 384220